NO OIL

PAINTING

Genevieve Marenghi

Burton Mayers Books

Content compiled for publication by Richard Mayers of Burton Mayers Books. Cover by Holly Book Design.

First published by Burton Mayers Books 2025.

A CIP catalogue record for this book is available from the British Library

ISBN-13: **9781917224123**

Typeset in Garamond

www.BurtonMayersBooks.com

To Pauline, my wickedly funny mother. A chain-smoking bookworm and people watcher, who taught me the value of manners, swear words and standing up for myself.

Still so missed after all these years.

Author's Note

I've always been fascinated by art theft. So when I learned that in 2002, Titian's Rest on the Flight to Egypt was found dumped outside Richmond Station in a stripy plastic bag, I couldn't shake such a compelling image.

I volunteered at National Trust property, Ham House, for many years. My passion for this Jacobean jewel on the Thames, together with my fellow volunteers' indomitable spirit, gave birth to Maureen, my unlikely anti-hero.

Most women start to become invisible from the age of fifty. Like my septuagenarian protagonist, I view this as a superpower. Unlike Maureen, I haven't used this to commit art theft. Yet.

I found all the staff at Ham House friendly, supportive and committed to their work. As this would have made for dull reading, they are nothing like the House team in *No Oil Painting*.

When I started out as a guide, some friends teased me about volunteering with a bunch of pensioners. One offered to buy me a plastic rain hat. But these written-off OAPs were by far the most interesting people I've ever worked with. Shrewd, funny, resilient, polite but irreverent, they were passionate about visitors enjoying Ham House. Without such dedication, the British institution that is the National Trust simply couldn't operate. This book is a tribute to its volunteers throughout the UK, whatever their age.

It is nothing to die. It is dreadful not to live.

Victor Hugo, *Les Misérables*

And now what can I do or what must I further do? But condemn my own mistaken measures which have proved so fatal…

Letter written in 1694 by Elizabeth Murray, the Dowager Duchess of Lauderdale, to her daughter, the Duchess of Argyll

Ham House Floor Plans

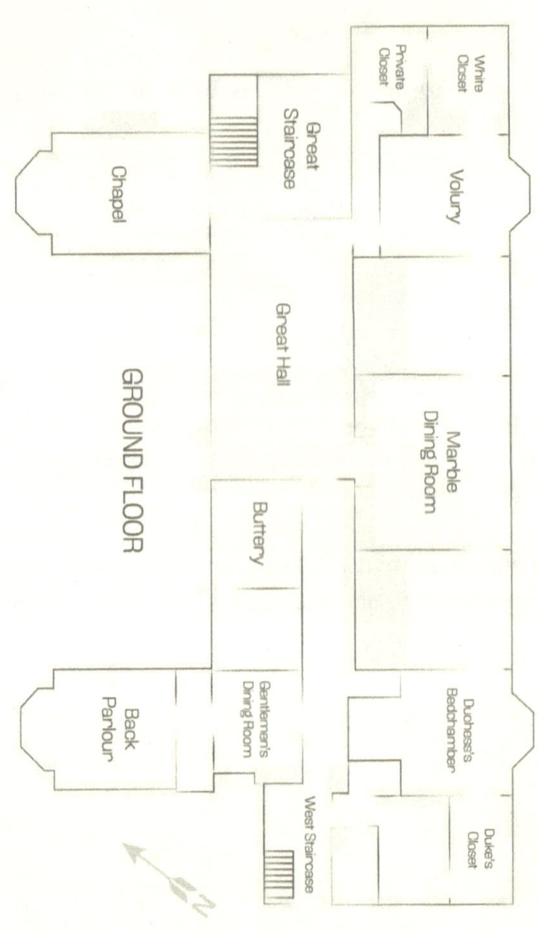

No Oil Painting

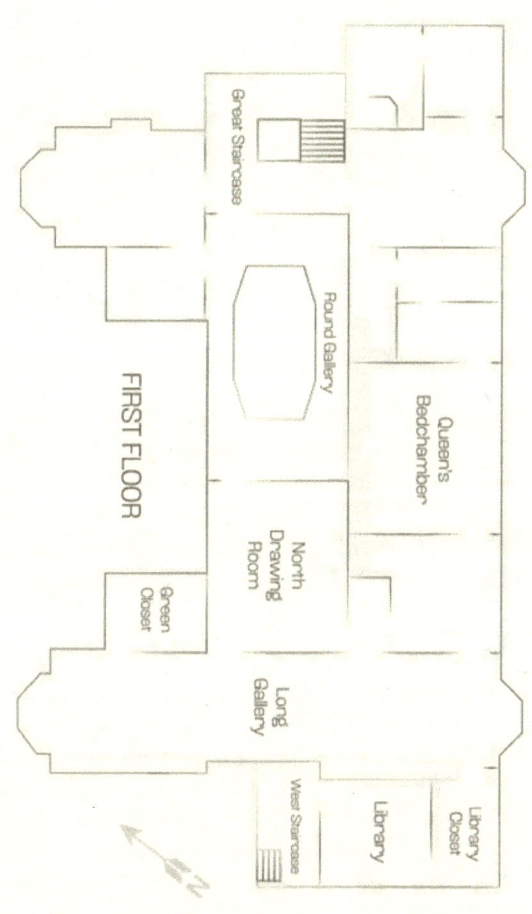

By Suzannah Leigh Design Ltd

Prologue
Tuesday, 21st November

You're a long time dead. That's what her mother used to say. Often to recruit her for some errand. *Never mind the lashing rain, you're a long time dead, now go on with you to Cullen's and fetch five Weights.* Without a flake of irony. After all, smokes were good for you back then, when Maureen was little more than an ankle biter. Now, seven decades on, she stopped herself blurting the very same battle cry. Instead, she upped her mother's mantra with, 'Oh come on, live a little!'

Vinegary wine slopped over her glass as she slammed it down harder than she meant. 'It's got to be an item worth stealing. Something that would land you a good few years inside.'

Virtual tumbleweed swirled round the New Inn's sticky carpet. She scanned her fellow Thursday guides. Deirdre's spinach-flossed gasp, Rhona's foggy specs, and Sanjay's torn paper crown flapping off his bald patch.

'Deirdre, you can nick dried lavender from the Still House any time.' Maureen puffed out sunken cheeks. 'More like the Van Dyke in the Long Gallery. Mind you, bit dicey to unscrew it with everyone rushing past.'

Thelma tapped her stick against the table leg. 'What's all this?'

It was several months since Thelma's hip replacement, and Maureen viewed her floral cane more as a lethal weapon than walking aid.

'We're playing a game,' said Deirdre, winding a strand of red tinsel round her wrist.

'The fire alarm's gone off in the House. It's not a drill. You've got minutes to steal something in all the panic. So what are you going to take?' Maureen congratulated herself. Finally, something to stall the endless debate on the virtues of crème brûlée versus salted caramel brownie.

Accompanied by strings, came Shane MacGowan's

rasping lament. He could have been someone. *Well so could I*, thought Maureen.

'The Duchess's teapot is rather lovely,' said Deirdre. 'And it's—'

'Chinese rare, white-crackled glaze porcelain with silver mounts.' Sanjay recited the Private Closet deets in nasal tones, oblivious to the blotches on his reindeer tie. 'Produced in the Zhangzhou kilns in the Fujian province, circa 1650 to—'

'Tricky. Way too tricky.' Rhona wiped her glasses on a stained napkin. 'It's on an alarmed pressure pad, so it is.'

'Well one would simply have to find something the same weight and swap it over.' Thelma spoke as if she performed this feat every other day.

'Like Raiders of the Lost Ark.' Sanjay now in schoolboy mode. 'Minus the giant rolling boulder.'

'Aye right.' Rhona sneered. 'Piece of pish to switch an object of identical weight within a split second, while dodging the House team. It's top of their *save* list.'

'You'd need inside help.' Maureen pulled at a hair on her chin, ignoring Rhona's eye roll and Thelma's pursed pink lips. In the brief lull, Kirsty and Shane belted out their chorus, recalling the NYPD's song of the Old Country.

'Kerry.' Deirdre clapped liver-spotted hands. 'She looks worn out since she's been on maternity cover. Twice the work for no extra money, and I heard—'

'Nah, too risky. The more people in on it.' Maureen spoke as if to herself, toying with the remnants of her mashed potato.

'Well, we all know who to send the police to when something goes missing from the House. Mind you Maureen, you're the very last person I'd suspect of masterminding a fine art heist.' Sanjay's guffaws launched flecks of spittle on to her bobbled cashmere.

Ting, ting.

Swaying between two tables, the National Trust co-ordinator tapped a fork against her empty glass. 'It's wonderful to see you all,' she said, as the lights flashed SOS on her Santa hat.

'Crême brulée?'

'Another year's flown by.' She raised her voice, as the bartender weaved in and out, slapping down the various desserts. 'First, I'd like to thank Sanjay for organising our Christmas lunch this year…'

But Maureen muted the chorus of cheers. She didn't respond to Rhona's mutter that it was still November for crying out loud. Nor did she register Sanjay's mock bow. Picturing instead a Jacobean stately home just over a mile away, where shutters were being closed and bolted, then lights extinguished, until the House was cloaked in near darkness. Save one second-floor window, which glowed in latticed squares as the sun dipped behind the cobbled West Courtyard.

Chapter 1

She Freezes Who Does Not Burn

Thursday, 23rd November

Art theft today isn't about people bulldozing through with an SUV, storming up some stairs, and bailing with some Vermeer or van Gogh. That's old school. The real action now is in fakes and forgeries, false attributions and shady provenance. That's where the money is in art crime. Forget the smash and grab, it's all about theft by deception…

Waiting alone on the marble floor, Maureen replayed the art detective's interview in her head. By chance, she'd caught it on the radio as she drove in, her mind still buzzing with that Christmas lunch game. Her waggish brainteaser had certainly livened up the festivities. In fact, they had all lapped it up. Even Deirdre had got there in the end. Plus, she hadn't seen Sanjay that perky for a long time. He'd been more subdued since his wife had moved into a care home. Dementia — the cruellest of exits. She shuddered, all too aware of the soaring stats for her age.

Doubly important to keep the mind sharp. What was that quote? *Procrastination is the thief of time.* And she considered her question again. It was an excellent one. What could you steal from Ham House? Puckering her lips, she scoped the majesty of the Great Hall. Its walls were heaving with goodies, but you couldn't just snaffle a Constable or Reynolds. Those arch countesses were hardly covert targets, and a trifle too large for her handbag. No, something more subtle would be required. Theft by deception, say.

Her train of thought was disturbed by a tapping noise from the West Passageway. The ghost of the Duchess with her ebony cane? Much worse. Thelma. Now advancing on to the monochrome floor, she narrowed her mascara-caked eyes as she clocked Maureen, already garrisoned by the closed shutters.

Leaning on her stick, the harridan lowered herself on to

the guide's chair, her greeting on a par with the standard House chill. 'You're in early today.'

'Yes, roadworks are gone, so no traffic.'

Thelma didn't respond to Maureen's fib, but rifled her way through the latest Antiques Trade Gazette, until the others drifted in. Thelma always arrived before anyone else and so had first choice of rooms, which were allocated on a first-come, first-served basis. Without fail, she nabbed the Green Closet, which needled the others. Not enough for them to arrive before 11:15. Today however, Maureen wanted to bag the Green Closet and so had signed in at 11:06. As if exempt, Thelma never bothered.

Of course, this didn't stop her old adversary from trying to elbow in when it came to dishing out rooms at the 11:45 briefing. But Maureen, maestro of the pass-agg apology, insisted with a gritted smile, that in fact, she had arrived first, and was bored of doling out ale samples in the beer cellar. Emma, the House Manager, handed over the pewter key and, avoiding Thelma's death stare, Maureen marched up the cantilevered Great Staircase.

Up past the carved panels of military trophies; the cannons, barrels of gunpowder and mounds of shot. Then shields and armour, blunderbusses, swords and spears. Along with dolphins, elephants and dragons — the whole, fuck-off, bronze effect Roman triumph. All crowned with gilded baskets of fruit, which she caressed on her way. Just occasionally, she mused, money is not wasted on the rich.

On the first floor, she sauntered through the Round Gallery and glanced down at the last guides still gossiping on the Great Hall's chequered floor. Rhona broke off cackling and acknowledged her pal with a wolf whistle. Maureen royal-waved over the balustrade and continued on her way.

At the far end, the Duke and Duchess of Lauderdale eyed her with disdain. As the King's head honcho in Scotland, the Duke flaunted his Order of the Garter star. He was a nasty piece of work: ruthless, greedy and utterly corrupt. Meanwhile, the Duchess wafted a gold hankie in a bored, calculating manner. Clad in a glam, low-cut nightgown, the notorious Elizabeth Murray must have been freezing her tits off. Another one too big to snag, Maureen thought, as she passed their double portrait, before entering the North Drawing Room.

Here, gilt barley-twist columns flanked the marble fireplace. Above this, chubby plaster putti clambered round a painting of more naked children offering fruit to a baby girl, in a rather fingers-up parody of Adam and Eve. The Stuarts didn't do minimalism. A clapped-out harpsichord and a carved ivory cabinet fanned the room's eerie grandeur.

Despite the oppressive atmosphere, the blinds were closed in here to preserve the tapestries depicting merry peasants working the land. They illustrated months in the agricultural calendar but were hung slapdash. Half a panel from another set had been hacked to fill in the edge of May, so that it ploughed into August, right before October. Perhaps part of May had been ravaged by moths, and this was considered the most practical solution back in the day. Regardless, it always reminded Maureen of her father's botched wallpapering. Except, assorted remnants of floral paper seemed a tad more expendable than eighteenth-century tapestries. Worth a bomb, but you couldn't exactly roll one up and whistle back down the Great Staircase with it over your shoulder.

It was a relief to emerge into the daylight splendour of the Long Gallery. King Charles II glared down at her, as if unimpressed with this shabby, grey-haired underling. His own thinning pate hidden beneath a long black, curly wig, doubtless also masking syphilitic sores.

'Hey Maureen, so you got the Long Gallery as well.' Sanjay stood a few portraits down, blowing on his hands. Maureen always forgot to dig out her long service badge, but Sanjay's pin glinted under the shell uplighters.

'Last week, Nigel was in here — got right on my wick.

Kept barging down my end to bang on about that hidden portrait of Mary Queen of Scots. You know, the one they found beneath Sir Whatsisface.'

'Classic Nige. No, I'm in the Green Closet today.'

Sanjay raised bushy eyebrows. 'Is Thelma not in?'

'Yes, but I think she took the Marble Dining Room.'

'What? She hates it in there. Says it's too cold with the front door open.'

'She's playing the martyr, 'cos I got here before her. Fancied a change today.'

'Good for you. Here, let me help. That lock's fiddly.'

'No, don't worry.'

But Sanjay had already snatched the key and was striding towards the dark panelled doors, tucked away on the Long Gallery's north end. Queen Henrietta Maria, wife to the intractable Charles I, stared down her long slender nose at them, pearl necklace touting her fertility. Mumbling something incoherent, Sanjay wiggled the key inside the ornate lock, and Maureen could just discern the odd cryptic word, such as *only, half* and *knackered.* On hearing the requisite clicks, he freed the right half of the double doors, then with impressive skill, released the floor and ceiling bolts of the left half, and pushed both wide open.

'There you go, all yours. Not my first choice. Too claustrophobic,' he sniffed, 'and musty.'

'Really? I think it's the best —'

'Hi Sanjay,' Emma called out from the other end of the Long Gallery. 'Can I speak to you about today's tours?'

Left in peace, Maureen placed the key, labelled 113, next to the folder on the windowsill, hung the room pager round her neck, and adjusted the blind. Then she tucked her quilted Chanel handbag under the steward's chair, looping the gold chain out of sight. It had originally belonged to her late sister, bequeathed to replace Maureen's scruffy satchel. Now, she never left home without it. Although, unable to cram everything in, she also lugged round a plastic bag for life, blithe to this fashion crime. As a rule, she wouldn't have dreamt of placing her cherished 1980s heirloom on the floor, but this was freshly buffed.

She paused by the mullion window and peered through a grille mired in birdshit, cobwebs flapping in the sharp breeze. Eyes crinkled, she gazed out across the Forecourt at the large, brooding back of Father Thames, his shaggy head wreathed in foliage. The river god reclined in the centre of the carriage circle, his right foot tucked under a brawny, weathered thigh. Small groups milled round Visitor Reception. They dumped nylon rucksacks on a bench beside the imposing wrought-iron gates. What would the Duchess have made of the mobile ticket office? She'd have torched it. Along with the welcome assistants.

Perhaps the more liberal 6th Earl might have approved; in a radical move, he'd opened up the North Front, pulling down the high garden wall that had hemmed in his ancestors. At last, this magnificent, red-bricked Stuart mansion was visible in all its glory, the gates now adjoined by a low parapet. The hipster Earl had punctuated this token wall with Coade stone pineapples, symbols of hospitality. In truth, they further rammed home his great-great grandmother's clear message of wealth and power.

Bloody champagne socialist.

Beyond the open gates, past the saggy bunting, she surveyed the far side of the Avenue. Through a gap in the near-leafless trees, she glimpsed smudges of blue and green; canopies for boats stranded by the annual draw-off between Richmond and Teddington locks. In the seventeenth century, roads were perilous dirt tracks and the Thames, wider back then, would have been alive with traffic. Like some bucolic, aqueous meld of the South Circular, A3 and A4, alive with the wiry forebears of London cabbies rowing courtiers upstream to Hampton Court and downstream towards Richmond Palace. Not forgetting Whitehall — the very seat of power — a mere four hours' commute with the tide behind you.

Maureen tried to visualise the gridlock of scullers, long barges and wherries, gruff, dexterous watermen jostling for position amid hazardous currents, in those precious hours when the tide worked in their favour. Today, the river was near deserted. Hammertons Ferry and the cruises had long since packed up for the season, while the rowers had all decamped upstream in search of deeper waters. Just a few dog walkers exploiting the frail sunshine. And the odd rider leading their coated steed down the avenue towards the stables.

Maureen's breath began to mist up the leaded glass. Patting her tweed pocket, she turned round and looked up at Flora larking with cupids among the clouds. The folder described this ceiling as being executed in tempera on paper, then pasted on to a linen backing. She often confused *tempera* — some egg-whitey mix — with *tempura*, those tasty Japanese fried bites, which her niece had insisted she try. Stunning though it was, the rectangular paper joins lent it a whiff of DIY. To be fair, the artist's work had been interrupted by the outbreak of the Civil War.

But she hadn't chosen this room for its Baroque inspired ceiling. Here, she had decided, lay the solution to her game poser — the perfect spot for a surreptitious art heist. Really, the only viable location in the House. A small cul-de-sac, teeming with pocket-sized delights, not all visible from the cramped area near the doorway. It was only possible to study all the miniatures and diminutive oils if you gained access beyond the rope barrier.

But first, she must pay homage to her secret jewel. And she stepped to the far end of the western wall, where it hung, shielded from view in the alcove on the other side of the chimney breast. Ambrosius Bosschaert's *Blackbird, Butterfly and Cherries*. Was it Ambrosius the Younger or Elder? She could never remember.

'What, that rough oil sketch. It's a waste of space,'

Rhona had scoffed, when Maureen had named it as one of her favourite paintings.

'No really, say what you mean.'

'Och, away. Why wouldn't you choose, say *An Alchemist* — you know, in the Duke's Closet? Now that's quality art, right enough.'

'Yes,' she had conceded, 'But Bosschaert also knew how to paint, and I love its simplicity. Plus, it's rare. Unusual for him to paint live birds.'

Her fellow guide had refused to budge. Too stubborn for her own good. At least, her great niece had better taste. Jodie had always loved *that little blackbird one*, when Maureen would let her sneak a peek, back when she was still excited by Auntie showing her the House's treasure trove. Now, it was just a boring, creepy old building.

Except when some *Made in Chelsea* celebs were doing a photo shoot there. The House had to shut early, which infuriated some of the volunteers.

'Never heard of them,' one had snapped, as if they were the target audience. But Maureen had recognised Binks, (or was it Bonks?), and had taken a selfie with her to send to Jodie, who was *well jel*.

But on the whole, it couldn't compete with YouTube and Roblox, hanging with your besties, listening to Sabrina and Tay Tay. Or that other Charli XYZ one. Something about a *summer brat*. Maureen tried to keep up. With less success than when Jodie used to set her *BTS* homework:

'Okay Auntie, what's Jin's star sign?'

'Virgo. No, wait. Let me think, Sagittarius.' Tick.

'So, who's just got ink, what is it and where?'

'Ooh, I know this one: Jungkook. *ARMY* on his knuckles.' Full marks. Natch.

But now, that was like, so ova. Maureen's *BYE* gag hadn't gone down well, post the K-Pop band's traumatic hiatus. Now and then, Jodie updated Maureen. Such as Jimin's latest relationship status with an actress, who'd been trolled mercilessly. And sometimes, Jodie would ask whether *her* painting was still there, tucked away in the corner. Maureen was more than happy to be buttered up, and to *help* with homework.

Maureen zoned back in on the *Blackbird.* Although not large — a mere peck less than a sheet of A3 — it wasn't handbag-sized. Particularly combined with its elaborate oak frame, which ruled it out of her theft by deception challenge. But it wasn't this fanciful border that transfixed Maureen, rather the arresting scene captured between the carved putti and fauna. A sunny, snatched moment on a stone tabletop.

On the upper left, a peacock butterfly hovered near a sprig of luscious cherries, attracted by their sweet fragrance. Stem trapped under foot, a shiny blackbird, stood mesmerised, as pulp dribbled from its sharp, yellow beak. Evidently, the exquisite pattern on the insect's wings, vied with the fruit for the bird's attention. The Dutch artist had captured a near carnal joy until his belle-laide smudge burst the idyll. A bluebottle had landed on the table's edge.

Maureen knew that flies represented mortality and wicked earthly desires, but also gave an excuse for artists to show off, as they were tricky little buggers to paint. The Dutch artist had certainly demonstrated his ingenuity, as this fly had a glossy, metallic quality. As though, with a blurring agitation of its gossamer wings, a living insect could buzz off at any moment.

She stepped back and tilted her head. All three creatures wanted to feast on the succulent cherries. Though quicker than their feathered predator, both insects were also in danger of being eaten, and they knew it. Providing they could resist the fruit's juicy charms.

'Welcome to Ham House!'

The front-door guide's greeting boomed up from the Great Hall, rousing Maureen from her trance. Today's coach party must have disembarked. They'd be up soon, so she hadn't got long to play. A few paces back to the door, she stuck out her head. There was Sanjay down the south end, reading through his tour notes. Maureen clicked the twisted rope back in place.

Pulling a small package from her pocket, she advanced to the eastern wall and held a dark, oval frame up near the miniatures pinned to its green damask. To and fro, up and down. The perfect size and, wait a minute. She placed it beside a miniscule portrait to the left of Henri II, Roi de France. Not bad. Not bad at all. A near exact match — even down to the tiny gilt ring from which it hung. She'd spotted it yesterday in an antique shop in Twickenham. More like a dusty junk shop, crammed with the pitiful detritus of solitary, expired pensioners. Sheltering from the rain under its tattered awning, it felt as though this window reflected her own not-so-distant future back at her. Then, a tiny picture of a dog caught her eye.

It wasn't the gaudy print, but the frame that had attracted her attention. Its size and embellished inner rim, conjured the Green Closet miniatures. She was right. Lo and behold, it bore an uncanny resemblance to the one encasing *Unknown Lady in a Yellow Dress.* Although said Lady would have been appalled at being ousted by this cheap bonneted beagle. Yet, she doubted if anyone would notice. This absurd stand-in would fool a careless glance a few feet away. Filling the gap amid the green silk swirls, its frame would blend in sufficiently to count as theft by deception, its canine model more a two-fingered salute than any splash of a forgery. Would those bastards even care, she wondered. In a way, these little gems were unseen. Unsung.

'Hello. What room's this?'

Maureen jumped, slipping the goofy hound back into her pocket. She turned to face a small group of visitors hovering at the doorway.

'You're in the famous Green Closet,' Maureen cleared her throat. 'One of the few surviving Stuart cabinet rooms. Designed by owner William Murray, as a sort of tribute to his friend, art-loving King Charles I. Its intimacy was designed to contrast with the bustle of the Long Gallery. Only the odd, elite guest would have been invited to view Murray's collection of miniatures by candlelight. His eldest daughter, Elizabeth, later a Duchess, left it largely unchanged.'

Polite nods, glazed eyes.

Come on, pull yourself together.

'Here, let me show you some beauties behind you.' She shone her torch on the most valuable miniatures by the door.

'This is a famous one of Elizabeth I, known as *The Mask of Youth.* She was getting on a bit when her court artist painted this, but you must flatter your patrons, and you couldn't afford to upset Queen Bess. Plus, it was a clever piece of propaganda.' *I may be old, but I'm still very much in charge and don't you forget it.* 'And if the recipient had any sense, they didn't. More permanent than social media, that's for sure. I doubt there'll be many posts that will survive four centuries.'

Having elicited the requisite laughs, Maureen felt in control again.

'These two locks of hair belonged to the Earl of Essex, Elizabeth's former golden boy. Got too big for his leather riding boots and was swiftly demoted. Then rebelled against her. A fatal mistake, which cost him his head. It was fashionable back then to wear a tuft of a loved one's hair, mounted on a jewel. These strands are thought to have been cut on the morning of his execution. I presume, with head still attached.'

'Eugh.'

'Imagine rinsing off the blood.'

'But this is my favourite. It's called, *A Man Consumed by Flames.* The Latin inscription on it reads, *Alget qui non ardet,* which literally translates as *He freezes who does not burn.* In other words, these are flames of love. We don't know the identity of the sitter, but he clearly had his eye on someone at court. Perhaps with a view to a lucrative marriage, or something more clandestine. The ultimate Valentine. It would have won me over, that's for sure.'

'Better than a text.'

'Like a Tudor Tinder.'

More laughter, interrupted by the insistent ringing of a handbell.

'Ah, that means it's time for the first tour. Don't miss out.'

The visitors shuffled off.

'Thanks, how interesting.'

'Wouldn't that be funny to wear hair as earrings.'

'Your ears are hairy enough George.'

'Bit dark that room.'

'No, not for me.'

Alone again, Maureen considered the dapper courtier once more. The ring of gold in his left ear, the slight smile gracing his moustached lips, unperturbed by the engulfing bursts of orange and gold. Talking of flames, this most definitely was an object worth stealing in the event of fire. His delicate-lashed eyes seemed to goad Maureen, confident that he was untouchable from beneath the alarmed, toughened glass case. No, that would be mission impossible — way beyond a smash-and-grab job. The art detective was right. Theft by deception was by far the easiest route.

Just then, a cry pierced the chatter in the Long Gallery. Unfastening the rope, she peeked out. A gaggle clustered round a white-haired woman, who lay motionless on the parquet down the far end, her anorak all bunched up. Sanjay knelt beside her, checking her pulse.

Standing in the doorway, Maureen experienced a sudden, weird out-of-body sensation. As if a cosmic pause button had been pressed. In this adrenaline-fuelled hiatus, was she the blackbird, the butterfly or the bluebottle? Later she told herself that in those protracted seconds, she'd agonised over her next move. But in truth, she didn't hesitate. *She freezes who does not burn.*

Stepping back into the empty Closet, she turned round one last time and checked. Huddles of visitors gawped at the dazed pensioner. Crossing the floor, she took out the mini pooch, and at odds with her thudding heart, swapped it for the *Unknown Lady*. With surprising deftness. She always wore gloves in the unheated House at this time of year, and she'd watched enough crime dramas to know that she mustn't leave fingerprints.

It was important to play this game properly, and it had proved so easy. Too easy by far. Most delicious of all, at this very moment, Maureen was a fine art thief.

Chapter 2
The Penitent Magdalene

'What are you doing, you loon? Are you off your trolley?'

Rhona, open-mouthed in the doorway, had clearly witnessed Maureen's switch. The guilty party stood frozen, cradling the *Unknown Lady* in her hand.

'Er, I was only... See, I bought this print and was comparing frames. Look, it's exactly the same as—'

'Well, don't just stand there. Put it back, you bampot! Thelma's on her way up to cover for your tea break.' Rhona tapped her forehead. 'That glaikit game of yours. Let it go, Maureen. See you down in the Mess Room.' She turned to go. 'Oh, and you're welcome, by the way. Imagine if the Empress of the Green Closet had caught you.'

Maureen was left, holding the disparate portraits in each hand, staring at the gap on the west wall. Then Rhona stuck her head back round and hissed, 'Quick, she's coming,' before disappearing once more into the Long Gallery. Maureen hesitated. As the final grains of sand trickled down the egg timer, she was even now reluctant to part with this little oval beauty. As if stalling a painful goodbye to someone she loved.

She heard a loud, forced exchange from outside.

'Well, it's all kicking off today, what with that poor woman fainting. What was it? Low blood—'

'Dehydration,' came the curt reply. 'We should all avoid it by drinking eight glasses of water a day.'

We should all avoid being sentenced for theft, more like.

And Maureen fumbled the yellow-gowned Lady back on the little brass hook. Once more claiming her rightful spot — beside King Charles XII of Sweden.

She didn't catch Rhona's retort, or the ensuing acrid backchat. Instead, Maureen met the sidelong glance of those beguiling eyes. Feasted one last time on her ringlets and coral lips. Near photographic realism, achieved with stippled dots of colour. She could almost hear the rustle of that gold lace dress, a clustered pearl brooch setting off the cleavage. Gilding the lily somewhat, but Stuart courtiers weren't renowned for their subtlety.

'What's that you've got there?'

A dark spectre filled the doorway, the severity of her walnut pageboy matching her expression. Thelma.

'Where?'

'In your hand.'

With a lurch, Maureen realised she was still clutching the ten quid, furry locum.

'Oh this.' And she held up Exhibit A. 'I picked it up from a local junk shop and was comparing its frame.' As if this was routine procedure. 'Just wanted to see if it stood up to any of these. Might have clinched a bargain.'

It was hard to tell if the old crow bought this. Her painted poker face exuded her standard disapproval. Yet she felt sure Thelma's right eyebrow had twitched.

'And does it?'

'Sorry?'

'Does it stand up?'

'Absolutely!' Rapid downplay. 'I mean, it would only work from a distance.' Hollow laugh. 'Without glasses.'

'You don't wear any.'

You're so sharp, you'll cut yourself.

'No, that's right. Not since my cataracts were zapped. Anyway, it's a little early for my tea break. What about yours?' Maureen fired back, although she heard her voice higher than normal.

'Already had it. I'm helping Emma with the storeroom inventory later.'

Well, la-di-bloody-la.

With rictus smile, she handed Thelma the pager. She found herself walking in slow motion back through the Round Gallery. Circuiting the banisters furthest from the windows, to avoid the coach parties, she stopped near the Great Staircase end. She needed to collect herself, so she paused to look up at the Duchess's final portrait.

Arguably her finest, as famous artist, Lely, had painted every inch. He hadn't farmed out her russet silk stole, or her hands, to studio assistants, as was standard. Neither had he gone overboard in flattering his friend and former patron. By now, well into in her fifties, with a double-chin and fleshy arms. Although, no danger of exposing bingo wings with those puffy sleeves.

The Duke had probably suffered a stroke by this point, the reality of their huge debt was kicking in, as well as their exile from Court. Their brazen extravagance and thirst for power had forged many enemies, leaving the Duke's powerful ally, Charles II, with no choice but to distance himself. The days when Elizabeth flounced around Holyrood Palace as if she were the Queen of Scotland were over. The It-couple of the 1670s were now social death. Was this why the Duchess wore her hair half loose, resting head on hand, in the classic Penitent Magdalene pose? Did she rue the choices she'd made? Or was this last portrait mere skilful spin? Both, suspected Maureen.

Although her breathing was still shallow, Maureen felt a little calmer, as if the menopausal Duchess had bestowed some of her steeliness. But also, her regret. *You totally screwed it up —your best chance.* Yes, Rhona had saved her, but she'd also spoilt the game. She knew she should be more grateful, imagining her panic if that ghastly print now hung on the western wall, with Lady Anon gracing the inside of her pocket. It was farcical to think of that frilled mutt rubbing frames with Europe's seventeenth-century elite. But also terrifying.

Yet, as she descended the Great Staircase, an anarchic idea leapt out of her subconscious. If it wasn't for her loyal friend and that accursed vixen, would she really have needed to swap the miniature back? Would anyone have even noticed? The staff seemed far more concerned with targets, membership sales and *emotional impact feedback*. Why shouldn't she glean some secret comfort from an intricate object, which few saw or appreciated?

She crossed the east side of the Great Hall into the narrow servants' passageway. Pushing open the sage door, she stepped into pitch darkness, before her motion activated the light. Clasping her sister's Chanel bag, she picked her way down the wooden spiral staircase, and berated her inner demon. But as she reached the dingy Basement, this thought still clung to the back of her mind, like one of those burdock seeds with myriad tiny hooks that stick to your clothes and can't be brushed off.

It was warm and noisy in the Mess Room. At the long central table, the garden volunteers rolled up mud-splashed fleeces, comparing scratches and other war wounds. They paid no attention to Maureen, who darted past them to the cupboard, and poked around for an unchipped, cleanish mug.

Rhona had already installed herself at the round table below the Basement window. A new volunteer sat knitting some dubious affair, with festive red and green balls of wool encroaching on Barbara's Tupperware. Foraging for unbroken biscuits in the Mess tin, Rhona raised her glasses skew-whiff on her platinum white crop. 'No sign of that new packet of Bourbons of course,' she said, scowling at the gardeners. 'Just Garibaldi and stale custard creams.'

The rhythmic clicking of knitting needles was unbroken as Barbara shouted through her crustless triangle, 'Any sign of that ambulance?'

But as Maureen ran the scalding hot water tap over a teabag, and drained the remnants of some pungent semi-skimmed, she registered only her internal clamour.

Rhona had abandoned the tin and scrutinised the accused with raised eyebrows. Maureen nodded in sheepish reply to that razor, blue stare.

What the hell had she been thinking? Total car crash if that beagle now adorned the silk damask for real. However well the frame matched, she felt sure Thelma would have sussed it at once. Nothing got past that eagle-eyed witch.

As it was, Maureen had looked decidedly shifty. Mouth full of egg and cress, Barbara persisted:

'Earth to Maureen. Earth calling Maureen. Do you receive? Over.'

'Sorry, what did you say?' Maureen sunk on to the armchair near the bookshelves, wedged a lumpy cushion behind her back, and sipped her dishwater tea.

'Has the ambulance arrived for that woman who collapsed?'

'Not yet, but it's on its way.'

'Get you in Her Ladyship's chair. First you bag the Green Closet, and now you've nabbed Thelma's spot. Is this a military coup?'

Rhona baited Maureen from behind a red length of knit and purl, which the newbie was holding up to the light. Unawares, Barbara came to the rescue. 'No quiche today, Maureen?'

'Not feeling that hungry. I'll grab one of these,' and she dipped a custard cream into her tea.

Wrinkling her nose, Barbara changed the subject. 'Busy today with that coach party. It's been dead this week, apart from that. Just as well they're closing upstairs next week.'

'What?' Maureen choked on a crumb.

'You know,' Barbara ignored Maureen's coughing fit; 'the annual deep clean. Only the Basement's open from next week. Oh, and the ground floor. They're decorating it in the style of a Restoration Christmas.'

Triumphant, Rhona fished out a jammy dodger. 'I'm not sure the Stuarts had flashing fairy lights.'

Barbara prodded her bouffant. 'Me and Rhona have signed up.'

Rhona and I have signed up.

'To help out with the cleaning.'

'Aye, help make it a bit maer Protestant.'

'Oh, I forgot.' Maureen's hands felt moist, and she put down her mug. 'Thought it was the week after next.'

'You okay Maureen? You're looking awful peely-wally.'

Rhona, merciless, as always.

'I'm fine, really.'

'Well tell that to yer face.'

'There are some nasty viruses doing the rounds,' said Barbara, scraping her chair further away.

Navigating her own private maelstrom, Maureen ignored Barbara's hypochondria. The Green Closet would be off limits next week. Praise the heavenly hosts. If she hadn't been thwarted in swapping miniatures, her secret wager would have backfired big time. How could she have been so stupid?

'You're not wrong there,' the knitter tutted, as she identified a dropped stitch.

'Would the Duchess's Bedchamber be okay for you when you've finished your tea, Maureen?'

Meera, the assistant House Steward, scarce older than a sixth form prefect, materialised with a clipboard. Brimful of hysteria, Maureen hoped nobody had noticed her jump.

'You're like the shopkeeper from Mr Benn.' Barbara laughed at her own dated kids' TV reference. 'Where did you spring from?'

Meera looked blank under her long fringe. 'I came in as the garden team left.'

Spying Meera's carrier bag bulging with fresh supplies, Rhona ditched her half-eaten dodger and sat bolt upright. Barbara held up a purse mirror and applied a dark brown lipstick — a shade favoured by the emo big sister of her great niece's BFF. No oil painting herself, Maureen didn't bother with lipstick anymore; it just bled into the myriad fissures and grooves round her mouth.

Her focus snapped back to Meera. Now wise to next week's first floor closure, Maureen was tempted to return to the Green Closet for possibly her last chance to case the joint. But it was unusual to steward the same room before and after tea, and she didn't want to draw attention, especially from Rhona.

'Er, yes. That's fine.'

Maureen employed her stock cotton-wool brain ploy. Saved also by the sudden entrance of Deirdre — a vision in beige. As always, she exuded a Julie Andrews brand of cheerfulness, which grated on the aspiring art thief. So, with a cursory rinse of her mug and some inane parting comments, Maureen picked up her bag, not unlike a pillowcase labelled SWAG.

By now, Deirdre had cornered Meera and was enlightening her on the merits and hazards of the number 65 bus route from Richmond. One of the Basement windows had swung open, and Meera eyed it with longing, as if by some latent superpower she could separate the iron bars, then hoist herself onto the gravelly South Terrace. Maureen slunk out via the normal route. It took three attempts to type in the correct code on the keypad.

'Come on, come on.'

Finally, the door to the servants' staircase unlocked, and she pushed it open, triggering the light. Blowing out long breaths, she rounded the worn, narrow steps back up to the Great Hall.

* * *

Tours complete, Sanjay had moved to the Duchess's Bedchamber, and was in full arm-waving flow, explaining to an incredulous couple that no, the imposing four-poster was actually six-foot-six in length. Its position in the alcove and its ten-foot height just made it look short.

'You're kidding? That's nuts.'

'What's the point of a painted ceiling, if you can't see it from the bed?'

As Sanjay handed over the pager to Maureen, he mimed a yawn.

'To impress visitors,' he said, his abrupt exit achieving the opposite effect. Somehow, he'd sniffed out the biscuit mountain in the Mess Room.

'In the seventeenth century, bedrooms of the elite doubled as offices during the day.' Maureen expanded on Sanjay's brusque explanation, again tucking her bag under the guide's chair.

'They copied the courts of Charles II and Louis XIV. Many political decisions were made in the King's Bedchamber. Of course, this sounds crazy to us. I mean, imagine the King, or the PM, holding key public meetings in their bedrooms.'

'I'd rather not,' grimaced a woman in a leather trilby.

'Excuse me.' A rotund man in mustard cords butted in. 'Aren't these naval war paintings a bit macho for a lady's bedroom?'

He looked pleased with his sexist, if historically accurate, observation.

'Well spotted.' Always best to flatter the smart-arse. 'In fact, this did used to be the Duke's bedroom, but after a few years, the Duchess made him swap. We think she wanted easy access to the bathroom, which she installed directly below us in the Basement. Guess he must have really loved her.'

'Or just wanted a quiet life,' said Mustard Cords.

'Isn't this meant to be the most haunted house in England?' Leather Trilby asked.

Okay, stop being ridiculous, piss right off the lot of you and leave me in peace. I need to plan a recce.

'Well, some say the Duchess has never left this House.' Maureen lowered her voice. 'Actually, she died in this very room.'

Leather Trilby clapped a hand to her mouth, and now everybody was paying attention.

'Some guides refuse to work in here,' Maureen lied, then quoted from her own ghost tour script. 'And it is said that if you look into her beautiful silver mirror, you might feel a sudden chill, a wave of despair wash over you. Some even claim to have seen the Duchess's face stare back at them.'

The room soon emptied after this. Apart from one man, rucksack on his front, baby carrier-style, who marched straight through to the adjoining Duke's Closet, pronounced it 'too small', and stormed out in disgust. Well, that got rid of them, she thought. But in truth, she knew it was the final lunch run on the Orangery, before the coach left.

From above the fireplace, a pair of dark eyes bore into her. This was Lely's first portrait of Elizabeth, after which they became lifelong friends. Here she stood, a fresh faced twenty-two-year-old, awkwardly gesturing to the waterfall behind her. A bucolic sunset highlighted coppery curls, which Lely had muted to strawberry blonde. She was considered a beauty in her day, despite her unfortunate hair colour, the fashion for redheads having died with Elizabeth I half a century earlier.

Certainly, her low cut, waistless satin dress and string of pearls were bang on trend. No accident of course that her gown was blue in colour, albeit an eggshell hue of indigo mixed with white lead. But Lely had nailed the brilliant sheen of her silk nightie with a finish of ultramarine. This, the period's most coveted pigment, was produced by grinding, blending and extracting lapis lazuli: a semi-precious rock, mined only in Afghanistan. Maureen had learnt all this from one of those National Gallery tours. Curious how she could retain such useless details but couldn't remember what she'd done the previous week, or whether she needed to stock up on Go-Cat for Pepys.

'European artists have robed the Virgin Mary in this familiar, deep blue since the fourteenth century,' their elegant Brazilian guide had told them. 'And behind this colour's compelling association with holiness and purity, is a clear message of wealth and power.'

It's all about the bling. Every bleedin' time.

Staring up at the portrait, Maureen couldn't remember what the shawl's umber tone symbolised. Affinity with nature; harmonious disposition; landowning status? Or maybe, she just didn't want to catch a chill. Maureen wasn't fooled by this demure depiction. With little interest in genteel feminine pursuits, Elizabeth had shown herself to be formidable — ruthless as well as brave. Clever too, navigating both sides in the Civil War to protect her family. And to retain ownership of Ham House. Dangerous times symbolised by those ominous clouds, which threatened to engulf the clear sky above her. Come to think of it, impending turbulence would epitomise her own predicament if her tacky canine had usurped that *Unknown Lady*.

Would staff have spied her drooling impostor during the daily House check? Maureen had no idea how thorough this was. If not, someone couldn't fail to clap eyes on it during next week's deep clean. And inevitably, it would have all pointed back to her; why she was so keen to score the Green Closet, that silly Christmas lunch game. Sanjay's words echoed round her head:

Well, we all know who to send the police to…

Elizabeth's raven eyes seemed to challenge Maureen. Wherever she positioned herself on the parquet, they pursued her with accusations of ineptitude and cowardice. *Get a grip*, Elizabeth's penetrating stare, seemed to command. You've got your ten years' service award badge. You've always been there when they needed help. Good, old reliable Maureen. Why would anyone doubt you? Again, she heard Sanjay's voice:

You're the very last person I'd suspect.

Like the lofty Stuart heiress, he made a sound point. It had been a large coach party. They would have been the prime suspects. Plus, how much was that miniature worth — seven grand? The police would have put it down to an amateur theft, and the insurance would simply cough up. Except, such a switch implied careful planning and an intimate knowledge of the House, or some previous scouting trips. Suspicion might even focus on that fainting lady, as an accomplice.

Maureen felt clammy under her thick tweed. Was she going down with something after all? Maybe she was experiencing a hot flush for the first time in years. Yet, by the twitching of her thumbs, she also sensed a new thrill stirring within. And she wasn't sure she could follow Rhona's advice on that *glaikit game*. She didn't feel able to let it go. Not quite yet.

'Of course,' she thought out loud, startling a keen bean, who had just landed from Tennessee that morning, and wanted to *do* Ham House before she checked into her Paddington hotel. Maureen joked about talking to herself being the first sign of madness. In fact, she'd just recalled Thelma's earlier boast about helping in the storeroom that afternoon. She cogitated furiously while reeling off the Bedchamber's former use as a nursery for Elizabeth's sons by her dull first husband. Unfair perhaps, but she knew little of him compared to the corruption, bad temper and excesses of husband number two, the Duke.

That's a shout, she told herself, (her great niece's slang was contagious), as the visitor exited to mainline some caffeine. She could page Meera and offer to cover for Thelma when she left the Green Closet. Claim that she'd dropped an earring in there. Glancing at her watch, she braced herself and turned towards the Duchess's mirror, but all she saw was her own lined, pensive face. If anything, she felt calmer in this room.

It took Meera sixteen minutes to respond to Maureen's pager, at which point, a woman bounded in, demanding to know, 'What's old? What's important in here?' while photographing everything in sight. She continued to bark questions, ignoring any replies. Maureen was tempted to tell her that the walnut, brass-mounted strongbox, with its secret drawers, contained the skull of King Charles I. But the demented visitor marched out, and Maureen heard her shouting down the West Passageway, 'Is this original? Are these buckets old? What's important?' like some existential lines from a Samuel Beckett play.

At last, Sanjay arrived as a cover guide, and Maureen hurried up the Great Staircase, honeybee stud in one earlobe, handbag glued to her side. Deirdre was now stationed in the Long Gallery but stood chatting with Barbara in the doorway to the Library Closet down the other end. Neither heeded Maureen.

She turned right, and almost marched smack into the gilt-edged panelled doors. The Green Closet was locked. She stared in disbelief, as if by doing so, the doors would swing apart of their own accord.

'Emma said there was no point in keeping it open after Thelma went to the storeroom. What with the House being so quiet now the coach party's gone,' said Deirdre, when Maureen bowled down their end. 'I'm not sure who has the key, but they're all in a meeting.'

Typical of the House team's pants communication, fumed Maureen. Although, she knew this was unfair; several staff had left in the past few months, so everyone was run ragged.

'You definitely had both earrings in at lunch, so you can't have lost it in the Green Closet.'

Thanks a bunch Barbara. Trust you to bloody notice.

'Will you be driving past Richmond station, by any chance?' asked Deirdre.

As Maureen descended once more to the lockers in the Basement, she reflected that her potential new career as an art thief was over before it had even begun. And if her hair were longer, she would have half loosened it in lament, like the weary Duchess in Lely's final portrait.

Chapter 3
Doomed

'Delhi Orchid — *authentic Indian cuisine.* GBK. Chez Lindsey. Coffee That. Ha! Like *copy that.* Funny. Must be new. Nando's. Nandoooooos…'

The wipers scraped the misted windscreen in Maureen's Nissan Micra, as they crawled towards the mini roundabout. The right arm was warped, creating a rhythmic scraping, which set her teeth on edge. Like Deirdre's singsong broadcast set to some weird beat. For a blissful few seconds, Deirdre paused her recital to grip the front seat as a cyclist sped past. Leaning inwards, as if that would create more road space.

'They race by from all directions these days,' she said.

Maureen hooted at the Land Rover in front, which whipped left over Richmond Bridge.

'I'm not a friggin' mind reader. Try indicating!'

Deirdre directed a watery smile at Maureen, but then looked back out of the window and resumed her light operatic solo.

'And So To Bed. Space NKaaaay…'

Catching Maureen's eye in the rear-view mirror, Rhona enacted blowing her brains out. Maureen emitted a strangled cough. Blinking, Deirdre turned to check that her chauffeur wasn't having a seizure.

'For the love of God, woman, button it!' Rhona snapped. 'You auditioning for talking Yellow Pages? We're in the future now, you know.'

This is why I love Rhona, thought Maureen. Never pulls her punches. Does not give a flying toss. Deirdre cleared her throat and sat ramrod straight, in a mercifully silent protest, broken only by the wiper's metric grating.

By the time they reached the station car park, Deirdre had reverted to her default chirpiness, announcing that she had just enough time to buy the latest Homes & Gardens, before her Reading train. Deirdre lived in Egham, which, as they all knew by now, was only twenty-five minutes from Richmond.

'Well, that's a huge weight off my mind, so it is,' said Rhona, waving as her fellow passenger trotted off down the stairs. 'Head full o'mince, that one.'

Maureen curled her lip in agreement, stumped by her friend's affection for that pound shop Mary Poppins. What must she have been like to work with every day? According to Rhona, she'd been a secretary, or *administrative executive,* at Ashford Hospital. Sterling efficiency, no doubt, but an unapologetic gossip, never bloody shutting up. Like death by a thousand paper cuts.

'Actually, I might jump out here as well. I'm getting the messages from Waitrose.' Maureen nodded, baffled by her friend's vernacular. 'Before I forget, Emma needs articles for the Bulletin, so maybe you could do a piece on security in stately homes?'

'For the last time, I was only checking to see—'

'You keep telling yourself that, hun.' Rhona leant forward and patted Maureen's shoulder before climbing out. A little way off, she turned round to wag her finger, before merging into a rainbow sea of umbrellas.

Relieved, Maureen watched her go. Too drained for further chit-chat, she certainly lacked the energy to handle awkward questions. Turning into The Alberts, she offered up thanks to any hovering gods. Hey presto — a generous parking space in front of her cottage. A rare and blessed gift.

Blue Christmas lights flashed in frenetic sequence outside Ollie and Will's. Way too early, she thought. It's not even December yet. Pace yourself, boys. Before long, the season of goodwill would vomit down her street, and it would blaze with sparring fairy lights. Her heart sank at the prospect. She would simply dig out her silver pinecone wreath and tie it to her front door. She'd bought it years ago from the National Trust shop. A bargain, with her twenty per cent volunteer discount. Every year, it shed more artificial berries, but it served as a token gesture. Pointless trying to compete. After all, hers was the only cottage without the mock Edwardian tiled path.

'I'll *never* waste my cash on that,' she'd vented to her niece. Not that she had could afford it. 'Completely wrong period for these cottages. And as for the scourge of plantation shutters…'

The gate scraped the path as she pushed it open, and her wobbly picket fence seemed to flick the *V* to all the railings and neat brick walls down her street. She took a grim satisfaction in lowering the general twee factor, not to mention the house prices.

From the landing, a pair of yellow neon eyes checked her. Pepys slunk downstairs, picking his way round piles of books. His tail vertical, the moggy threaded and mewed round her ankles. Stooping to stroke his black and white fur, she grabbed a bunch of flyers. She skimmed pizza discounts, estate agents' brags and scam antique valuations, still reeling from what might have been; a certain madame zipped into her handbag, instead of pinned to the Green Closet's east wall. She shivered and clicked up the thermostat.

At the kitchen sink, she donned Marigolds, and ran piping hot water over her clenched fists, thawing her frozen fingertips. Enjoying a bonus facial steam, she recalled her mother's quip:

'With ice blocks like those, never mind the warm heart, you should be a pastry chef, so you should…'

Maureen believed that life was too short to make pastry, and truth be told, would have preferred higher blood pressure and non-reptilian hands. John had always likened them to mini glaciers, as they sought his warmth in bed. But that was a lifetime ago. The hit was already fading, and she peeled off the mildewed gloves.

Not long after, as Pepys crunched on some dry chicken bites, Maureen dipped stale bread into a bowl of soup. Not the most inspiring meal, but she was too distracted to care.

Right now, she could be dripping broth onto stolen artwork, as she ogled that mysterious *Unknown Lady* on her kitchen table. A gross insult to the court belle, and yet, an intoxicating thought.

Pepys leapt on to her lap, startling her out of her reverie, purring and kneading his claws into her stretch-waist trousers. Pushing her half-empty bowl aside, she opened her laptop, a birthday present from her niece. They'd been upgrading them at Laura's work — some fancy PR firm in the West End — and her boss had let her keep it.

When Laura had joked to Maureen's neighbours that her aunt would soon be silver surfing her way into the twenty-first century, Ollie and Will had insisted on giving her their Wi-Fi password. Most of the terraced cottages down their road had thin walls, so Maureen could easily access their broadband. 'After all,' Ollie had assured her, 'we pay the same whether you use it or not.' Perhaps they felt guilty about their noisy dinner parties. They needn't. Maureen really didn't mind the music and raucous laughter. It made her feel less alone. Mind you, she could have done without the frenzied yapping of their pug, Britney, who erupted whenever the postman, or some poor sod delivering leaflets, darkened their door.

Maureen had been touched by her niece's kindness but doubted that she would use the laptop. Resolute, Laura had set it all up for her, and with heroic calm, had shown her how to send emails, log onto websites and look up stuff. Pretty soon, Maureen wondered how she'd ever coped without the internet.

Laura had also made her join Facebook, much to Jodie's amusement, who sneered that she was about the right age for it. In truth, Maureen felt baffled by the whole concept of social media. Why did people feel the need to share every aspect of their lives? Showing off about where they could afford to eat, or go on holiday, right down to the more mundane: *A bird just shat on my washing and I've got a parking ticket #Ihatemondays, sad face.* It reminded her of her former infant school pupils, jostling for attention. It was almost as if an activity didn't count any more, unless everybody knew about it while you were actually doing it.

Maureen had become very close to her niece, since her beautiful Kathy had died of ovarian cancer, over a decade earlier. She still missed her outrageous big sis, so cruelly snatched before her sixtieth. No, not snatched. In the end, she'd starved to death. It had been slow and terrible.

Nor had she *passed away,* as everyone phrased it these days, in hushed tones, as if it was somehow distasteful. Kathy hadn't passed wind, or slipped into the room next door, like that nauseating poem. It's not nothing, seethed Maureen. Death is very much something, and newsflash — it's going to happen to us all, so fucking well call it by its proper name.

She pounded the keyboard and logged on to myvolunteering. Just on the off chance. She needed a plausible excuse, as she never room-guided on Fridays, and the lost earring ruse was too flimsy. Laura was right about the shoddy website — it took ages to load. Her heart sank; next day's rota was fully booked. Buggery bollocks. Her final chance down the swanny.

Idly, she checked out her *Unknown Lady* on HH Resources. Enamel on copper blah blah. As it turned out, said Lady wasn't anon, but had been pegged as the *beloved* sister of Charles II. *I bet she bloody loved dogs, and far from being insulted, would have been right up for a switch. Just temporary, of course. A covert prank.*

Sighing, she closed the tab and spotted a new email from Meera announcing that some specialist was gracing Ham House next week.

'We are delighted that Fothergill's Fine Art Gallery will be sharing their extensive expertise and that they will take the opportunity to inspect our renowned collection of miniatures in the Green Closet!'

Curious, she logged on to Fothergill's. Mesmerised by a

video of the debonair owner pacing through his triple floored gallery, showboating high-end landscapes, portraits and still lifes. Judging by some of the miniatures, her nearly acquired princess was worth a lot more than she'd thought. She chewed her lower lip. Possibly more than double.

She stared at the miniature portraits of brigadier generals, duchesses, vicomtes and actresses, advertised three in a row. Pairs of stern, dreamy, aloof and beseeching eyes all vied for her attention. Like some high-end Stuart or Queen Anne dating site.

That was it. Game over then. The Green Closet was closed from Monday, for the first-floor winter clean. And its contents were due to be inspected by boffins, who would instantly clock her dog-in-a-hat surrogate.

A very close shave indeed. Bless her pal, Rhona. What state would she be in now, if she really had enacted that ludicrous theft by deception challenge? She knew full well that some *spontaneous dare gone wrong* story wouldn't cut any mustard. And as if in reply, a catchphrase from Dad's Army, one of Jodie's favourite TV shows, popped into her head:

We're doomed! Doooomed.

She closed her laptop.

'Oh, do be quiet Frazer!' she said out loud to the empty kitchen.

Chapter 4
The Education Room
Tuesday, 28th November

Maureen had nailed a parking place overlooking the Cherry Garden. These days, the fretwork of privet hedges enclosed only santolina and lavender, which hummed with pollen-drunk bees in summer. Right in the centre, stood Bacchus, now masked by black thermal cladding to protect the decadent Roman god from frost damage. Like some puritanical edict against boozy parties. No more fun. Stick to the rules, or we'll send Thelma round.

As if coloured in by a child, the sky popped blue and cloudless between the House's umpteen chimneys. These rose tall and grandiose above the grey-slated roof, like the freestanding pillars of some ruined temple. Yet this sublime backdrop failed to lift her spirits today, as she trudged past skeletal lime trees, their naked twigs clawing the crisp air high above. On reaching the West Door, she pressed the buzzer, angling her face towards the doorbell camera, before the latch was finally released.

The staff entrance served as a cluttered porch. Gardening gloves and muddy walking boots abandoned near a fire extinguisher. Above a dormant, cast-iron radiator, a white cupboard secured the House keys. A ring binder lay perched on top. Staff were supposed to use this Key Log to record which keys they'd taken and when. No surprises, they didn't always bother, and the interim General Manager had cracked right down on such sloppiness. Hence her unofficial title, *The Enforcer.* Recently, Maureen had heard panicked radio requests for keys to the Library or Green Closet. Did all staff have access to the magic tabernacle, she wondered. What about room guides?

That bloody game of yours. Let it go, Maureen.

Well, allow me some fun, at least.

Mid-imaginary tiff with Rhona, she almost tripped on

some plastic shoe covers, discarded inches from the *CAUTION SLIPPERY FLOOR* sign. Cursing, she snatched them up, and stuffed them in a low shelving unit, which housed the signing-in book. Barbara always moaned about the broken pencils and lack of working pens provided. *All visitors must sign in and report to the duty manager upon arrival*, a sheet of A4 decreed. Maureen resented these *Polite Notices* or *Gentle Reminders*; their superfluous adjectives injected a menacing tone. Better to cut the crap with: *Do this right now or be kneecapped.*

'I mean, I get our visitor numbers aren't great for November, but we smashed half-term, despite the rain. Now Lorna insists that we hit our December targets. Falling short's not an option, whatever the weather throws at us.'

Emma continued to rant, as Maureen dithered outside the office door, in the gloomy West Passageway, like a delinquent waiting for the head teacher. Although, by the sounds of it, Lorna give-me-solutions-not-problems, filled that role.

'Insane,' soothed Meera. 'Is that why she's called a strategy meeting tomorrow?'

'Must be. How do they expect us to manage the volunteers, keep on track with the deep clean, and implement the Christmas programme, when we're so understaffed? I'm supposed to just fill in as House Manager, while they get round to interviewing. And I know I'm not in the running. Lorna can't stand me.'

'Not sure The Enforcer likes anyone.'

Giggling followed Meera's use of Lorna's nickname.

What am I doing? They need me, remember.

With that, Maureen pushed open the top half of the stable door. 'Sorry to interrupt.' She wasn't. 'I'm here to help with wrapping gifts for the Visit Father Christmas dates.'

'Oh, hi there.' Emma sprang into managerial mode. 'Cool, the more the merrier. Let me radio and find out where they are.'

As Emma shouted into her handset, Maureen stepped into the cramped office, noting the chaos. Loosely pinned lists flapped above desks strewn with files, torches, clipboards and half-eaten sarnies. On the floor, tangled tinsel spilled out from boxes, wedged against brollies and more stray boots.

'Hi, Kerry here. They're all down in the Education Room. Over.'

'Sounds ominous,' said Maureen.

Emma looked puzzled.

'You know, like they've been sent to Room 101.'

'No, the rooms aren't numbered, Maureen.' Emma's radio crackled again:

'It's Visitor Reception here. Thought you should know Lorna's just driven in. I repeat, The Enforcer is back. Over.'

Maureen pretended not to hear, as she closed both halves of the door behind her. She pretended not to see Emma sweep empty crisp packets and a tea-stained copy of OK! into the bin, then start hammering her keyboard, while Meera stapled piles of papers with impressive speed.

Outside, a guide was explaining to a visitor that the row of suspended leather buckets had served as a seventeenth-century fire extinguisher.

'But how did they get the buckets down?'

'With a long pole.'

'What, full of water?'

'Nooo.' The volunteer could barely disguise her impatience. 'They took the buckets down, *then* filled them with water.'

'I believe they contained sand,' said Maureen. She couldn't stop herself.

'But that would have made them even heavier…'

The Tuesday guide mouthed a sarcastic thanks, which Maureen returned with a fatuous smile, then retreated down the Passageway, through the Staff Only door.

Turning right down the remaining wooden stairs, she opened another hefty door to the Basement. As she crossed the flagstones, she could hear Sanjay in the Kitchen, blaring his Below The Stairs tour.

'…important guests, such as King Charles II, dined at Ham. The chef was expected to display his skills, and justify his huge annual wage of around thirty-seven pounds… a cardboard ship sailing on seas of salt, firing canons with real gun powder… red wine pouring from an arrow in the side…'

The dim Basement with its uneven, grubby walls, was one of the warmest parts of the House. Doubtless due to the insulation provided by said thick walls, the low ceilings and general lack of ventilation. Which explained the flaking plaster and damp. She pushed open the door to the Education Room. Straight on to Rhona, who, plate of iced gingerbread Christmas trees in hand, was serenading off-key:

'Stille Nacht, heilige Nacht
Alles schläft, einsam wacht
Nur das traute hochhei—'

'Ssh,' Maureen hissed. 'Sanjay's doing a Basement tour.'

Rhona dismissed this with a wave, exposing sticky tape along the sleeve of her Fair Isle jumper.

'Shut the door then pet. So here's the thing — the only German I can remember from school, is the whole of Stille Nacht. Except, *meinen Vater ist sehr dick*. I remember our teacher saying, *Rhona, you're just gauny have to get used to the German for father…'*

'Sellotape,' ordered Barbara, pressing an orange manicured finger on a flap of winter woodland paper. Judging from the stacks on the grimy tablecloth, this year Santa was doling out colouring-in books and mini felt tips. Rhona complied by ripping a piece of tape off her sleeve to free Barbara's finger.

'Now there's fluff stuck to it.'

'Like the kids are going to notice. Or care.'

At a loose end, Maureen had offered to help, following an appeal in the latest HH Bulletin. This had featured some out-of-focus shots of the sparkly Christmas tree in the Great Hall. There slouched Sanjay, sporting the obligatory red suit and straggly white cotton wool beard, looking about as enthusiastic as a pupil on detention. Plus, some faux cheery updates from the Head Gardener and Visitor Experience Manager. The latter, Kerry, squeezed in the most exclamation marks, in a vain attempt to convey how the House was *buzzing* with excitement at the arrival of Father Christmas. They were all urged to keep their eyes peeled for him in the Mess Room, *as even Santa is entitled to a break!* The final year's round-up came from Emma, as acting House Manager, with her loaded sign-off:

'I think one of the biggest success stories has been the House team's sheer tenacity to keep going and remain so positive, no matter what this year has thrown at them!'

Finally, *a very warm invitation* from the GM. Once again, the surplus adjective made it sound like a veiled threat. This was captioned with a mugshot of Lorna's unsmiling, contoured face. More sinister than cuddly, in her festive hat.

'Wishing you all a very happy Christmas, and hope to see as many of you as possible…'

All absentees will be noted.

'…at the volunteers' Christmas Party — one of our calendar's highlights…'

It's a right pain in the backside.

Beneath the Basement bay, someone had dumped a crate stuffed with broken crayons, dried glue sticks, scraps of paper and empty egg cartons. Outrage had erupted amongst the arts and crafts volunteers, when The Enforcer had banned loo roll tubes, in case of residual germs. As if they were donated smeared in faeces. Health and safety gone mad, people whinged. Honestly, what was wrong with a dose of cholera and the odd tapeworm, for goodness' sake? Everything's too clean these days. No one had allergies when we were kids. *No, they just snuffed it.*

'Maureen, can you make a start on the rubber ducks?'

Aware the question was entirely rhetorical, Maureen

pulled up a wobbly chair.

'Note how Babs is giving you the awkward ones to wrap,' quipped Rhona, through a mouthful of gingerbread.

'Note how Rhona is busy stuffing her face and not helping.'

'Aye well, a certain control freak told me that I wasn't folding the paper right. So, Yours Truly is providing snacks, sticky tape and entertainment.'

Maureen lacked the will to join in so, like Switzerland, she remained neutral and focused on wrapping the inconveniently-shaped toys. Usually, she was buoyed by the camaraderie. Usually, this damp, dingy servants' hall, with its peeling paint and exposed brick, took on a warm, homely feel. After all, this was where the junior servants had eaten. A modest little sanctuary with its Spode Chinese Rose tea set, brass candlesticks and copper kettle glinting on the dresser. Maureen liked to imagine that they had moaned and gossiped by the cavernous stone fireplace, snatching brief respites from their daily grind. But today, she just wasn't in the mood. She felt restless, somehow. Scratchy.

Deirdre burst in, heaving a cotton tote. Maureen's heart plummeted. She couldn't face that woman's perverse cheerfulness right now.

'Looks like you've cleared out the gift shop, right enough,' observed Rhona, tearing off more sticky tape.

'The crackers are great this year. They're themed on the Twelve Days of Christmas. And I bought this sweet bark candleholder. Look, it's decorated with cherubs.' Rhona pulled a face, as she extracted the hideous item. Undaunted, Deirdre continued.

'Plus, I bought this silver pinecone garland, some holly tea towels, with some matching oven gloves for Gary. He's on Turkey Watch. And this advent calendar was reduced…'

Maureen felt obliged to fake murmurs of approval, which only increased her ill humour. Especially as Rhona remained silent. Barbara's only contribution:

'Thirsty work all that Christmas shopping.'

About as subtle as a falling lump of plaster.

'Good idea. Would anyone like some tea?'

After double-checking the various orders, Deirdre scooted down the long, dreary passage to the Mess Room. Barbara also nipped out to *spend a penny*.

'How does Deirdre do it?' Maureen griped. Adding, in response to Rhona's raised eyebrows, 'Her glass isn't just half full, it's spilling over. She must be on something.'

Nobody was that happy. It was exhausting.

'Come on, she's no that bad. What's up with you?'

For once, her friend's reliable bullshit detector was switched to standby. While Rhona never dialled back with Deirdre, Maureen had noticed that she was also weirdly protective of her. True, they had been at Ham a few years longer than her, and she knew opposites could also attract in platonic friendships, but still she wondered at their tight bond.

As ever, she began to overthink it. Deirdre was harmless enough, she supposed. Yet she found her neatness, her incessant cheerfulness, all so cloying. Probably even her farts smelled like synthetic air freshener. Did she resent Deirdre's affinity with her Scottish pal? Perhaps Rhona's wicked vitality helped fill the Kathy-sized hole in her life. Rhona sorted the remaining gifts into neat piles, ruffling her pixie cut. Maureen often marvelled how she made her silver hair look on trend. But then, among her many former lines of work, including TV props manager and fundraising for various kids' charities, she had once been a hairdresser. Any client dumb enough to wave a picture of some actress's glossy locks, always incurred the classic Rhona riposte:

'I've got scissors, hun, not a scalpel.'

Impossible not to love her.

Enter Barbara, with freshly backcombed perm, who freed Maureen from her own private Inquisition.

And soon, the four women were ensconced in a present-wrapping production line round the PVC tablecloth, slurping diverse hues of caffeine. All talking over one another. Or rather, Barbara, as self-elected supervisor, interrupted Deirdre's babbling with curt instructions, while Rhona delivered acid one-liners and despite everything, Maureen tried not to spit out her tea. In what seemed like no time, they were tackling the final pile of snow globes and dinosaur stickers.

'Of course, now my daughter's vegan,' Deirdre went on, 'I'll do a nut roast, while Gary sorts out the turkey. I'm thinking cranberry and pistach —'

'Jamie Oliver?' asked Barbara.

'Yes, I found it on his web—'

'Sellotape, Rhona.'

'Sorry Your Grace. I do apologise for the delay. Won't happen again.'

'Does your daughter always come over for Christmas lunch?' Maureen interjected, wearily assuming her role of UN ambassador.

'Not every year. But she really wants to be with us this Christmas, as it's twenty years since Jack…'

Deirdre trailed off, appearing to scrutinise a miniature T. Rex. Brows knitted, Rhona leaned towards her friend. Even Barbara paused in her paper folding.

'Since… Well, since my son died.'

She looked up at last, her knuckles white from gripping the table. More terrible silence.

'Dee, why didn't you tell me it's the twentieth anniversary?'

No sarcasm in Rhona's tone now. Deirdre didn't register the question, just stared ahead and smiled.

'Such a handsome lad, my Jack. All the girls fancied him. Took a gap year, went travelling in South America with his best friend.' She faltered. 'Their plane crashed in Peru. They wanted to see the Nazca Lines. Jack loved history. He was so excited that…'

She peered into the depths of her *KEEP CALM AND DRINK TEA* mug, as if searching for the end of her sentence. Maureen also found herself unable to speak. Rhona squeezed Deidre's hand. And Barbara rooted in her bag for a tissue. Then Sanjay flung open the door and flopped onto a creaking chair.

'Well, that lot were hard work. Not sure about my Visitor Enjoyment feedback. And you saw I'm roped into being Father Christmas? Kerry made me an offer I couldn't refuse. Just need to find some elves. Any offers?'

He puffed out his cheeks, swiped the last gingerbread tree, and finally, sensing the tension, glanced round at the seated women. His nervous crunching reverberated round the flagstones. Mouthful of biscuit, he asked, 'Er, have I in—'

'I'll be an elf,' Deirdre piped up, moist eyes lit with a manic grin.

'Excellent,' said Sanjay, relieved that normal service had resumed.

Indeed, they all beat a hasty retreat into light banter. They finished wrapping the last of the toys, while Deirdre listed the best places to buy green tights, and which denier would be most suitable for an elf. Maureen avoided eye contact. All too aware of the agony of loss, she winced at her earlier spite. Two empty mugs in each hand, she fled the Education Room, which had once again adopted its mantel of forlorn drabness.

Chapter 5

Press for Champagne and Ibuprofen

Wednesday, 29th November

She didn't often drink during the day, but Laura was treating her to lunch. It was one of those swanky restaurants where Maureen felt she could happily take up residence in the palatial, mosaic-floored loos.

Set into the wall of their leather-upholstered booth, gleamed a brass button, labelled *PRESS FOR CHAMPAGNE*. Laura insisted it would be rude not to. As if by magic, a pink-jacketed waiter materialised with a bottle in an ice bucket. It washed the duck shepherd's pie down nicely. The brass lamp-lit interior kindled a touch of Orient Express in the heart of Soho, and Maureen relished its obscene opulence. She half expected to see that rotund Belgian detective tap his cane past their table, as those Brut bubbles tingled on her tongue, turning her little grey cells muzzy. She focused back on her niece, who was scowling at her phone.

'Sorry,' Laura plonked it, screen down on the gold-edged table. 'Some needy client chucking his toys out the pram. I'll let him stew.'

Raised right eyebrow, same devastating bone structure, it could be Kathy leaning forward to whisper that a certain famous actor was being fêted in the booth behind them.

'Just been caught playing away.'

'Plus ça change.'

Laura had triumphed over adversity, as Maureen often liked to remind her. A year ago, she'd been promoted to senior account manager. Not bad for a single mother. Kathy had never lived to see her granddaughter, or even hear about her existence as a bunch of fast multiplying cells. Laura had only discovered she was pregnant just before her mother died. The day after the funeral, she'd made an appointment for a termination, having already split with the embryo's father. He'd promised to support her no matter what. This entailed flying back to his well-heeled girlfriend in New York, to resume his role as creative director for some leading ad agency. In the end, Laura had decided that a baby would be the best antidote to grief. Unlike that spineless bullshit merchant, Maureen had never once voiced her misgivings but promised she'd be there to help. At the very least, she'd owed it to Kathy.

Maureen had no children of her own. In her twenties, a doctor had declared her fallopian tubes as blocked, or *incompetent.* In response to his stern interrogation of her sexual history, she'd been tempted to tell him that she was on the game but had recently upped her prices. Instead, she heard herself thank him on her way out. Reeling. Although, more surprised than bereft, as she still had periods, albeit irregular. Kathy, who'd suffered several miscarriages before Laura, had been more upset, despite Maureen's reassurance that she spent every day teaching snotty-nosed brats, and was more than happy to escape child-free at the end of the day.

'Christ, I have my fill of the little buggers at school,' she had told John afterwards. His arm round her, swearing that it changed nothing. But in the very next twinkling of his eye, he'd upped and left her for a more fertile prospect — a cheap blonde with unfortunate ankles. In quick succession, her sub, Brenda, supplied the requisite son and daughter. The last she'd heard, they had moved to a semi-d in New Malden, where she liked to imagine they all bored each other shitless.

After John, there'd been a steady succession of men. Well, it was the 1970s, and while the Pill had become available to unmarried women, it wasn't as if she had to worry about contraception. But those racy encounters failed to exorcise her inner void.

Maureen had acquired a certain reputation down her road. Many an Austrian blind had twitched when she'd performed that dishevelled walk of shame, stumbling over the flares of her lamé jumpsuit. Not that she cared. It all just stopped being fun. Her boyfriends became controlling bores, and the sex no longer interested her, despite her faked enthusiasm. Most of all, they weren't John. Their embraces lacked real comfort. They didn't brew their own beer and she missed his woody scent of hops. They didn't wash her hair in the bath or make her laugh. Plus, the albatross of her infertility weighed heavy, so she always ended it before things became too intense. Anything to avoid *that* conversation.

One or two had even asserted their needs without her consent. Since when did a drunken floozy tell a man what to do? Pushy tarts needed to learn their place. Even now, there was a small piece of her that felt culpable for those unspeakable violations. That she had somehow deserved it. There were no more men after that.

Yet all those years later, when her furious great-niece catapulted into the stark glare of the delivery room, Maureen couldn't deny that this hairy froglet had plugged the cavernous, barren hole in her own life.

Increasingly frustrated by the endless box-ticking, Maureen decided to give up teaching when Jodie reached six months, so Laura could return to work part-time. Like the proverbial iceberg, retirement had been looming ever nearer anyway, and the sociopathic new head could barely contain his delight. To him, Maureen was an unmalleable, mouldy old fart, who refused to abide by lesson plans. Behind the times and naïve. Doggedly fixed on stoking the imagination of curious young minds, irrespective of the school's ranking. Maureen was more than happy to swap shitty nappies for *quick chats* with that patronising prick in his shiny suit and slicked-back hair.

And now, another life-changing projectile had been launched in her direction. Laura had been offered another promotion. But that was great news. Wasn't it? Why hadn't she accepted it yet? Oh. Maureen's stomach contracted. Now she understood. The position was based in their New York office. Dear mother of God, no. Not that. She grasped that Laura was waiting for her to speak.

'Well? What do you think, Auntie? Be honest with me now.'

Her niece folded and smoothed the linen napkin, her black gel nails glistening in the lamplight. But before Maureen could digest this bombshell, and gather her thoughts into some coherent reply, Laura blurted:

'You've been so good to us. Couldn't have coped without you. We'd really miss you, but you can come and stay with us any time. You must. Just such a good offer, and it would give Jodie a chance to see more of her father.'

How often had Maureen dreamt of storming into his swanky Manhattan office, to scream one of her favourite Angela Carter lines at him: *There's more to fathering than fucking!*

'Of course you must take the job. Wonderful opportunity for you both.'

Despite her best effort, she heard the brittle note in her congratulations, as she toasted her niece's impending move to The Big Apple. This time, it was Maureen who pressed the Champagne button.

* * *

Later, on automatic pilot, she descended to the Piccadilly Line, gripping an old, wooden tennis racket. Laura had handed over Kathy's *lucky* racket after lunch. Still in its faded Dunlop case, she had unearthed it going through some boxes, designating their contents for storage or charity shop. 'Mum would have wanted you to have this.'

Scaling the ranks of the County Ladies' Doubles, Kathy had been obsessed with tennis. What was the name of her partner back then? When it came to sports, Maureen had been the polar opposite of her big sister, and tennis bored the pants off her. Although, talking of which, she did have a thing for that ice cool Swede, Björn Borg, back in the day; piercing eyes that bit too close together, flowing blonde locks tamed with his trademark stripy headband. He'd definitely made Wimbledon worth watching.

She changed over to the District Line in a wobbly daze, dodging the fractious museum school outings on the platform at South Ken. From the many school trips that she'd overseen, she knew only too well how an insidious out-of-class delirium took root, but her whirring head eclipsed all empathy for the frazzled teachers, counting and recounting their mutinous charges. Lost in the 1970s, she caressed the brown leather-bound grip. Fiddling with the zip, she noticed a white corner of paper poking out from the case.

A square, blurry snap of two tanned women on a sun-drenched tennis court. Maureen's sister on the left, blonde ponytail thrown back in laughter, her sleeveless tennis dress indecently short. The other woman in a sun visor, smiling up at Kathy through oversized shades. Sifting through dusty memory files, Maureen couldn't recall the brunette's name, or even having met her. Outside of teaching, Maureen had been too busy partying to pay much attention to her sister's sporting prowess. *The Dream Team* was scrawled on the back and underneath, the letter *K*, with a short horizontal line scored atop its vertical spine, like some bizarre cult symbol. Maureen studied the yellow photo some more before zipping it back into the case, but the image of the smirker in her polo shirt and mid-thigh skirt, only faded as the train drew into Richmond.

Back home, after downing a glass of water, she spied a voicemail and listened to Jodie's breathless gush: *living in New York's gonna be sick… all my friends are dead jelly… it's been like so hard to keep quiet 'til mum told you…* And Maureen felt her heart plunge to the very soles of her balding moccasins. She couldn't face calling back right now. Couldn't trust herself to sound sufficiently upbeat. Instead, waiting for a caffeine and Ibuprofen cocktail to work its magic, she collapsed in front of *The Chase.*

Unable to focus on The Governess hounding Rory, Nu and Alans' seventeen step lead, her mind strayed from the red-lipped sangfroid of Anne Hegerty, back into the playground for school pickup.

* * *

'Anyone not bought tickets for the Denim, Diamonds and Dallas night?' a PTA fascist barked at the wary huddles of parents and childminders.

'Think I'd rather chew razorblades,' muttered Maureen.

A nearby mum in joggers and wedge trainers spat out laughter.

'Sorry?' said the ticket tout, looking anything but.

'Think I better check with Laura.'

Swishing fiercely ironed hair, the PTA rep stalked off to menace a hollow-eyed woman, leaning on a pushchair, stuffed with nappy sacks and empty juice cartons, oblivious to the seated toddler pushing a Wotsit up his nose.

'You're Jodie's gran, right?' asked Ms Wedge Trainers. 'She says you work at Ham House. Love that place.'

Maureen had started volunteering there a year or so back, on one of her childcare-free *days-off* and had grown to love that place too.

'Actually, I'm—'

'Hi Tamara,' a trouser-suited woman raced towards them. 'They not out yet?' she said, catching her breath. 'Parked on a double yellow…'

Maureen was always happy to leave her granny status uncorrected. Equally happy to opt out of playground politics: the fierce one-upmanship on reading book levels and after school clubs, the standard catwalk bitching:

'I mean, has she dyed her hair for Comic Relief?'

'Does she get dressed in the dark?'

'He's a bit lush. How did she score him?'

Despite her childfree status, not long into her teaching career, Maureen considered that Sartre had got it wrong. Now, waiting the other side of the classroom door, she knew she was bang on. Hell is other parents.

'Auntie!'

Jumping up and down, her great niece often grassed up her infertility. But rounding the corner, as Jodie squeezed her hot little hand into hers and asked her to do the voices of her favourite toys —Monkey and Stripy Cat — Maureen cared not one jot.

* * *

And your time is up… Team, well played, Bradley was congratulating the trio on their fourteen-grand win. Maureen switched off the sour-faced Governess, and pressed *Call Jodie* on her phone.

'Hey.' Loud music, long pause.

'Bad time?'

'Perfect time. Doing my English homework.' Long exhale.

'What's it on?'

Longer pause. In the background, a girl whispered over bass drums that she was a baaad guy, interposed with a camera click.

'Sorry, Auntie, couldn't break my snapchat streak. Me and Melina have reached 377!'

Melina and I.

'Impressive.'

Maureen was entirely clueless on this front, but didn't want to spoil the moment.

'So, I've got this essay on Macbeth. Oh my God, Shakespeare is such a snooze fest. Like every word 'sposed to have five meanings. Bet even he didn't know that. Most of it wasn't written by him anyway.'

Maureen laughed. 'Well, put that in your essay then.'

'Serious?'

'You can pretty much say anything, so long as you back it up. But Macbeth's a good one, no? Blood, ghosts, witches.'

'I guess,' Jodie yawned. 'Thought you didn't believe in ghosts?'

'I don't, but they're still fun.'

'You doing any ghost tours at Ham House?'

'Of course. Want to come on my next one?'

'Er, no way, freaked me out last time. Hope you're looking after my blackbird painting.'

'Don't worry, it's safe in the Green Closet.'

'What's it worth?'

'Not sure. A lot. Why? Are you planning to steal it?'

Jodie converted her giggle into a groan.

'Kill me now, I've got to finish this essay. At least I'll miss seeing Macbeth. Haaate the theatre. We'll be in New York by then.'

'I know. How exciting.'

'Super cool. Except, mum's stressing out all the time. Like shouting at me, over literally nothing. And we've been given sooo much homework. Not fair, cos mum says I still have to do it. Like, why? She won't even help me with my French — just keeps saying *check your adjectival endings*. God, French is *the* worst.'

'Would you like me to do it?'

'Omg, that would be amazing.'

'Sure, send it over.'

'You're the best. You're… *too full o'the milk of human kindness*.'

'Nice. See; you've nailed Macbeth.'

Another pause. 'Just sent it.'

'I won't correct it all — that's a big giveaway. I'll do it now. But listen, not a word to your mum.'

'You're a queen. And Auntie…'

'Yes?'

'Gonna miss you.'

'I'll miss you too, sweetheart.'

Like you wouldn't believe.

Chapter 6

Best Unsung Hero
Wednesday, 6th December

Soon after hours, darkness obscured the Gardens. Welcome shards of light radiated from the Orangery, now rammed with volunteers. They descended on the catering staff like a flock of gannets, stripping white plates of squash tartlets and cranberry brownies at breakneck speed.

'I'll have me some dainty wee pieces.' Rhona grabbed a plate of finger sandwiches from the hot new café assistant. 'I'm awful parched. Any mulled wine left, son?'

'Yes, but it's going fast,' the Adonis advised from under long lashes.

'I'll grab us some,' said Maureen.

'Let me give you a hand,' said Deirdre, trying to detach a snowman earring from her scarf

Mouthful of white bread and salmon, Rhona parked herself on a stool, claiming its neighbour with her orange puffa. 'I best stay here then. Oh, hiya Babs.'

Untoggling her duffle coat, Maureen left Rhona wrestling a plate of sausage rolls from Barbara's iron grip. Yet again, Barbara's lippy an identical shade to her espresso-tinted hair. Meanwhile, Deirdre, still fiddling with her earring, remained glued to the spot.

In the main doorway, Maureen spotted Carmella, a former Thursday guide, who now did Tuesdays to accommodate an art course. Tantamount to pure treachery in Barbara's book. Kitted out in silk blouse and velvet flares, Carmella stood out from the scrum of matching coats and scarves — also useful for masking turkey neck. Most adopted the practical uniform of jeans and fleece, with the odd bomber or leather jacket thrown in. Rhona fell into this last camp, while Maureen went old school with tweed, cashmere and Eau de Mothballs.

By contrast, Carmella exuded jasmine and myrrh. She branded Maureen's cheeks with lip gloss. 'You look well, but why don't you dye your hair? Take years off you mia cara and it would bring out your eyes. I'd recommend Gino at Colour Lab.' She breezed past. 'A dopo.'

Talk about a shit sandwich. Pretty sure I couldn't afford Gino. And I can't be arsed to dye my hair, but maybe she has a point.

In the main café, Maureen bumped into Kerry, a walking cactus face with a Christmas pud beanie. In a tepid exchange, Kerry asked how her first Christmas ghost tour had gone, eyes sweeping the room for someone, anyone, more important. Before Maureen could reply, Kerry shot off towards Lorna — every inch The Enforcer, in black jacket, jeans and boots.

Glowering after her, Maureen turned and elbowed her way through the sweaty hordes. At the counter, a pink-haired handed waitress doled out a glass of liquid carmine, swimming with cloves and orange peel.

'Maureen!' Sanjay beckoned her over. He looked older with uncharacteristic silver stubble and hunched shoulders. Ironic, given that his jumbo cord trousers and plaid shirt were now hipster apparel. Possibly not the penguin tank top. According to Deirdre, his wife no longer always recognised him when he went to visit her. But tonight, at least, he was in his element, regaling his elves with some Santa horror stories.

'Can you believe it? She handed it straight back and said, *we don't give plastic to our children.* Bet she drives one of those huge Chelsea tractors. I told her the ducks were biodegradable.'

A diminutive elf shook her head in mock rebuke. 'But the NT claims to be fully eco these days, so maybe she had a point.'

'Well, they were a right bugger to wrap, let me tell you,' said Maureen, flinching at the mulled wine, which tasted like some vile herbal tea.

'On the subject of box-ticking,' Sanjay lowered his voice. 'I heard they're gonna stop us parking on-site.'

'You are kidding. There'll be a volunteers' revolt,'

gasped Elf One.

'Orders from Head Office, so reckon it's a done deal. Although of course,' Sanjay paused to make air quotes, 'they'll *consult* us. Then completely ignore our responses.'

Noises of solidarity.

'That'll be tricky for me,' said Elf Two. 'My osteoporosis makes long walks quite painful.'

Elf Three piped up, 'I mean, look at our average age. Some of us won't be able to come anymore. And Ham House is such a lifeline.'

'Don't I know it,' said Sanjay under his breath.

'Suppose they have to be seen to do the right thing,' Maureen sighed, 'but it is a longer hike, especially from the bus stop. Not much fun on a dark, rainy afternoon in winter. Most of us car share anyway.'

'Just greenwashing, with some health and safety chucked in.' Sanjay slurped the dregs from his glass, splodging crimson down his penguin's white abdomen. 'They're happy enough to allow huge lorries and trailers on site when they're filming.'

There was more chat about the latest Trust edicts and rumoured redundancies. Uninterested in their conspiracy theories, Maureen manoeuvred a tray of dribbling glasses back down the corridor.

'…and Meera made a big song and dance about giving out hand warmers, but they don't last long. And the House was dead. All rather pointless.' Barbara wiped some cream cheese from the corner of her mouth. As Rhona distributed the plonk, Maureen finally shed her duffle, then wolfed one of the remaining sausage rolls.

Raucous peals exploded from the neighbouring table.

'Typical snowflake generation,' roared Nigel, his double-chin wobbling above his wax jacket.

'What's he blethering on about now?' Rhona shook her head. 'Mind you, that Friday lot are lapping it up. Can't understand why, he's such a prick.'

'He's not that bad,' said Barbara. 'He just—'

'Likes the sound of his own voice?' suggested Rhona. 'Thinks he's the cat's pyjamas, that one.'

'Those Friday guides are so cliquey.' Barbara turned her chair to face away from Nigel's red-denimed manspreading. His fan club spewing tripe like, 'I mean, we all coped, didn't we?' And 'Women just want it all these days. Haven't we got enough now?'

Rhona curled her hands into mock strangulation.

'Hello everyone. Er, if I could just have your attention…'

Emma stood at the top of the steps leading into the snug, clutching her hand-held microphone. Over Chrissie Hynde warbling *2000 Miles* on a festive playlist, she thanked them all for coming, over-egging how great it was to see 'so many familiar faces.'

Beside her, Lorna stood poised. Watchful. A smiling assassin. Emma handed the mic to her boss, who received token applause, rings clinking on glasses.

'Thank you, Emma,' withering smile, 'can we turn the music off now?'

Hush imposed, Lorna launched forth, while Maureen dialled in and out.

'It has been an absolute privilege getting to know you all…'

'On the odd occasion I've seen her, she can't wait to skedaddle back to her office,' Rhona hissed.

'…some exciting changes in the New Year…'

'I can hardly contain myself,' Maureen whispered back.

'...announcements to follow shortly…'

Emma and Meera exchanged glances.

Barbara shook her head. 'Here we go again — some new manager with a big idea and suddenly it's all change. Do you remember that hideous red sculpture they put up in the Gardens last year?'

'…delighted to announce we're acquiring another very special portrait of our Duchess, Elizabeth Murray. This one painted by Elizabeth's friend, Joan Carlile, one of the first British female professional artists. It currently hangs in Thirlestane Castle, which as I'm sure you all know, was the Duke's Scottish residence. In return, they get our Bosschaert — the *Blackbird, Butterfly and Cherries.*'

What? But we've already got a Joan Carlile portrait of Elizabeth in the Back Parlour. Why the hell do we need another one?

'… like a stately home, fine art game of Pokémon!'

Maureen looked around. Apart from some forced laughter — mainly from staff — nobody seemed in the least phased by this travesty. More concerned with refills and leftovers. In dire need of her own sugary solace, Maureen pounced on a lone mince pie, stranded among the crumbs and scrunched napkins.

This is Ham House's legacy, not some stupid game! You can't just evict my favourite painting like that. Chrissakes, I promised to keep an eye on it for Jodie.

Maureen wrestled an urge to sweep crockery on to the floor.

'This unique exchange takes place in March,' Lorna continued. 'You'll be aware, Thirlestane Castle isn't owned by us, but all Ham House volunteers can get free entry for one year.'

I'm basically never going to see it again.

'We could go visit some time,' said Rhona, alive to her friend's fury.

Okay, so maybe once before I die.

'That'd be fun, but I'm not sure,' said Deirdre, cheeks flushed, empty glass.

'How no?' said Rhona, jerking her head towards Maureen.

'Well, it is quite a trek.'

Maureen licked her fingers, while Lorna droned on with further announcements: a few days' closure for a big filming project in the New Year, some new displays, and various half-baked ideas to increase footfall.

'More importantly, we'll be looking at ways of breaking

down barriers, making Ham relevant to *all* parts of our local communities and in general, broadening our visitor and volunteer profile…'

Still smouldering, Maureen was only snapped out of it by a sharp elbow from Rhona. 'Aye, we could do with some more colour round here, right enough. Apart from Sanjay, we're a sea of pasty old stagers. Brace yourself. For what we are about to receive.' She crossed herself before resuming Word Trip on her phone.

'Now we come to *your* favourite part of the evening,' Lorna couldn't have sounded less interested. 'The volunteer awards.'

Deirdre had spent the whole journey speculating on the likely contenders. An expectant hum rose round the Orangery, particularly from the non-designated drivers.

The stilted ceremony began. Although, the first prize recipient elicited loud cheers: Best Tour Guide was awarded to Sanjay. He returned, clutching a jar of Gooseberry & Coriander Chutney, his back straighter, and grinning like a Cheshire cat. Deirdre, who sometimes helped in the shop, patted his arm. 'Nice. We always sell out of that one.'

The applause for Best Pop-Up Talks was more muted. A ruddy-faced Nigel waved a jar of horseradish in the air, and like Buster Gonad, strutted back to his groupies.

'Best Tube, more like,' said Rhona.

Next up, Carmella tottered up to collect Best Dressed Guide. Despite Thelma's wolf whistle, many of the women appeared less effusive. Barbara's hands remained glued to her sides.

'Well, she does always look fit, but not the most PC category,' observed Rhona.

In a brazen display of Continental affection, Thelma congratulated her glam young friend with several light kisses on each cheek. Carmella whispered something in Thelma's ear, who turned to smirk at her confidante.

Now that the wine had dried up, the mob were restless.

People talked over the announcements. A tall, wiry man from the property care team, received only cursory acclaim for his graft as Best Miracle Worker.

'I've been told this next award goes to someone who can always be relied on to step in at the last moment, a safe pair of hands in a crisis. So last, but by no means least, it's my great honour to award Best Unsung Hero to …'

Rhona eyed her empty glass. 'Get on with it.'

'… to…' Lorna peered at her list. 'Maureen Goodwin?'

Rhona whooped over the table-banging. After a shove from Sanjay, Maureen made her way up to the steps in a daze. She half expected Lorna to tell her this was a joke, some unfortunate mix-up. But she handed Maureen a prize, her red lips moulded into her trademark eat-shit smile, while behind her, Emma and Meera clapped hard. The Alice In Wonderland effect fuelled by Lorna's stiff hug, and a whispered command to 'keep up the good work.'

'Waddya get, waddya get?' asked Rhona when, after multiple slaps on the back, she returned to their corner.

'Em.' Maureen read the label at arms' length. 'Chocolate honey spread.'

'Sounds disgusting.'

Barbara, as usual, full of the joys.

'No trust me, it's sheer heaven,' said Deirdre.

Maureen didn't care what was in the jar. She'd never been picked for anything in her life, apart from first prize in a school poetry competition. Without fail, Maureen had been the penultimate choice for any rounders or netball teams. Always her and the generous sized girl with the sweaty upper lip. But in the Orangery that evening, there was no prospect of Fat Pat status. No longer insignificant, or a burden, she was aware of a sensation that she hadn't experienced in a long time. She felt esteemed. Wanted. And for now, she glossed over the *Blackbird's* northern migration and basked in this warm alien glow.

Despite the clattering of smeared glasses and plates

being cleared away, the volunteers showed no inclination to leave. If anything, the volume crescendoed, as it bounced off latticed windows and the grimy floor. Lorna, who'd been working the room at full pelt, was forced to interact with the Thursday crew, blocking her escape route. After congratulating herself for a successful do, Lorna glanced at her smart watch, and announced that she had an urgent appointment, as if she'd been summoned to a COBRA meeting.

'Surely you don't have to go back to work now?'

A maternal edge to Deirdre's incredulity.

'This *is* work.' Lorna replied, unsmiling.

'At least you get paid for yours.'

In the ensuing frosty silence, Maureen both berated and lauded herself for thinking out loud. Although really, she wanted to scream that Lorna would be swimming with the fishes if she dared lay one finger on her Bosschaert.

'Are you turning into me?' enquired Rhona, after the bristling Enforcer had bolted, not unlike a pantomime villain.

After being turfed out of the Orangery, Sanjay once more commended Maureen on her award.

'Well, you definitely can't steal anything now.' His plump finger in her face. 'I was just telling the others about your Christmas lunch game, but that's off the menu. You've got a new accolade to live up to.'

As they strolled towards the terrace's arched gate, he started badgering her about a petition for on-site parking. As luck would have it, she'd forgotten her trophy. Doubling back in the hoary shadows, she swerved round the dawdling clusters. Unseen, she slipped past Nigel pontificating to Barbara down the corridor. Maureen snatched up her prize, then pulled up sharp by the doorway, ears pricked, much like Pepys at Britney's approaching snuffle.

'Who, Maureen?' Loud bellows from Nigel. 'Barely got the gumption to get herself out the House in the event of fire, let alone nick something from the Collection. She probably thinks you can just lift a painting off the wall. As if they wouldn't be attached with some anti-theft, springlock device. Let's face it, that old bag couldn't wangle a piss-up at Majestic Wine, never mind pull off a fine art heist!'

'Well quite,' simpered Barbara. 'And as for that award, I wouldn't mind, but she doesn't exactly contribute much. Apart from the odd stale tour. I mean, she's such an airhead. So insipid, and frankly, I fail to see how she landed the votes.'

'Reckon they felt sorry for the poor cow…'

Maureen had heard enough and darted out, head down. Gloating over Nigel's misogynist ignorance and Barbara's sour grapes of envy. If they only knew how close she'd come to walking out with some *lifted* fine art in her handbag, it would blow their tiny little minds.

In your jowly face, Nigel.

It had turned out a memorable evening. Half an hour later, Maureen deposited Deirdre at Richmond Station. Soon after, she dropped Rhona back to her yellow-bricked Victorian semi, on the lower slopes of Richmond Hill. Her friend once more insisting that Maureen come over for Christmas lunch, seeing as Laura and Jodie were flying out just before.

'Here's the thing. My eldest is off skiing with his lemon, and the Prodigal will be smoking weed on Bondi Beach. That'll leave me and David rattling round our manor like a pair of wee Krankies.'

Maureen's brother-in-law, Frank, had also invited her. But this meant enduring the strained joviality of his latest girlfriend, while the master chef sulked at the head of the oak table. Frank, claiming he'd overcooked the turkey, thanks to that mockney Jamie knob, when he should have listened to the soft porn queen of cuisine, Nigella. Steadily drowning himself in brandy, in a futile attempt to douse his rage at Kathy's absence. She couldn't face it this year, so Maureen grabbed her inebriated pal's lifebuoy with wholehearted thanks.

As Rhona wobbled up the steps to her front door, she turned and held a fist to her ear, extending her thumb and little finger, then waved as Maureen hooted and drove off. Again, she experienced that peculiar tingling. The neurons in her brain firing in an unfamiliar sequence, venturing down an overgrown pathway, creating that luscious, chocolate honey sensation of feeling loved. She chucked the impending loss of her *Blackbird* on to her mental compost heap; Lorna might have moved on by then, she told herself, and the whole ridiculous gambit would be ditched.

As for Barbara's earlier betrayal, she refused to let that curdle her mood's velvety ganache. No, this pitiful exchange was too inconsequential, too ridiculous to qualify even as a flea in her ointment. She wouldn't let them spoil her moment of triumph; she had been voted Best Unsung Hero by her fellow guides, barring that turd brown-haired shrew. Icing on the cake, she'd been invited to Christmas lunch by a *true* friend, who possessed that rare gift of making her belly laugh. Cherry on top, there was a parking space right outside her house.

But indoors, climbing the book-lined staircase, the sting of Nigel's laughter fanned another spark.

'That old bag couldn't wangle a piss-up at Majestic.'

Oh, couldn't I?

And as for that perm-fried hypocrite, Barbara, toadying to that pompous prat.

Insipid, am I? Damn right, I play the airhead card when it suits. Trust me, you bitch, I can pull off way more than the odd tour.

How little they knew. How. Little.

And in that moment, it struck her how much she craved some excitement. A flight from the humdrum. Now over a decade since retirement, her surrogate grandmother services were soon to be further demoted. She needed a new sense of purpose. A challenge. Gripped by some peculiar eve-of-life crisis, she yearned for a dash of danger. Instead of resuming her stock septuagenarian role as mere bystander, she could exploit her very unnoteworthiness to become a player.

For once, she could relish her worthless status as an eccentric spinster. To be humoured and patronised at best, to be relied on when needed like the Best Unsung Hero, but mainly, to be ignored. Cold-shouldered even, as some bothersome bed blocker. Her *poor old dear* label, her invisibility, she now saw, carried an exhilarating power — the ability to hide in plain sight. Like a secret ninja.

Those arseholes! I could steal a painting if I really wanted to. I nearly swiped a miniature right from under their snooty noses. It would have been so damned easy. But I might just do it this time. Yes, maybe I will. And what's more, I'll go bigger. I'll show them. I'll show the whole fucking bunch of them.

Chapter 7
Farewells and Fag Ends
Thursday, 21st December

Maureen didn't accompany Laura and Jodie to Heathrow; airports were too fraught for big farewells. Instead, the night before, she treated them to a meal at the Quality Fish Restaurant in Richmond. Next door to The Open Book, this vintage gem had served excellent fish'n'chips for as long as she could remember. Its décor hadn't changed one iota since the 1970s, when she and John used to stroll there, lured by the waft of malt vinegar down King Street. Now, it was like walking onto a time warp lino of hexagonal tan and beige. Past the sizzling fryers and heated counters, they pushed through saloon doors and slid into a dark Formica booth down the back.

Crisp battered rock, fat golden chips and proper mushy peas — with that lurid green, as if they'd been harvested just outside Chernobyl. Maureen wiped the grease off her fingers, relishing Laura's mock cries of horror, as Jodie spurted a swirl of B-movie blood ketchup onto her baked beans. In return, her great-niece feigned gagging, as she pointed to Laura's tartare sauce. Raising the bar, Laura moulded a wedge of lemon rind over her teeth, and looked up with a yellow, pock-marked smile. Even goofing around with no make-up and hair scraped into a messy bun, she was still knockout. It was all so Kathy, it hurt.

Later, sipping her tea, Maureen marvelled how Jodie could demolish a Knickerbocker Glory, straight after scampi, chips and beans.

'Where exactly do you put it all?' she said, prodding Jodie's ribs.

Jodie wriggled on the sticky banquette. 'Stop it Auntie, you're tickling me.'

'Oh, am I? What about now?'

As she broke off from tormenting her convulsed victim, she caught the sadness in Laura's eyes, like a punch to the solar plexus. For a few seconds, Maureen struggled to compose herself, twisting her paper napkin, mumbling a request for the bill, as the waitress came to clear the debris.

Much too soon after, outside her crooked gate, Maureen hugged them both tight, logging their scent into her memory bank, reluctant to let go. Jodie, shivering in her teddy jacket, bored with the incessant list of promises, hopping from one unlaced Converse to the other. Yes, they would ring as soon as they landed. Maureen really didn't need Rhona to keep an eye on her. (The very last thing she wanted.) The next few months would flash by. Of course, she remembered how to FaceTime. Laura, hood up against the drizzle, unable to maintain eye contact. Both adults trading banalities, buying just a little more time, floundering on those jagged, treacherous rocks of the unspoken.

The marvel of kids, living only in the present, blind to the enormity of some goodbyes. Maureen waved hard until the red taillights disappeared round the corner. Off to spend their last night with friends, Laura's own little house off Twickenham Green already occupied by new tenants. Had they clocked the graffiti in the cupboard under the stairs yet? The jagged lines of biro marking Jodie's growth spurts between the ages of two to ten. An invisible, icy hand wrenched Maureen's cardiac muscle, extracting a primal gasp of anguish into the night. She stood there alone on the pavement, pure feral, waiting for her young to return, and wiped the stinging sleet from her eyes.

* * *

In general, Maureen was allergic to enforced jollity, particularly the stifling ritual of Christmas lunch. But this was proving a welcome deviation. In her teal Shaker kitchen with the obligatory bifold doors, Rhona dished out some M&S pre-stuffed turkey and all the trimmings, with minimum fuss. Plus, a Tudor Crust-cum-giant-porkpie for David, who claimed that turkey was one huge, flavourless con.

'Awkward bastard,' said Rhona, 'bit like Henry VIII.'

'We're all entitled to our views,' David protested, doling out honey and mustard parsnips. 'I mean, you're a quinoa-denier.'

'Well, I reserve the right not to eat bird food.'

David pulled a cracker with Maureen, making sure he won. Playing the gent, he offered her the mini set of screwdrivers, then read out the joke:

'What did Adam say to his girlfriend the day before Christmas?'

'Er, don't—'

'It's Christmas, Eve!'

After more artery-clogging fare, namely chocolate log with extra cream, washed down with assorted wines, they abandoned the wreckage. Rhona blocked Maureen's paltry attempt to clear up with, 'That's no your job.' And she jerked her head towards David. 'Leave it to the butler.'

The man in question had insisted on watching *The King's Christmas Broadcast*, while Rhona muttered dark oaths about dusting off guillotines. David's paper crown had drooped over his face and was now billowing in the wake of some impressive snores. In short, he looked the very antithesis of a hot-shot TV producer.

Beached on a Heal's sofa, watching Doctor Who wield his sonic screwdriver, Maureen suddenly missed Jodie so much that she felt a stabbing pain. But then again, it could have been indigestion. Either way, she was glad that Rhona talked over the Christmas special, airing some vague notion of getting fit in the New Year.

'Dee keeps banging on about Pilates.'

Maureen cringed at the thought of attempting a class, alongside a bevy of honed Millennials.

'Last time I went, I lay on this manky floor doing endless pelvic tilts, while the woman next to me farted,' said Rhona, massaging her food baby. She switched over to a *Morecombe and Wise* repeat, slurping coffee from her *Breaking Bad* mug. This was a Christmas gift from

Maureen, adorned with the head of that iconic baddie, Walter White. Inscribed beneath his black hat and sunglasses, his famous boast that *he* was the one who knocked. Rhona had recently binge-watched all five series and so the present was a no-brainer. Little did Maureen know just how prescient it would prove.

'I did try one of those spinning classes at that new wee gym round the corner. Walked like John Wayne for a week. Does it count if you just sit on the bike and watch telly?'

Their gales of laughter made David snort, open one eye and fall back into his food coma, as they reminisced about shiny leotards, leg warmers and Jane Fonda workouts back in the hairspray mists of the early eighties.

All in all, Christmas lunch had far exceeded her usual low expectations. Standing outside Rhona's front door, myriad hues of flashing lights vied for their attention.

'So here's the thing.'

Rhona dug sparkly nails into Maureen's arm, more to steady herself than emphasise a point.

'What you need pet is a New Year's project. Sssomething to keep you busy. Anything'll do, right enough, but it musst be something.' She paused, flailing for coherence, 'Sssomethingtodistractyou.'

* * *

Back home, Maureen FaceTimed her niece. From the off, Jodie's father butted right in, his boot polish hair as unconvincing as his hearty greetings. Laura finally prised the phone off him. 'He's overplaying the dad routine, but at least he's trying.' She sighed. 'Anyway, Jodie's happy and that's the main thing.'

True enough, her great-niece was bouncing off the walls, her words tripping out so fast that Maureen couldn't keep up. But too soon, she was called away by that loud-mouthed oaf, and the call ended abruptly.

Looking out of her bedroom window, Maureen was dazzled by the huge buttermilk moon. Almost as though she could reach out and grab a chunk off the luminous giant cheese. Its hypnotic glow bathed the slate rooftops, silhouetting the mesh of old aerials that trembled from crooked chimney stacks.

Odd how right then, she recalled her lonely walk back from Richmond Station after her final exchange with John on Platform 2. All those years ago. Torrential rain had flattened his mullet, highlighting those infuriating cheekbones. She had screamed at him to fuck off, and off he had fucked. Right out of her life. And now here she was, alone again.

When she woke the next morning, in those first serene moments of amnesia, she puzzled over her sense of emptiness, before the answer pressed down on her like a great weight. It felt as if that demonic imp, Incubus, had sat on her chest in the middle of the night, and repulsed by her wrinkles and woeful lack of oestrogen, had tried to stop her breathing.

In the seventeenth century, people feared the hours after sunset — when evil spirits roamed free. Maybe, like Catherine of Braganza, that reviled Catholic queen, she should have sprinkled her pillow with holy water. Or dug out the necklace that John had bought her, as red coral was believed to offer protection against malign forces. She'd also read about Stone Age charms but doubted that wolves' teeth were available on Amazon.

Perhaps she'd gazed too long on that moon, and some of its rays had pawed at her sleeping face between unevenly drawn curtains, through which right now, the stark grey morning barged. She hugged the duvet round her, summoning the will to get up. Lured by the prospect of porridge, she left Pepys in a determined ball and hauled herself out of bed. Further rallied by *Woman's Hour*:

'… well done, you've survived the festivities thus far into Boxing Day…'

Good point, it is damned impressive.

Clattering round her drab, decidedly non-Shaker

kitchen, she absorbed snatches of some headline-inspiring women.

'... and we'll ask, if there is any actual reason to celebrate, as we stagger towards next year...'

Nope. Sweet F.A.

Maureen hankered after some of that chocolate honey. Long since consumed, due to her penchant for eating it straight from the jar, by the regular consoling spoonful. Instead, she lavished her gruel with Demerara sugar.

Some twenty minutes later, she was dressed. Impressive, when all she wanted to do was crawl back under her duvet and block out the earth's orbit on its ever-grinding axis. Meanwhile, those brave women were still speaking out against upskirting and sexual harassment.

'... so here we find ourselves, right at the fag-end of the year...'

Don't I know it.

Kitchen straightened, Maureen hung the tea towel on the radiator. She smoothed out the wrinkled, damp cloth, inspecting the scene printed on its coarse cotton. Minus its wild, fanciful frame, her favourite little Dutch Golden Age oil. The tea towel had been a Christmas present from Jodie, who had slyly secured inside help. Explaining why Rhona had looked so furtive exiting the gift shop the other week.

As the presenter began thanking all her guests, Maureen turned off the radio and considered Rhona's kindness, how her generosity smashed a wrecking ball through that cheap Scot trope. Having once divulged that where she grew up, they had to fight for *every wee scrap.* this was doubly impressive.

In the drear light, Maureen tilted her head and studied Jodie's present from a different perspective. The cherry stork snared under the blackbird's scaly foot, those succulent cherries, as Rhona's slurred farewell rang in her ears:

'What you need, pet, is a New Year's project...'

Sound advice indeed, dear friend.

The bluebottle had been cropped out of this crude reprint, and in that moment, Maureen was oblivious to Bosschaert's shiny fly landing on the table's edge.

Chapter 8
Ocean's One
Tuesday, 26th December

Traditionally, this was the day for Pepto Bismol shots, family meltdowns and ransacking the sales. But Maureen was pioneering a new Boxing Day pastime — planning a fine art heist.

Now that the first floor was closed until Spring, her only way to access it was during one of her tours. Ideal for a reconnaissance mission. She double-checked the rota to confirm that her last Christmas ghost tour fell on Thursday. In essence, this was her last chance saloon.

At first, she considered using the evening event as cover to execute her New Year's project. Perfect — only one of the House team present, acting as tour shepherd. Aside from the second-floor flats, of course. For insurance reasons, there was always at least one resident staff member on site, but they only surfaced outside their work rosters in cases of fire, armed siege and plagues of locusts. Or when Lorna mislaid her car keys. Then, as if she could hear Rhona's snide tones, she came to her senses.

Brilliant. That wouldn't look at all suspicious. A painting mysteriously disappearing the night of your tour.

No, she would have to conduct *Operation Blackbird* in the New Year before it was sequestered to Thirlestane Castle in March. Christ knew how. In fact, she would need to dial up some divine intervention. But in the meantime, she could scout out her target. In which case, she needed to get into the Green Closet at some point on Thursday night, but how the bejesus was she going to manage that?

Earlier that year, Trevor — one of the more incongruous employees, with his inked biceps and Brizzle accent — had conducted the annual fire evacuation training. Some of the other guides had stared at Maureen when she'd asked if the policy was to shove visitors aside and shout, *Save yourselves!*

Towards the end, Nigel had brought up the subject of alarms, doubtless as an excuse to hear his own voice. Trevor, always affable and a mine of information on the House, had explained that all the doors were alarmed after hours. They learned that the House was brimming with pressure pad alarms, and wireless sensors behind the most valuable paintings. Not forgetting the infra-red motion detectors and air pressure sensors, which, when triggered, allowed the monitoring company to hear any noise within range. Unchecked, Trevor and Nigel switched into full geek mode, while everyone else sloped off to retrieve their will to live.

Yet, on her last shift, Maureen overheard Emma tell Kerry that it might be simpler if the alarms were switched off during the post-Christmas ghost tour. So often these days, others barely noticed when she was in the vicinity. But now Maureen viewed this as an unexpected kind of superpower. The possibilities were intoxicating.

She probably thinks you can just lift a painting off the wall. As if they wouldn't be attached with some anti-theft springlock device...

The memory of Nigel's taunt snapped her back to the coalface. His words had stung, because he was right; she was entirely clueless on this front. She resolved to remedy this with some basic research. But a pro would never leave a shady search history on their own laptop. She would have to wait until tomorrow, to use the computers in her local library. Again, to avoid any digital trace, she didn't pre-book a session. Anyway, unlike pubs, she figured that libraries were generally not mobbed during the Christmas hols.

* * *

As predicted, excluding a couple of bored staff, the library was empty apart from a woman plainly struggling with homelessness, who sat hunched on a pouffe in the children's section. Head-phoned at the PC furthest from reception, Maureen's mind soon boggled with Ryman plates, bridge brackets, spring inserts and keepers. A simple set of screwdrivers might not suffice, after all. Several videos later, it became clear that she'd need to order some special spring lock release tool. That would raise a massive red flag, she thought. She gazed out over a windswept Richmond Green, wondering how else she could get hold of one. Frank would know, but she could hardly just drop it in conversation. And this was assuming the *Blackbird* didn't require a special number-recorded key to remove it.

Unlikely though, for a less well-known painting, out of public reach. There must be an outlet somewhere in London, where you could walk in and buy such a lock release gadget with cash. It turned out, there wasn't an Art Thieves R Us, for precisely that reason. About to abandon her project, she saw an advert *for all your art, framing and accessorie's supplies* on an industrial estate near Isleworth. Together with the bad grammar alert, she noted the details, and on her way out, placed a Kit Kat by the woman, now curled snoring on a red sofa.

* * *

'We usually just deliver to trade online,' the man explained. Like some over-invested method actor, Maureen had been careful to use her landline and pre-fix 141 before dialling. Undeterred, she trowelled on her plummy, out-to-lunch accent and said that she needed to secure an ancestral portrait. A Christmas present, she rambled on. Probably not worth much, but sentimental value yada yada. He finally relented. Just to shut her up.

'Fabulous. I can drop by in twenty minutes.' All prepared, she'd been to the cash machine on her way back.

'Er, we don't open again until the New Year. Your call was diverted to my mobile.'

Fuckshitwankbollocks

'Sorry, didn't catch that.'

'Understood. You've been most helpful. Guess I'll see you next year!'

She over-chortled and rang off. No choice but to assess

the required tools on-site.

* * *

Maureen stretched out beneath some bath bubbles. She'd made vague noises about replacing her avocado suite, but Jodie had begged her not to, and even Laura had described it as vintage. 'Bit like me,' Maureen had laughed, knowing that she could no more afford a new bathroom than she could fly to the moon. She usually did her best problem-solving in the bath, but doubtless due to yesterday's binge-fest, she sank into a dreamless doze.

The water was lukewarm by the time Maureen stirred. The foam had evaporated into iridescent swirls highlighting her white expanse, now even more crinkled. Her nipples had migrated towards her withered biceps and protruded above the oily film like sea buoys. Tiny air bubbles coated her silver-streaked pubes, which wafted near the surface, like some petrified coral reef. Why did women put themselves through such pain and expense to remove them? She raised her right leg out of the water, making a *good toes* point. One of the great mysteries of life: no matter how carefully she shaved her legs, she always seemed to miss a bloody-minded clump on her knees. Although surely, the bigger mystery was why she continued to shave her legs at all. Who the hell was ever going to see them?

She examined the network of blue veins on her calf, an unattractive purple bulge at their epicentre, and almost regretted the cataract surgery a few years earlier. Thanks to the NHS, this miraculous procedure had rendered several pairs of glasses instantly redundant, but now she could view her mileage with horrific clarity. She couldn't help but mourn her once decent set of pins. Not as long as Kathy's of course, but then she'd always skulked in her older sister's shadow, part adoring, part resentful. All her boyfriends had fancied K. Apart from John.

Anyhow, your siren days are long past. More like The Kraken Wakes.

She yanked the plug and stood up, so that half the bath water seemed to run out of her down the squawking, rusty plughole. Note to self, must use fabric conditioner, she resolved, as she dried herself with a thin towel, the texture of a scouring pad. Still, cheaper than the body polish treatment advertised at the local spa.

If she were the Duchess of Lauderdale, her maids would massage her with herbal potions prepared in the Still House. Enveloped in linen, she would then drape herself alluringly on a four-poster, piled high with quilts. As the Delft-tiled hearth blazed, she would sip some fortified wine, allowing her skin to absorb the fragrant oils.

That brazen Duchess knew how to live, maybe because of the dangers she'd endured during the Civil War. They must have been horrific times, Maureen thought, shivering. Even afterwards, with wealth and status renewed, life was tough. Both Elizabeth's parents had died by then and only five of her eleven children survived. There were no funeral records for the lost babies. She supposed that infant deaths were so common, they weren't considered noteworthy.

Elizabeth adopted all the latest fashions to plug her hard-fought status. But then, wealth has always represented power. Perhaps, surrounding herself with exquisite art proved some kind of antidote to all the darkness. Beauty changes nothing, but it can at least provide the illusion of comfort. Then wasn't Maureen just taking a leaf out of the Duchess's book? No, not taking, she reasoned, but *conserving.* After the Duke's death, Elizabeth had arranged for cartloads of his possessions to be stripped from Thirlestane Castle and despatched to Ham. Lauder legend described how incensed locals only arrived in time to halt the fifteenth wagon.

With this strong, cinematic image in mind, Maureen pulled on a baggy jumper. Now more than ever, she felt sure she had the Duchess's blessing and was strangely soothed.

Chapter 9
One Key To Rule Them All
Thursday, December 28th

'What are we going to do? I can't go and tell twenty-six visitors the tour's cancelled 'cos half the friggin' lights are off!'

Maureen was crouched behind the doors to the pitch-dark Long Gallery, fumbling for the catch in the wainscot. Her tour shepherd, Daisy, giggled by way of reply, and Maureen felt hysteria begin to take hold. This most certainly wasn't part of her plan.

At least the House was empty. The rest of the team had left ages ago, including Kerry, who had exited like a bat out of hell, having ignored Maureen's emailed list of requests. To be fair, this hadn't specified leaving the lights on, as she hadn't realised that she needed to state the total bleedin' obvious. Just as well she'd arrived with over thirty minutes to spare.

They'd already wasted precious time in the Great Hall, trying to turn off the festive playlist from under the Christmas tree. Crawling on all fours beside the fireplace, Daisy had twiddled various knobs and cables, yet still '*Santa Baby*' blared out from the speakers.

'I know there's an easy way to do this,' said Daisy, pine needles sprinkled along her French plait.

After grouching about the lack of a simple on/off switch, Maureen suggested they turn the volume right down. 'Why on earth did they leave it playing?'

'They said it'd be nice and festive for the tour.'

'Brilliant. I mean, Mariah Carey's the ideal soundtrack for a ghostly anecdote.'

She knew the House team loathed having to work late and shepherd the evening tours. Maureen had witnessed first-hand their groans and eye rolls. Never mind that *it's only a ghost tour* generated direct revenue for Ham House. Irritated, Maureen glossed over their depleted staff levels and how often they worked overtime for no pay. She'd forgotten the treadmill of full-time work, how she used to be on her knees by the end of term. Instead, she continued her internal rant. Doubtless, the new girl had been sold this evening as part of her induction. With minimal briefing. But despite this farting around, Daisy's inexperience was exactly what Maureen had banked on. It was bloody perfect.

The Doc Martened and mini-skirted recruit was the new Retail Supervisor. All the heady excitement of stocktaking and pricing William Morris scarves, salted caramel fudge, rosemary hand cream, beeswax candles and plaid picnic rugs. On a minimum wage. In fairness, those rugs were excellent, and she was often tempted to whip out her discount card, whenever she went in the shop. She usually ended up buying more pointless postcards, after lingering over the sticker books that Jodie had loved so much. Maureen often dropped in now if she knew Deirdre was helping out. Her fellow volunteer had grown on her these past few weeks; her Pollyanna routine didn't chafe as much. If anything, she found it contagious, though it wore off pretty sharpish.

'Here we go.'

At last, Maureen's fingers felt the catch, and the rectangle of wainscot swung open. In the torch's faint beam, she located the switches. Instantly, the Long Gallery's dark gilded panelling was bathed in a soft glow. Opposing rows of Stuarts, Murrays and Maitlands glared down at her from their ornate, gold frames, as if both annoyed and amused at being disturbed at this hour.

'Is there anything else?' asked Daisy, switching off her torch.

For a few moments, Maureen was lost in the magic of seeing the empty House lit up at night. That's what made these tours so special. Although, the plastic crates shoved under a fold-up table down the end somewhat tarnished the grandeur. All part of the new Trust ethos; granting access to its properties three hundred and sixty-three days of the year and letting the public see conservation in action.

'Let me think,' she ticked the prep list off her fingers. 'We've opened the Chapel, the Spaniel skeleton's already below the portrait in the Round Gallery…'

Trevor, the real unsung hero, had retrieved it from the Storeroom earlier that afternoon.

'Fake candles. We need some on the Great Staircase and in the Marble Dining Room. *And* the Duchess's Bedchamber. Plus, you were going to look for the Duke's clay pipe.'

'Riiight,' Daisy looked clueless. 'Not sure—'

'There should be some spare candles. Let's go down and look.'

As they descended the polished staircase, the clicking of their shoes echoed round the House. They came to a standstill on entering the Great Hall, stunned by its majesty, as if seeing it for the first time. Suspended high above them, the chandelier in the Round Gallery remained switched off, so that the Hall was lit only by fake candles and the lights on the towering Christmas tree. Plaster statues of Mars and Minerva guarded the mantelpiece. Their white faces, modelled on Elizabeth's parents — William Murray, 1st Earl of Dysart and Katherine Bruce of Clackmannan — gaped down from the shadows, while smoke-effect steam rose from the fake coals glowing in the grate.

'It almost makes you feel warm,' said Daisy.

'Yes. If I could still feel my toes.'

As though in a cathedral, they spoke in hushed tones. Maureen shivered in her thick wool coat — an elegant, double-breasted heirloom, infused with the vanilla and cinnamon musk of her sister's Shalimar. Bit tight over her boobs, their southward migration hoisted up by an old bra, which dug into her ribs, but overall, a pretty good fit. Some of the other ghost tour guides donned floor length capes, but Maureen only wore black. 'You'll need to pay me, if you want me to dress up,' she'd told Kerry, who had dropped the subject pronto.

They stepped out of the Great Hall into the West Passageway. Here, the floor was festooned with empty boxes, tastefully wrapped in brown paper and gold ribbon, matching those under the tree. Daisy peered into the grungy depths of a cupboard, crammed with a hoover, a set of storage drawers and some mops and feather dusters splayed in a bucket. Not that Maureen cared about the absence of candles; she'd just needed this cupboard to be locked. *Why isn't it locked? It's always locked.*

'No sign of any here, and there's none in the office. We could use some of these.'

Daisy pointed at their feet, where different sized candles flickered amongst the bogus presents.

'Not sure Kerry would be happy with us moving them,' Maureen stalled. 'But reckon I know where the spares are kept.'

Despite her snap change of plan, she managed to sound calm and authoritative. It was clear that Daisy considered the volunteer's route-dressing way over the top. Maureen suppressed an urge to add:

You try taking round a large group for an hour. Tickets cost £29. Some have trailed from the other side of London. After work. You better damn well deliver the bacon.

But the older woman held her tongue. A high Trip Advisor rating and her self-respect weren't top priorities tonight. She needed Daisy on side. Above all, she needed Daisy to open the key cupboard. Time was slipping away, and her willpower was starting to flag. What if her intel was dud? Why exactly was she doing this? Was she having some sort of breakdown? The younger woman stood waiting for instructions. Maureen dialled up the bravado. 'I remember seeing Kerry fetch some candles from that store cupboard past the Gentlemen's Dining Room.'

Daisy hesitated, then followed Maureen into the

modest, panelled room at the end of the Passageway. This was where the senior servants would have eaten. Bit of a squeeze, she thought. All it contained now was a black lacquered table with floral motifs, a row of chairs and the 9th Earl's infamous wheelchair, which was said to move around of its own accord at night. Maureen now omitted this anecdote, after an ex-resident confessed that she'd caught her kids wheeling the chair down the corridor to spook next day's staff.

The walk-in cupboard was situated in a small, dark vestibule between the Gentlemen's Dining Room and the grander Back Parlour beyond, where the senior servants would have relaxed. The Parlour doors were now locked, so Maureen couldn't squinny at Joan Carlile's stilted portrait of Elizabeth, standing between her long-suffering first husband and her younger sister. Recent infrared imaging showed that the artist had originally outlined the two sisters beside a large tree. Joan had then painted over the tree with husband number one, dressed in black, bending his elbows in an odd, jig-like pose. Hard not to assume that he'd muscled in on the portrait in a feeble display of authority. *I'm the one in charge here, honest.* In truth, his wife always called the shots. She didn't strike Maureen as capable of obeying anyone. Inspired by Elizabeth, she screwed her own courage to the sticking place.

'It's locked,' she groaned, tugging at the cupboard door, as she wedged the bottom with her black boot. *Don't look up. Please don't look up.* At the top, lurked a simple turn latch holding the doors shut, concealed in the unlit corner.

'We can get the key from the key cupboard.'

Maureen did her best to sound breezy, like this was all standard practice.

'Okay, I'll go and get my key to open it.'

Daisy sounded resigned, if baffled by this bonkers pensioner. Torn between wanting to see where she kept the key, but not wishing to look even more weird, Maureen tapped her foot in the corridor, as Daisy ransacked the small office. Not a moment too soon, the recruit emerged with the one key to rule them all.

Inside the West Door, Maureen held her breath while Daisy jimmied the key in the cupboard lock for a few agonising seconds. She had just over ten minutes before she needed to go over to the Orangery, introduce herself to the punters, run through the rules and grant them a last lavvy stop. She converted her sigh of relief into a cough, as the tabernacle's small white door swung open above the cold radiator.

Inside, umpteen keys of various shapes and sizes hung on neat rows of hooks. Small unobtrusive office keys; rusty double-sided ones, silver tubular ones with black plastic bows; shiny barrels; chunky, antique brass skeletons, bright gold Yales and long, bronze Chubbs. All enumerated. Those hanging inside the fixed recess were labelled with green plastic tags, denoting ground floor status. While the first-floor keys bore blue tags and dangled inside the open door. Frowning, Daisy studied the attached inventory.

'Hmmm. Bit weird, that storage cupboard's not listed here. Hang on, this green key hasn't got a number. Reckon it's worth a try.'

And she plucked a burnished gold key from its hook. Maureen was fast warming to Daisy's sweet-natured resolve. Particularly, as her angelic helper now leapt up the steps, leaving the cupboard wide open. Pausing at the *Gentle Reminder sign-in-or-die* notice, Daisy turned, surprised to see the tour guide rooted at the bottom of the stairs. Maureen stood steadfast by the radiator, ready with phone in hand.

'Always mute my phone too soon.' Brows creased. 'Just missed a call from my niece. Her daughter's not been well, so better check my voicemail. Be with you in a jiffy.'

'Sure.'

Daisy looked down as the grey-haired biddy squinted and stabbed her forefinger on to various parts of the screen. Grinning, she disappeared into the West Passageway.

Silly old bird skit done, Maureen listened out for Daisy's retreating footsteps, as the heavy staff door swung shut. She pocketed her phone and scanned the rows of keys, as if speed-reading a large book. No need to check the first-floor list, the Green Closet key number was imprinted on her brain. But disaster, hook number 113 protruded naked on the bottom row.

'What the hell?'

In desperation, she double-checked the green section, praying that it had been put back in the wrong place. No such luck. In her panic, she was drawn to the jumble of discarded keys at the bottom. Among the medley of dark metal, a corner of blue plastic. Jubilant, she fished out a familiar, oxidised key with an elaborate, crown-shaped bow. Yes, labelled 113. Paying silent homage to Hermes, Mercury and any other gods of trickery and thieves, she buried it in her left coat pocket. It clinked against her torch, just as Daisy burst back through, squawking radio in hand.

'Turns out the cupboard wasn't locked, after all. Only a turn latch at the top. Anyway, found some spares, so I've left the box outside the office. You can put them where you want.'

Daisy sped down the stairs and opened the West Door.

'Apparently there's a couple at the gate who've forgotten their tickets and aren't on the list.'

'Okay thanks. I'll head to the Orangery after I've sorted the candles and double-checked every…'

But Daisy had already stepped outside and slammed the door shut. For a few seconds, Maureen froze, unable to believe her good fortune. She had the House entirely to herself, with Green Closet key in pocket *and* the cupboard remained unlocked. There was no time to lose. Despite her arthritic knee, she charged up the West Passageway. Grunting, she scooped up the cardboard tray of candles, which Daisy had dumped alongside the empty parcels.

Don't panic! Don't panic Captain Mainwaring!

This time, ignoring its festive grandeur, she crossed the Great Hall to the front door and crouched to grab her handbag from the cubbyholes. As she looped it over her shoulder, something caught her eye. Changing course, she strode towards the fireplace, as if to warm herself by its orange coals.

Mounted at the centre of the marble mantelpiece was a shiny mascaron. Its bronze face and hairstyle mirrored that of Queen Henrietta Maria. Hard to resist the theory that this was William Murray sucking up to his royal, demi-god chum. In contrast to the rest of her delicate gold features, HM's nose was blackened by a constant stream of visitors throughout the ages rubbing the regal snout for good luck. Alone in the candlelight, she was enthralled by the splendour of this Jacobean mansion. And although cynical by nature, she reached out her hand to trace a finger down the worn, slender nose.

Then, shaking herself back to business, she about-faced and marched up the Great Staircase. At intervals, she stooped to deposit candles on random steps. Not forgetting the wooden sills of those long windows which, when un-shuttered, overlooked the Cherry Gardens. Despite the chill, she was sweating now under Kathy's coat. Rushing into the shadowy Round Gallery, she nearly keeled over the minstrel banisters, as disembodied voices crackled the silence. After her initial shock, she realised they emanated from a hand-held radio, abandoned on a window ledge in the Hall below. It was transmitting a loud, incoherent exchange between Visitor Reception and harassed Orangery assistants.

'Er yeah, we're expecting at least four more … couple here. Just waiting for Dais... Ah, she's on her way... Over.'

'…complaining… sausage rolls and the coffee machine's… Over…'

Composing herself, she placed candles round the glass

box encasing the spaniel's bones, beneath Lely's double portrait. In the obscure light, both Elizabeth and the Duke appeared peeved at being ignored by this strange attendant, who, eyes down, just zipped through the North Drawing Room. The 1st Earl and his wife might have whipped off the dustsheet for a singalong with Charles I, round the battered harpsichord in that tapestried ante room. His son, Charles II might have been thrashing some of his courtiers at billiards in the Long Gallery, while various mistresses promenaded along the parquet. Still, Maureen wouldn't have noticed. Perhaps if she'd paused to inspect the 2D, Van Dyck copy of Queen Henrietta Maria, above the Green Closet doors, she would have discerned the upward curve of her lips. Almost as if this unpopular Fille de France was relieved that her daughter's miniature had not been usurped by a tacky beagle and might just deign to reward the rubbing of her bronze nose. Or maybe, it was a trick of the art nouveau style uplighters.

Instead, head lowered, Maureen dropped the box of candles at her feet. Unleashing some impressive profanities, she jiggled the key around in the unyielding gilt lock. How effing typical this was, how things only ever worked out half right for her. Having finally managed to secure the key, it now turned out to be useless. What the effing Norah was she doing this for anyway? A ridiculous scouting mission. Then she stopped and put a hand to her head, as if prodding her memory. Hadn't Sanjay mumbled the word *half*, on that fateful day when she'd chosen to steward the Green Closet? Hadn't he burbled something about the key being half knackered? No, surely, he'd said *only, only half*. And not knackered, but *knack*. That was it! *Only halfway, that's the knack*. Sanjay had meant only put the key halfway into the lock. And on cue, the readjusted key turned once and then twice with a satisfying click.

'Clever boy.'

But in that instance, her elation was doused by a powerful wave of dread. Heart racing, she dithered, the doors still closed. Just how reliable was her info that all the alarms were off? Earlier, when grappling with the light switches, she had fished for confirmation.

'All we need now is to activate the alarms in the Long Gallery.'

'Don't worry, they're all off,' Daisy had replied. 'I'll switch them back on after the tour.' Maureen did a virtual fist pump.

Not sure you should have told me that.

Yet still, she hesitated on the threshold. The moment of truth. Should she brave it? This was her only chance to assess the target. Almost criminal to back out now. *She freezes who does not burn.* Bracing herself, she nudged opened the right door, to be greeted with… deafening silence. Now it was Daisy's turn to receive Maureen's eternal gratitude as she struggled with the ornate bolts securing the left door.

Sanjay, less helpful here, had described the catches as *these round thingies on either side of the sticky-outy bit.* Only one of these released the shaft from the hole in the floor and in order to retract the ceiling bolt, she needed to press the round thingy on the opposite side. She could never remember which way round and the ensuing trial and error wasted valuable time. At last, she mastered it and pushing both doors wide open, took a step into the stale darkness.

For some reason, the light switches were located in the lift vestibule off the Long Gallery, but she couldn't risk any more faffing. Plus, Maureen couldn't be sure how well the blind would mask the lights in here, and she didn't want to advertise her presence to Daisy at the front gates. Instead, with the aid of her slimline pocket torch, (vital ghost tour kit), she unclipped the green cord in a peculiar, disembodied trance. As if in league with the congress of ghosts that had haunted this house for over four centuries, she tiptoed to the far side of the west wall.

Ignoring her previous quarry, the doe-eyed *Unknown Lady*, she directed her torch into the secluded alcove, catching some vibrant specks of red and yellow. Like a hit of laudanum, she stood, transfixed by the Holy Grail itself. The *Blackbird, Butterfly and Cherries*. Somehow, it dazzled her even more in the deserted gloom. The beam highlighted the bird's sharp beak and the ambrosian cherries on the sunny, stone ledge. So tantalising, she wanted to reach out and taste their sweet juice. Such delicious, forbidden fruit.

She stepped closer and plucked some latex gloves from her bag. With torch clenched between teeth, she extended one arm, then both. This might be her heart's desire, but it wasn't a Reynolds or Van Dyke, and despite Trevor's low-down, she felt confident that this smaller, remote painting wouldn't be alarmed. Holding her breath, she placed her hands either side of its auricular frame. Slow and gentle. Then gasped, as the painting wobbled slightly beneath her gloves. What the fuckety heck? Bosschaert's still life clearly had no springlock device of any sort. It wasn't even screwed down.

You know nothing Nigel Herbert. Turns out, I could just lift this right off the wall.

No time to lose, she whipped out her tape measure. The Collections website only listed the painting's surface area, and she needed the full dimensions, including its substantial, carved frame.

'Maureen! Maureen, are you there?'

JesusMaryandJoseph

She leapt away from the *Blackbird.* Daisy's shouts resounded from the Great Hall. Tape measure rammed back in handbag, Maureen reached the door in an adrenaline blur, fumbling with the rope barrier behind her. Nearly tripping headlong over the box of candles, she dropped her torch amongst them, and loudly recited her tour script, in a vain bid to muffle the re-bolting:

'And in 1661, he was crowned King Charles II of England.' *Which side is this stupid frigging catch? Got it.* 'And there he is behind you,' *now the top one*, 'in Lely's portrait.'

Why the hell did I bother with these shitting bolts? 'Looking a right dandy,' *too bloody noisy*, 'in his long, black curly wig…'

Now the right door was closed, and she twiddled the key anti-clockwise.

Come on, come on. 'The fashion for men wearing wigs,' *just halfway in remember*, 'was started by his,' *bollocks*, 'cousin, Louis XIV of France.' *Job done…*

Key thrust in pocket.

Gloves woman! 'Syphilis…'

Latex gloves scrunched away.

'…was rife in the seventeenth century.' *Thank the Lord…*

Tray scooped up with one hand.

'Both Louis and Charles probably suffered from it. Hair loss was a common symptom…'

Lit torch held in other hand, pointing to the Restoration King's portrait.

'So the wigs were.' *Yes!* 'Oh, hi Daisy. A godsend. Just practising my first stop.'

All too aware of her own shallow breathing, Maureen beamed as her panting shepherd scudded into the Long Gallery.

'Sorry, were you calling me? My hearing's not as good as it used to be.'

Daisy stared open-mouthed at this cuckoo volunteer.

'Yes, but never mind. Listen Maureen, they're waiting for you in the Orangery.' Adding, with laboured emphasis: 'YOU — BETTER — GO — TO — THE — ORANGERY — RIGHT — NOW.'

'Oh, are they waiting for me? Sweet baby Jesus, look at the time! Completely lost track. Be a lamb and shove these out in the Private Closet and Duchess's Bedchamber.'

And sweeping past Daisy, she handed her the box.

'Er, sure—'

'Also, can you put the Duke's pipe in the Marble Dining Room. Did you find it okay?'

'Yes, I saw it in—'

'Don't forget that photo of the graffitied second floor window,' she shouted back over her shoulder, as she raced back through the Round Gallery. 'I'll need it when we go outside near the end.'

Daisy remained stupefied, clutching the last few candles. Now she understood why this gig had been traded round the office like a compostable cup of Novichok tea.

Chapter 10
Most Haunted

Standing on the Orangery terrace, perfectly accessorised with freezing fog and, less so, with the un-Jacobean roar of the Heathrow flight path, Maureen assembled and recounted the group. Still euphoric from her clandestine encounter with the *Blackbird.* True, she hadn't measured up, but she could work that out online later. All in all, mission accomplished.

But as she extracted the torch from her pocket, her fingers grazed an unfamiliar metal object nestled in its lining. Deep, inward groan. She'd only forgotten to put the sodding key back in the sodding cupboard on her way out. Its absence would create one unholy row. She needed time to think, but the expectant party stood before her now, fidgeting, exchanging nervy gags, making ghostly woo sounds into the sharp night air. She snapped into teacher mode:

'Okay everyone, please follow me and I'll lead you into the House.'

Clustered outside the imposing main entrance, they sniggered and gasped as the embellished door creaked open in response to Maureen's theatrical raps. On entering, some peered behind it and jumped when they saw Daisy hiding there, as if more shocked to find a living person.

Once again, Maureen buried her handbag out of sight in the cubbyholes. She would need to *forget* that later, she decided. The group ogled the candlelit Hall, as she conducted her preamble on the dais by the Christmas tree.

'First, I'd like to introduce you to Daisy, a member of the House team, over there behind you.'

Her saviour raised a tentative hand to the few that turned round.

'Daisy will be locking up after us as we make our way through the House, making sure no one gets lost...'

Although she bloody better not have locked the key cupboard, as I need to return an important key that I nicked, before anyone notices. You see, I'm an amateur art thief as well as a volunteer tour guide.

Maureen paused, imagining their reaction if she had said that all out loud. Instead, she lauded the *fabulous* festive decorations. Then, buoyed by her moment of authority, launched forth.

She acted as a benign dictator on these tours. Woe betides those who didn't mute their phones as instructed, with *we mustn't upset the ghosts*, accompanied by genial smile and trustmetheghostswillbetheleastofyourproblems eyes.

There were certain things that she couldn't control though; a helicopter circling overhead during the garden stops, or the blood-curdling screams issuing from a staff flat during a teenage sleepover party. But this evening, the punters seemed tame enough. No drunken hecklers to quash. Her teaching experience often came in handy for this. There was one nutter though. There was always one.

In the Round Gallery, the visitors took turns to peer down at the canine's delicate, brown bones. These had been unearthed in the Kitchen Gardens; purportedly its furry ghost had been spotted scampering round the House. At any event, this doggy yarn proved a reliable crowd-pleaser. Some took it a little too seriously. A woman in beanie and red-framed glasses marched up to Maureen.

'Excuse me, is the spaniel ghost see-through, or is it like a normal dog that vanishes into thin air?'

Illuminated only by Daisy's torch, the Duke and Duchess stared down at the woolly-hatted intruder with gratifying menace. Maureen was tempted to push her over and claim temporary possession by Elizabeth's spirit.

'I've never seen it myself.' *Because ghosts don't exist!* 'But I've been told it looks like a living dog that disappears through walls.'

Satisfied with Maureen's improv, she backed off to join her friend. Pre-empting any further brainless questions, Maureen ploughed on with Elizabeth's story; the rumours that she had poisoned her first husband in order to marry rising star, husband number two. Doubtless, just malicious gossip. By the time, number one had shuffled off his mortal coil in Paris, Elizabeth was already cosying up with the soon-to-be Duke. And although she may have been ambitious, ruthless and corrupt — vital qualities for any aristocrat worth their salt — Maureen didn't buy her murdering the father of her five children. Still, who wasn't drawn to a dirty scandal? Who hadn't scrolled down the Mail Online's sidebar of shame?

'There was even talk of her being a witch. Back in those days, women with red hair, and a basic knowledge of herbs, were thought to possess evil powers.'

Ignorant, misogynist pigs.

'It was often fatal just to be accused of witchcraft. One of the *tests* was known as *swimming the witch.* Basically, your hands and feet were bound together, and you were chucked into the nearest pond or river. If by some fluke, your clothes filled with air and you rose to the surface, then you were guilty. Proof that you'd embraced Satan, and the waters of baptism were rejecting you. So, if you didn't drown, you were then taken to be hanged, pressed to death under a heavy weight, or burnt alive.'

Yes, thought Maureen, basking in their rapt attention, don't we all like a bit of darkness with our custard creams? And then, more like a sheepdog, Daisy herded them along to the Great Staircase.

'You are now standing in the most haunted part of Ham House.'

At this, Red Glasses nearly wet herself, and Daisy rounded big eyes.

Get a grip.

'The spaniel that I mentioned earlier has been seen running across the landing here. Sometimes, when the House is quiet in the late afternoon, staff hear footsteps going up these stairs.'

Maureen paused to provide sound effects with slow

stamps on the wooden step, suppressing an urge to burst out laughing.

'These footsteps are often accompanied by a very strong scent of roses. On rare occasions, their source has been glimpsed; a small lady in black silk can be spied wandering here. Is this Elizabeth, our Duchess? Almost certainly, as I'll explain later.'

It took them forever to meander down the candlelit stairs, which resounded with their prattle and discordant footfall. Situated off the inner hall, the small Chapel was the ultimate ghost tour set, with its dark panelled walls, crimson velvet hangings, and electric candles. During opening hours, visitors could only peer from the rope barrier, but Maureen insisted they be admitted between both sets of box pews. This way, they could fully absorb the Chapel's gloom, as she continued her tale from the altar's black and white marbled dais.

Get your grubby mitts off those pews. She phrased this in a more polite-notice manner, and waited as a mother nudged her son. As if suffering from exhaustion, he obliged, removing his elbow from one of the ledges. Over the clamour of Daisy locking up the first floor, Maureen outlined the nosedive in Elizabeth's fortunes.

'The Duke overplayed his hand. He'd fallen out with his mate Charles, and it wasn't the wisest move to argue with a powerful Stuart King. All their *A-lister*, so-called friends vanished. The parties stopped, and Ham House fell silent.'

We love our wayward heroes, but like a baying mob at a public execution, we also relish their downfall. And Maureen kept them gripped as she described Elizabeth, grief-stricken and bankrupt following the Duke's scurvy-induced demise in 1682. The infamous couple had lived way beyond even their lavish means, and at long last, the tower of embossed cards had collapsed.

'The Duke had left her with huge debts.'

As if Elizabeth hadn't played an enthusiastic part in amassing them. Still, I'll conform to the sexist narrative by painting her as hapless victim. Never let the truth get in the way of a good story.

'So, she had to sell his vast library of books, all her jewellery and beautiful silk dresses, in an attempt to clear some of them.'

At this, the girl with black hair and purple lipstick flinched. Granted, the Duchess hadn't exactly been left homeless and starving, but she was forced to pay an eye-watering £5,000 for his funeral.

'That's equivalent to around one million in today's money.'

This, combined with all the other debts, meant that she buried la dolce vita, along with the love of her life.

'Now you can see the relevance of the lady in black that patrols these stairs at night — a bereft widow, who's also been glimpsed kneeling here at this altar,' Maureen gestured to the carved rails. 'Sometimes a man in dark robes hovers behind her. Perhaps her chaplain trying to comfort her?'

It would have been handy if both could have materialised on the marble step at this point, but instead, Maureen made do with *strange goings-on.* As they left the Chapel, Maureen overheard Red Glasses whisper that she could definitely smell roses.

'Bet it's one of those plug-in air fresheners,' said her friend.

Bracing herself for further ghostly autosuggestion, Maureen led them into the Marble Dining Room.

'Unlike the former Great Dining Room upstairs, used to entertain Charles II and his entourage, this was more for everyday fare with close family and friends. After meals, the Duke would relax in here with a glass of claret and a pipe of his favourite Virginian tobacco.'

Shining her torch on the clay pipe that Saint Daisy had placed on the gate-leg table, she told them that many had detected pungent pipe smoke in this room. As if on cue, Maureen caught Red Glasses sniffing the air. About as subtle as a brimming chamber pot. Maureen hastened through to the Duchess's Bedchamber.

Here, the only light emanated from some fake candles and a battered, angle poise lamp by the shuttered bay. Tilted inwards, it shed a yellow spotlight on to a cast iron radiator — that same reptilian breed as the one by the West Door.

Wedged into the darkness, the imposing four-poster loomed over them from behind the barrier. The group seemed to lack the concept of personal space and Maureen found herself pressed against Emo Girl, nose to septum ring. Streaming colds must be a nightmare with that through your nostrils, she thought, imagining everyone's reaction if she got hers pierced. The canopied bed cowed the shadows, with dusty ostrich feathers cascading out of urns aloft each corner. On revealing that Elizabeth had slept in this room for some twenty years, a few craned their necks, as if the old Duchess still lay there, part-shielded by the red and black curtains. She directed her torch on to Lely's portrait above the fireplace:

'Here we see Elizabeth as a fresh-faced woman of twenty-two, right before her first marriage. What a contrast to that picture of her as a Duchess in her late forties, upstairs in the Round Gallery. Even more so with her last few years, when she was confined downstairs by gout, walking with the aid of her ebony cane.'

Some, she claimed, heard footsteps with the tapping of a stick, down the Passageway and across this Bedchamber, followed by the slamming of the servants' door, which leads to the bathroom in the Basement.

'None have dared investigate the source of these noises, and I can't say I—'

Brazen, Red Glasses' pal was typing on her phone, complete with audible keyboard haptics. The white glow bathed her saliva-stranded yawn, until meeting Maureen's filthy stare, she pocketed the offending device.

'Blame them.'

You dare sabotage my finale, and I'll have you dragged to the nearby shooting range for target practice.

'During her last few years, Elizabeth must have been very lonely. She had little money at this stage, only one or two servants left. Her sisters were dead, her younger sons had been killed in battle and her daughters lived in Scotland. She wrote to one of them: *I am but a prisoner in my beloved Ham House, and I don't think I shall ever leave here.* And do you know, she never did. In fact, she died in this room on the fifth June 1698.'

A spine-tingling hush prevailed. It nearly always did at this point. Even seasonal pissheads were awed by the intrepid Duchess. After all, her skill in navigating both sides during the Civil War had preserved Ham House intact *and* in her name. She'd given birth to eleven babies. Yet in middle age, could still hold her head high among King Charles II's court darlings.

Maureen reflected on this during her brief hiatus, once more exchanging eye contact with the red-haired, vivacious woman in the portrait, who had ended her days alone, embittered and insignificant, a fate Maureen considered the most terrible of all.

Shuddering out of the waning seventeenth century into the twenty first, she dared them brave Elizabeth's silver mirror on the lacquered table. Trigger warning: they might be confronted with the icy stare of the Duchess herself, as some *deluded halfwits* had claimed.

'I don't feel comfortable lingering here at night, so I'll meet you back in the Great Hall.'

Various batches idled round the slanted chess board floor, some enticed by the fake smouldering coals. Maureen positioned herself by the front door, taking care to forget her handbag.

'Of course, we don't just have ghosts indoors here at Ham, we have them outside in the Gardens as well.'

Drawing back the stiff iron bolts, she pulled open the giant door, carved with royalist inscription *Vivat Rex*, and marshalled the party outside into the biting cold. To avoid small talk, particularly with those boasting paranormal gifts, she paced some way ahead. Down the stone steps, past the neatly clipped yews twinkling with white lights, until they rounded the carriage circle to the east.

The Cherry Garden entranced in the moonlight, as they crunched through the tunnel of hornbeams. Wisps of mist unfurled round privet cones and box hedges, while tiny crystals encrusted domes of lavender, conjuring giant ice cream scoops. A veritable fairy tale setting. Or at least, the backdrop for some dry-iced, 1980s pop video. Maureen half expected a synth soundtrack and a ball gowned woman dashing down latticed paths, pursued by trenchcoated men with dodgy sideburns.

Shivering on the south front, her charges had become distracted, lured by cosy pubs, centrally heated homes and prime time TV. So, she raced through an improbable suicide fable —one of the basic rules of public speaking: always follow a violent death with a cheery, festive tale — and congregating outside the brightly-lit Dairy for the last stop, Maureen rattled to the chase.

'…They jumped up to answer it, but to their surprise,' wry smile, dramatic pause, 'no one was there. And it is said that the 9th Earl crosses the Courtyard every Christmas Eve, to knock on this door.' She rapped it with her knuckles. 'But you can only hear him if you're inside this former cottage.'

No chance as the Dairy will be locked, and the whole thing's made up anyhow.

'That brings us to the end of this tour. I do hope you've enjoyed it.'

Feel free to tip. Seriously, the cash would come in handy.

Maureen savoured their genial applause, aware that it was part motivated by the prospect of escaping the cold. It was standard to invite questions at this point, but she needed to return the wretched key, while her shepherd escorted everyone off the premises. So, she whispered to

Daisy that she was such a wally, but she'd left her handbag in the Great Hall. Careful to dodge any laggards, she trotted over the cobbles. Followed by Daisy, who was gushing over Maureen's sick tour. Normally, she would have lapped this up, but yet again, she needed rid of her shepherd.

'Well, you better make sure this lot bugger off.' Maureen stepped through the West Door. 'Especially that stand-in from *Most Haunted*.' She inclined her head towards Red Glasses, who was roaming round the Courtyard, snapping random photos. 'See you at the front gates in a bit.'

With the door closed firm, she discovered at once that Daisy had locked the key cupboard. Her pride in pulling off the casing assignment dissolved. *Not so clever now, are we?* After several more useless tugs, she grabbed the Key Log and flicked through to check who had taken out the Green Closet key that day. Meera, who had also signed its return. Curse The Enforcer's clampdown. What now? She might as well scout out the office before retrieving her handbag. Maybe she could place the key somewhere out of sight, as if someone had misplaced it there. Assuming the office was unlocked. She pressed her shoulder again the Staff Door, thanking both Daisy and God, that the downstairs lights were still on, along with the flickering fake candles. Furthermore, that the stable door yielded to her nudge.

There had been a serious tidy-up. The half-open boxes were gone, the bin had been emptied, food debris removed, and the desks were pretty much devoid of clutter. This was a total bastard, as it meant there was nowhere obvious to hide the key. She swivelled round on an ergonomic chair, and opened some drawers, rifling through post-its, staplers, paper clips and biros. Her usual stationery kleptomania overwhelmed by more pressing considerations. She could leave it in a drawer. Not very plausible, as Meera had recorded putting it back. Surely there were duplicate keys. What if this was the only copy, and no one could find it tomorrow? Maureen envisaged the staff's panic, Emma's blanched face.

This hadn't been part of the plan at all, but it could work in her favour. What would happen if she just kept it? But again, she pictured the furore. Could she imprint its pattern on a bar of soap? *What is this — a prison break? Anyhow, only antibac liquid wash these days.* What if she—

Maureen sprang off the chair. She could have sworn she heard footsteps. *Christ on a Brompton, is that Daisy back already?* Dredging up excuses to warrant her presence in the office, she listened at the door. Silence. *I really am losing it. Better grab my handbag.*

Once more in the Great Hall, she darted to the cubbyholes. Then it happened. Sniffing, she picked up her bag. She sniffed again. It took a few seconds to place, but then, unmistakeable. And she registered the hairs on the back of her neck stand up, like Pepys's fur, when cornered by the plump silver tabby over the road. The heady scent of roses. Drenching her airways. Another footstep. Distinct this time.

'Hello?'

Maureen heard her futile question echo round the minstrel gallery. Her voice sounded faint, somehow disembodied beneath the pounding bass of her heart, as if the plea had been uttered by someone else.

She fought the impulse to look, but she knew she would. She knew she had to. Clutching her handbag with rigid fingers, she raised her head in the soft candlelight, and dragged her horrified stare away from the bogus smoke rising from the amber coals. Away from the shining Christmas tree, and inch by inch, towards the darkness of the Great Staircase. There, in the shadows, immobile on the wooden steps — an indiscernible silhouette. Maureen's mouth was dry, but she dared not swallow. She dared not blink. Rooted on the marble floor, her grey eyes locked in appalling paralysis on an ethereal being. This was no illusion, no trick of her mind. Even before her vision adjusted to the dusky stairwell, she knew. She'd known as soon as she'd inhaled that weirdly familiar fragrance. Like a camera coming into focus, the amorphous outline assumed the unequivocal figure of a woman in a long, black dress. A gaping silk hood part obscured the pale face and a pair of dark eyes that met her own frozen gaze.

Mocked by her tour script, Maureen was enveloped in an icy wave. She saw her laboured breaths cloud in the glacial air before her and became aware of a repetitive clicking noise. After several protracted seconds, she realised this was her own teeth chattering, and it was hard to judge whether this was triggered by cold, or sheer terror. But stronger than the fear, and more awful, was the slowly tightening grip of a bottomless, abject despair.

Chapter 11
Valediction

Biding in the cold candlelit hall, eyes still fixed on this blood-curdling spectre, Maureen's flight reflex suddenly kicked in. She span round and hurtled down the West Passageway. Past the open office. Not looking back. Never daring to look back. Wedged against the other side of the staff exit, she struggled to steady her breathing. She more or less fell down the stairs and shot out of the West Door. Slammed it shut without any regard for the blackened key lining her pocket. Safe at last, she exhaled into the raw night, purging any vestige of roses from her lungs.

At the front gates, Maureen wheezed if Daisy was okay to lock up. Scarce waiting for the younger woman's blasé assent, she screeched off down the leafless avenue. Headlights at full beam, failing to swerve the mounds of horse dung, jolting her Micra's suspension, as she took the speed bumps too fast.

Back in the sanctuary of number fourteen, she dipped a Rich Tea into her whisky nightcap. An excellent combo. Her brain throbbed with ideas and discarded solutions to the gunmetal, key-shaped problem she turned over in her hand. Towards the end of her teaching career, she had scorned the diktat to replace *naughty* with *sad choice.* But right now, she conceded that she had indeed made a very sad choice.

Admitting defeat, she climbed the stairs, scraped a toothbrush round her receding gums and dragged on some flannel pjs. At last, she fell in and out of a twitchy, duvet-tangled sleep. Visited once more in her dreams, by the wraith in silk mourning dress, looming in the dim stairwell. But this time no longer silent, the Duchess's manic laughter jolting her awake.

She reached out for the comforting lump of Pepys, his teeth clacking on some wild feline adventure. He yowled drowsily as she stroked behind his ears and reflected on the evening's surreal twist. What could it all mean? A terrible portent, or some strange, sisterly affiliation spanning the centuries? Some sort of message, even. Then it came to her, as if she'd been struck over the head with the Duke's Book of Common Prayer. A remedy so glaring, that she half expected a lightbulb to materialise above her head. The definitive solution. And with that, she plunged into the sweet sleep of the righteous.

Chancing her arm first thing the next morning, Maureen drove over Richmond Bridge. As she turned off Twickenham Green, she experienced a sudden sting, like the scab being scraped off a fresh wound. This was Laura's old stomping ground. Or their ends, as Jodie would say. Left, past the Sally Army Hall, and just after the pebble-dashed bungalow. She wasn't expecting the converted garage to be open. Almost suspicious, during the holidays, but best not question the augurs. Aware there was always Timpson's on the corner by Barclays, she favoured this small, independent locksmith.

Yet again, she worked her barking old dear routine. A cheery middle-aged man in faded overalls examined the key's coronet. She was sufficiently unbarking to have removed its blue plastic tag.

'Haven't seen anything like this for a while.'

In response to Maureen's vapid smile, he added that if he couldn't copy it from the machine, he could ask another locksmith to cut it by hand, which would be expensive. Mindful that would scupper her plans, she let the goddesses of fate decide.

'Bring it back if you have any problems with it,' he said, as he handed over her change.

Thanks, but that'd be tricky.

'Will do.'

And with that, she zipped this shiny new toy with its tarnished twin into her Chanel handbag and reversed out of the driveway. Despite her miraculous possession of the Key of Doom, plus duplicate, she still faced one almighty stumbling block. How could she return the original unseen? Only too aware of the Armageddon that would unleash once it was discovered missing, she had no choice but to drive straight to Ham, even though it was Friday.

She popped into the office off the West Passageway — already a shambles again — and played the eager airhead. Knowing full well that the rota was booked, she claimed to be just passing. Did they need any extra guides? Meera thanked her, but no, today's shifts were all sorted.

Meera smiled at the muddled pensioner. 'Less rooms to cover, now the first floor's shut.' Also, Sanjay was standing in for the Architecture Tour. Another loner with time to fill. 'We're quite short tomorrow, if you're interested?'

Maureen promised to check her blank diary back home and let her know, tatty bye. Meera ogled her a few seconds. Who needed to check on *paper* what they were doing the very next day? As unfathomable as only being offered cow's milk in your macchiato. Bless those barmy Boomers. As it happened, Maureen had been born on the very rump of the Silent Generation.

Although the shutters were closed, the House had mellowed in the filtered daylight. Nevertheless, Maureen avoided the Great Hall like the plague, and scuttled back down the Passageway. She had timed her arrival well before 11 am, so the West Stairs were deserted. Seizing her chance, she placed the key on the filthy mat directly below the cupboard, half hidden beneath the cast iron radiator.

Her logic was to simulate the key having been dropped the night before, after Daisy had rifled through the cupboard. A clumsy solution. But how else could she return it without arousing suspicion? In fact, despite her fitful night's sleep, she couldn't deny a certain smugness. Especially as its silver copy now furnished her Chanel inner pocket. But she also knew that it could land that warm-hearted recruit right in the Eartha Kitt, depending on who found it. But shy of further excuses for loitering, she left. No longer triumphant, but uneasy, with a liberal sprinkle of guilt.

* * *

'What did you do?' asked Deirdre, leaning forward like a fidgety child between the Micra's front seats.

'Just legged it, right out of there as fast as I could. And did *not* look back.'

'Had you been on a bevy sesh with your Neighbourhood Watch pals?'

Maureen stared ahead at the bus inching forward, refusing to dignify Rhona's jibe. At her suggestion they help Meera out this Saturday, both had jumped at the chance to escape further festive internment with spouses and extended families.

'Well, I believe you,' said Deirdre, reclining once more in the rear seat.

'I'm not saying you made it up. Just think you've lost the plot,' Rhona creased up. 'Come on, I didn't mean anything by it. You'd been blethering about ghosts for the past hour. Your mind was playing tricks on you.'

From the corner of her eye, she caught Rhona gesture downing a drink at Deirdre, who promptly changed the subject. 'Barbara reckons that Lorna will be made permanent GM.'

'Hope not, she's pure nippy sweetie.'

Maureen tuned out of their gossip and relived those minutes alone in the empty Great Hall. The intense chill, those coal black eyes fixed on hers. Why this supernatural experience now, after ten years, without so much as a trace of tobacco in the Marble Dining Room?

'It's green!' shouted Rhona, as the van behind hooted.

Maureen pressed down on the accelerator and sped off, flashing her hazards to the gesticulating driver.

'Unusual for you to hang back like a fart in a trance,' said Rhona.

Deirdre spent the rest of the journey speculating on which staff might be axed in the New Year, while Maureen focused on her driving, aware she was now under scrutiny from her front seat passenger.

As Deirdre jabbered on, Maureen wondered for the umpteenth time how long it had taken for someone to spot the key. Fretting, she swung her Micra round, bonnet inches from a towering lime.

Claiming to want first dibs on room choice, she left Rhona and Deirdre ambling towards the shop. In truth, she needed to gauge the prevailing staff mood. And as she speedwalked across the Forecourt, she had to admit, it added a decent pinch of spice to the day.

In the Mess Room, Thelma was ensconced in her usual armchair by the bookshelves. What was she doing here on a Saturday? For the first time, Maureen considered that Thelma might be lonely too. Did she have any family, she wondered? Unsmiling, the Medusa studied Maureen from above her bone china mug. Apparently, she'd once been some big fish in Mole Valley District Council. Admirable to have smashed through that glass ceiling. Other than that, she knew very little about her. Best keep it that way.

At the main table, Daisy and Trevor sat side by side.

'Hey Maureen, I was just talking about your cool ghost tour the other night.'

Trevor grinned at Maureen, although his eyes flitted straight back to the lush retail supervisor, who slapped a hand to her forehead.

'Except afterwards, I must've dropped the Green Closet key as I was locking the cupboard.'

'Easily done,' said Trevor, who had never done any such thing in all his years at Ham. 'Anyways, at least *I* clocked it — well, trod on it — and not She-Who-Must-Not-Be-Named.'

Hallelujah!

Daisy wiped the back of her hand across her brow. 'Think I better stick to the shop for now.'

Mentally mimicking Daisy's gesture, Maureen had to restrain herself from hugging Trevor. In her head, she leapt up on to the table for a victory strut, imagining

Thelma's face.

For a second, she contemplated sharing her mysterious, ghostly sighting. Reflecting on Rhona's earlier taunts, she decided against it. Had Daisy sensed anything that night on returning to the House? Surely not. If she'd caught so much as a spectral whiff of roses she'd burst with excitement. Then there was the Dark Lord seated by the window to consider. Maureen mumbled something about nipping to the shop, and exited with a virtual backflip, like the burgeoning maestro cat burglar she was.

Although, she conceded, Lady Luck had played no small part. Lady Luck, or possibly even Her Grace? Yes, that might explain the Duchess's manifestation. Despite scaring the baggy pants off her, maybe it signified some sort of endorsement. A valediction.

Chapter 12
An Unlikely Heroine
Saturday, 30th December

She'd rather overdone the mulled wine. Far more palatable than the brew doled out in the Orangery, it oiled her attempts at small talk. But most of all, it numbed her inner void. This was a savage time of year. Lightheaded, she stepped back from the wood burner, nearly knocking a plate of smoked salmon blinis out of Ollie's hand.

'Oops, Britney would've hoovered those up. And you're on a diet, missy.'

He wagged a finger at the pug licking his brown ankles beneath the rolled hem of his jeans. In response, she raised dark tragic eyes, strands of drool seeping from velvety jowls on to her *HO HO HO!* neckerchief. As Ollie continued to mingle, Maureen dropped her canapé on to the oak floor. Snuffled in a trice by Britney, who panted for more. Maureen couldn't take too much rich food these days. My reflux is your diet-wrecking Christmas bonus, she thought, as she stooped to ruffle the wrinkled, doleful diva.

She sought sanctuary in the upstairs bathroom. Fixing her daft-old-bat grin, and ignoring the empty downstairs loo, she elbowed past the couple from across the road, who always blanked her. Earlier, Ollie had introduced them as Rich and Trudy.

'Actually, it's Rick,' he'd corrected, flicking his mutton-dressed-as-lamb bob.

'Is that Rick with a silent *P*?' Maureen had managed to refrain from asking. The man in question stood anaesthetising Will about his crucial work in IT. Will nodded with emphatic disinterest, trying to make eye contact with Ollie, who was screeching in the corner with a man in a paisley shirt and reindeer antlers. Next to Rick, stood Trudy — *actually, it's Face Ache* — kitted out in sequinned top and pleather trousers. She met Maureen's gaze in the Art Deco mirror; dead behind the eyes.

Headbutting paper lanterns in the hallway, Maureen smiled at a glum woman with blue-streaked hair parked on the striped stairwell, her Santa Baby jumper stretched tight over a distended belly. Or was it just a cushion? Maureen squeezed past with whispered apologies.

'When's it due?' Seema asked.

'March 12th,' said Ms Blue Streaks, balancing a near empty bowl of Kettle crisps on her bump.

'Spring baby!'

Delighted by this inconsequential detail, Seema beamed up at Maureen, who grimaced back from the landing. Seema knew everything that was going on down their street, rendering the local Neighbourhood Watch scheme redundant. Her generosity compensated for her brash nosiness. In truth, Maureen suspected that the former was cover for the latter. Nevertheless, she liked Seema, and found her raucous laughter infectious. She kept nagging at Maureen to join the TAGs — The Alberts' Girls. This dreadful female social club met to drink Prosecco, discuss house prices and any sexual shenanigans that took place in this network of narrow Victorian streets. Originally built for railway workers, these cottages had once been dirt cheap, but now sold for exorbitant sums, despite their bijou proportions. Over eight hundred grand, according to Seema. How in tarnation could anyone afford the deposit these days?

Although she'd inherited her cottage decades earlier, Maureen had paid a bitter price for her good fortune. Her convivial, tireless father had keeled over one sunny day with a massive heart attack. Snuffed out without warning in his sixth decade. Bernie, her Irish chain-smoking mother, was left utterly adrift. Having no Stan to cook for, scour junk shops and bicker with, she lost interest in everything apart from gin and the *Antiques Roadshow*. Within a year they had lowered Bernie's coffin into the double burial plot that she had insisted on securing, to lie forever with her soulmate. According to the death certificate, she'd died from double pneumonia, after a severe flu epidemic had swept the country that winter. But it seemed to Maureen that in different ways, both her parents had died from broken hearts.

Neither daughter could bear the thought of selling their ramshackle childhood home, even though house prices had shot up, fuelled by the soaring inflation of the 1970s. Maureen had offered to pay half the value by taking out a mortgage, but Kathy had just wanted her to have it. Frank's antique shops were doing a roaring trade, and he'd even built a swimming pool at the end of their huge garden in Weybridge. Maureen had insisted. In the end, they agreed a reduced sum in exchange for some of the contents. Frank and some of his removal lads loaded their British Leyland van with a couple of button-back chairs and a corner cabinet along with its Staffordshire contents, wrapped in pages of the Evening Standard. And they managed to squeeze in the grandfather clock with the rotating sun and moon faces. They left her the rest, including her father's oak writing desk.

These days, the tiny back bedroom that she used to share with Kathy, served as a guest-room-cum-dumping-ground. Although, the small, stencilled bed hadn't been slept in for ages. Not since Jodie started secondary school. Her feet would stick out the window if she lay on it now. Time to invest in a futon.

Maureen perched on an upcycled milking stool, resting her elbow on the roll-top bath with its clawed feet. A breathy cover version of *The Power Of Love* wafted up through the cracks of the distressed floorboards, and her head swam as she gazed at the wall of shimmering mosaic tiles. Now she regretted that last glass of mulled wine.

So much better once she'd flushed away the contents of her stomach, discharging lavish squirts of some *parfum d'intérieur* round the gleaming bathroom. According to the glass bottle, it scented the air with the *perfect fragrant blend of blackcurrant leaves and Bulgarian rose*, but her sinuses were still burning from acid bile, so it might as well have been fly spray. Next, she gargled some garish blue mouthwash by the sink, to preserve a shred of dignity. She imagined Rhona carping, *Last time I was that steaming, my parents had an empty.*

Nobody appeared to have clocked Maureen's lengthy absence. Downstairs, she braved the throng with a glass of Pellegrino and a lighter heart — buoyed by the memory of Laura's parting promise to pay for return flights. For the first time, Rick deigned to speak to her, but Seema, ever the humanitarian, rescued her from a detailed itinerary of his winter ski break.

Face Ache was quizzing Paisley Shirt about a stolen Manet. Apparently, he was some fine art bigwig at a London auction house. Had he heard the recent news that it had been found dumped under a tree in Hyde Park, not far from the Russian Embassy? Her neighbour had imbibed a little too much of the hosts' quince gin, and her attempt to sound sophisticated in front of the Richmond Hill resident, now minus his antlers, fell a tad flat.

'Oh, that turned out to be a hoax. A publicity stunt by a street artist about the nature of truth or something. Doubt they'll ever get the original back now. Probably been destroyed.'

Oblivious to Face Ache's deflation, Paisley Shirt tackled Seema's arch enquiry: had he ever come across any lifted paintings? He shook his head.

'You can't sell high value stolen art through any kosher auction house. Everything's checked against the Register.'

'I suppose they're just stolen to order for the head of some criminal gang. Or an oligarch,' snorted Face Ache, eager to ingratiate herself back into the conversation.

'Bit of a movie myth that art's stolen for its beauty. It's unlikely there's some evil villain's lair, heaving with masterpieces by Goya and Matisse. Stolen art's usually traded between criminal gangs for a fraction of its worth, say to finance arms or drug deals. Sometimes, it's shoved under floorboards as a bargaining chip in case of arrest.'

'So, it's not worth me breaking into the National Gallery to pay for our Verbier trip then!'

Joining their group, Rick chuckled at his own lame intervention, eliciting a scowl from his wife. An awkward lull descended, broken only by Britney erupting at some sozzled newcomers and Ollie's boomed introductions. Maureen's chance for an unobtrusive exit.

The cottage felt cold and shabby on her return. Even Pepys had abandoned her for some nocturnal, feline revels. What on earth was she going to do now? With Laura emigrating to the US, she would, in effect, have no family left. Apart from Rhona, she had few close friends. She yearned for something to fill the chasm. Why shouldn't she buck the trend? It wasn't hard grubby cash that she craved, but rather, the consolation of skilled craftsmanship, of transcendent beauty. The sweetness of forbidden fruit.

Slade's jaded chorus wafted through the wall, as she warmed her hands round a mug of tea. Not everybody's having fun, she thought. Riding a surge of fury, she wrestled a sudden desire to throw open the flaking French windows and howl at the moon. She wondered how Face Ache and Seema would react, or whether anyone would even hear, and an unbearable, suffocating loneliness pressed in on her.

* * *

She woke to an invisible vice gripping her skull. After several minutes, she flung on a men's navy dressing gown over plaid pyjamas. Padding down her narrow staircase, she stepped between lop-sided stacks of dog-eared paperbacks. *Jaws* (best score), *The Godfather* (that horse's head bit), *The Hound of the Baskervilles* (Jeremy Brett always), *You Only Live Twice* (toffs' Alastair Maclean), *Riders* (well thumbed), *Zen And The Art Of Motorcycle Maintenance* (abandoned), *Rebecca* (unbeatable intro), *To Kill A*

Mockingbird (the divine Gregory Peck), *Feel The Fear And Do It Anyway* (fuck off), further spineless best-sellers and some disintegrating guidebooks. What was it that Japanese multi-millionaire, neat freak banged on about? Laura, bemoaning the prospect of packing, had mentioned something about her. Only keep the things that *spark joy*. She loved every single one of those books, except *Zen And The Art Of Motorcycle Maintenance*, plus *Feel The Fear And Do It Anyway*.

Maureen needed a more palpable form of detox. Head-butting her shins, Pepys purred in protest at the tardiness of his breakfast. Always secure your own oxygen mask first. Watery-eyed and yawning, she swilled a couple of paracetamol. Dazed, she tore open a pouch and squeezed some dubious, jelly-smeared chunks into a bowl, daubed with paw prints and a spidery *Jodie, 7 years*. Then, slumped over a plate of marmalade slavered toast and a Votes For Women mug of milky tea. An irregular, silvery trail glistened with bravado on the lino floor. Weren't snails supposed to hibernate in winter? As Pepys gnashed his food, head tilted to one side, she relished the day's first, and always the best, cuppa.

She needed to get dressed. She needed to clean the house. She needed to go to Sainsbury's. Instead, brushing burnt crumbs off the kitchen table, she opened her laptop. There were the usual phishing emails inviting her to earn thousands trading on Bitcoin, demanding her personal details so that an important package could be delivered, or even enquiring if she needed a f**kbuddy. She also ignored several Facebook notifications, a TAGs invite for Xmas Drinks at The White Horse, and a Neighbourhood Watch summary.

Waiting for the acetaminophen to enter her bloodstream, she downloaded the latest HH Bulletin and perused the headlines. A riveting update on the quarterly pest check, photos of the winter clean in action, and a request to steward the House during a major filming project in early Feb. Unable to stand this level of excitement, Pepys shot through the cat flap, coating the sides with more tufts of his black fur.

About to shut the laptop, her attention was lured to an article on seventeenth-century female spies. Intrigued by the description of an auburn, pockmarked agent, who had used her links with the royal laundress to smuggle over one thousand, seven hundred pounds of gold into the exiled court at Oxford. Inside barrels of soap. The consignment had even included fresh hosiery for King Charles, with whom she was rumoured to have serviced in other ways. Although the evidence for this appeared to be mainly based on the agent's gender.

Maureen conjured the eye roll emoji so often favoured by her great niece when texting to complain about her mother's latest totalitarian edict. Evidently, the stresses of emigration were taking their toll. Not wishing to dwell on her own slice of empty nest, Maureen fixated on the article.

Headache receding, she read how this low-born agent had employed many daring ruses to divert funds to the royalists, as well as relaying intelligence between Charles and his supporters. As if typed in bold caps, certain words leapt off the screen — *smuggled; riches; laundry.* Odd how this image of an obscure woman smuggling riches with the help of a royal laundress struck a chord. An unlikely heroine. And just like that, the faint germ of a plan sprouted in her anaesthetised mind.

Chapter 13
Be Prepared
January

New Year's Eve came and went with barely a chunder in her direction, followed by interminable bitter nights with Pepys curled beside her for warmth. Somehow, Maureen dragged herself through those bleak January days. She had to dig deep — into her kitchen cupboards for cake and gin. Then there was her New Year's project to keep her occupied. Who knew planning a fine art heist could be such a hoot?

The PCs in her local library were busier now with the digitally excluded underclass that eked out an existence even in the most affluent boroughs: the black hole of computer-illiterate pensioners, desperate universal credit claimants and disadvantaged school kids clawing their way out of the widening poverty gap. Or just to sit somewhere warm. Brushing these unpalatable truths aside, Maureen knew she couldn't risk any unwelcome attention. Besides, browsing the NT Collections website from her own laptop hardly constituted a damning digital footprint. Thwarted by Daisy the night of her ghost tour, she took a ruler to the actual screen and measured the width of the painting. Next, she measured the width including its asymmetrical, oak frame. It proved fiddly and took several goes. Just as well she was in the privacy of her own home.

Re-booting her arithmetic muscle memory, she divided the second number by the first to calculate the ratio. After much effing and jeffing over a calculator, she used this to work out the complete width and height, thus determining the life-size surface area of the *Blackbird, Butterfly and Cherries.*

The name's Pythagoras, Maureen Pythagoras.

Arts and crafts were never her bag. She'd always dreaded that part of her teaching timetable; the sticky mess of coloured, scrunched tissue, the squabbles, the tears, the endless bloody clearing up. The Head Tosser's insistence that the clumsy artwork be *corrected* prior to parents' evenings. Nevertheless, whiling away this foul January afternoon with her own bizarre cut-and-paste session proved good sport.

Fished out from the recycling, she had cut and taped together several cardboard packs of porridge oats and savoured a *Blue Peter* moment of satisfaction. Then, stripping the single duvet off the spare bed, she'd rolled it into a tattered old laundry bag. Using the one-she'd-made-earlier model and guesstimating the ornate frame's approximate depth, she was able to establish whether the Dutch oil could be concealed inside. She had to trial several different folding techniques before she convinced herself that it might work. Thus, a laundered duvet would provide the perfect camouflage, while also cushioning the precious artwork from any knocks and bumps. All this inspired by the guile of that obscure, seventeenth-century female spy.

Now all she needed was a new, sturdier holdall. Nothing untoward about ordering one online, she decided. With no availability in plain white, it had come down to a choice between the standard check patterns. She chose a blue plaid, scored with red vertical lines.

Well, that's totally going to blend in with the House décor, eye roll.

Another trip to the library was required for yet more anonymous online searches. She worried that she was becoming a regular fixture, but she needed to research how to package antique oils in transit. The last thing she wanted was to damage Her Precious. She immersed herself in the water and grease-resistant properties of acid-free glassine paper. This had no chemical interaction with any object it touched and was recommended by most art shipping services.

After checking out the value of some of Bosschaert's other works on various auction house websites, she decided to buy some of that glassine stuff from a supply store in Covent Garden. Pullingers Art Shop in Kingston would have been more convenient, but best not shit on her own doorstep. Besides, she could drop in on the National Portrait Gallery and have gander round the Tudors on the second floor. More to the point, their café also served excellent cake.

Ham House was due to be closed for a few days' filming in early February. Already listed on the Project Conservator rota, she figured that the overall chaos triggered by the cast and crew, would create optimum conditions for her mission. In essence, her one and only chance.

Due to popular demand, volunteers could only sign up for a single session, which meant just one bite at that varnished Dutch cherry. With no guarantee whether an opportunity would present itself, she had decided to comply with the Scouts' motto, to *be prepared.* Although, she doubted that Baden Powell had art theft in mind when he devised that maxim, using his own initials.

Not that she considered this *proper* theft. It was more of a game really. The most stressful, exciting game that she'd ever played, but one that had given her more sense of purpose than she'd experienced in a long time. At least, since she had retired from teaching over a decade ago. Discounting some Post-its from the school stationary cupboard and the odd loo roll, she'd never stolen anything in her life. Yet, right now in her pathetic, empty little world, it was precisely the element of criminal danger that propelled her.

It was nearly time. Time to dust off her figurative, balaclava and black Spanx jumpsuit. Time for the white-knuckle ride of her threescore years and ten.

Chapter 14
And Action
Monday, 5th February

'Standby for a take. Tuck in please.'

'Rolling. Quiet everyone! Thank you.'

From her hidden vantage point, Maureen watched a pony-tailed lad in an Idles T-shirt, raise a microphone attached to a long pole, dark patches under his arms.

Earlier, a well-built man with hair in immaculate cornrows, had introduced himself as Martin, the commercial director. In addition, he was shooting cast interviews down in the Kitchen. In a faint German accent, he explained that Mr. Idles was the boom operator. He'd tried to outline the various roles and hierarchies within the umpteen crew members. The guy in the Arsenal cap used a laser rangefinder to measure the camera focus, then burbled something about checking the actors' marks. While behind them, the muscular girl with hennaed hands taping down cables, was known as a grip. Some red-bearded bloke discussing lighting with the Supreme-hoodied DOP, was called the gaffer, whatever that meant.

Maureen had strived to take it all in but was distracted when a squat man with shaved head, sauntered past, shouldering a tripod. Its three feet, shod in split tennis balls, grazed one of the gold Sutherland frames. Venetia, the NT filming curator had shouted a belated warning, and on seeing no harm was done, closed her eyes and inhaled.

'And action.'

The Long Gallery had been transformed into an Hercule Poirot film set. A Persian rug was rolled out over the parquet floor, dotted with pot plants. Side tables displayed Art Deco lamps, silver-framed sepia photos and a domed Bakelite radio. At the south end, a large writing desk had been placed near the Library Closet, complete with inkwell, an old-fashioned typewriter and piles of leather hardbacks. Unrecognisable.

The camera swung round as an actress in puff-sleeved blouse and tailored skirt, sat down at the desk and sliced open an envelope with a paper knife. Brushing chestnut curls off her alabaster forehead, she pulled out an engraved invitation and arched a pencilled eyebrow. A gangly, clean-shaven man in Fedora and trench coat burst into frame, and she thrust the card into a drawer.

'Captain Hastings, this is a surprise!'

'Cut there.'

Maureen stuck her head out of the Library Closet, as the crew sprang back into action, wiping camera lenses, moving props, lowering booms and whipping out phones. The spiky-haired director addressed the man in the Fedora in a low voice, waving his hands around. Maureen recognised Mr. Fedora from various TV dramas but couldn't recall his name. Laura would have known. A woman with a tousled bob dabbed a sponge round the actress's retroussé nose, a dizzying array of make-up brushes protruding from her pouch. Meanwhile, a fleece-clad assistant sealed the invitation into an identical envelope and placed it back on the desk at a precise angle to the inkstand.

The crew exuded a relaxed, jovial feel: banter about hangovers and football results. Mr. Idles produced a bag of jellybeans, clocked Maureen and grinned, before stuffing them back in his cargoes. This was one of Maureen's officially assigned roles — ensuring no food or drink was consumed in the House. Strictly capped bottles of water only. Of course, Maureen also had another very specific agenda, and this was totes unofficial.

As Maureen headed off on her break, the lead actress, parka flung over red silk dress, arrived on set amid a flurry of air kisses.

'Cup of tea, please Mand. You know how I like it.'

A strawberry blonde girl with rolled spreadsheet sticking out the back pocket of her ripped jeans, rushed off down the Great Staircase.

Leaning over the Round Gallery, the glam Ms Luvvie sprinkled a few drops from her bottle of water onto the head of Mr. Fedora, now reading his script in a director's chair below. Gratified by her own jolly japes, she caught Maureen's eye and winked.

'I know, I know, shouldn't spill water, but it only went on Si.'

She batted long lashes in defence.

'Well, it's more that the bannisters aren't really safe to lean on,' Maureen replied. 'Though I suppose an accident would create huge publicity for the film.'

And close down Ham House.

The actress threw back her head and roared, although she was also quick to stand back from the balustrade. A woman with a French braided bun approached, armed with a clear zipped case of rollers and hairgrips, with various brushes and combs fastened to her belt bag.

'Time for my perm already?'

'Yep, and your sexy hairnet.'

The stylist turned and addressed Maureen in conspiratorial tones.

'Is it true, there's loads of servants' passageways in this place?'

'Yes, they were put in when—'

'Are there? Oh my God! I bet this place is haunted,' Ms Luvvie cut in, 'I mean, how old is this house?'

'Over four hundred years.'

Ms Luvvie tried to raise eyebrows but was foiled by colonies of paralysing bacteria.

'Didn't they used to burn witches back then?' the hairdresser persisted. 'My daughter's doing a dissertation on witch trials.'

'It's true, many women were convicted of witchcraft. Hundreds were hanged. Not round here though, I don't think.'

Maureen left them exchanging ghoulish stories, resisting the urge to launch into a private ghost tour. Or to mention the wheels and petalled circles scratched into the Buttery panelling, to deter evil spirits and witches.

Except, they haven't managed to keep me out.

Descending the Great Staircase, she passed Meera and Venetia steadying a tall stepladder. A crew member wobbled on top, trying to cover the not-so-1930s flashing red lights on the alarm sensors. The resident staff often moaned how these were triggered by Huntsman spiders skittering over them during the night.

'I've already phoned the monitoring company to say the alarms are off for filming today,' she overheard Meera explain. They seemed distracted by the task at hand, and Maureen passed by unheeded. *Ta for the heads-up.*

She picked her way through the Great-Hall-turned-obstacle-course, its chequered floor masked by a patchwork of overlapping grey mats. As if performing some odd dance routine, she swerved round fold-up chairs; TV monitors; lighting tripods with the requisite tennis ball feet; incongruous red foam edging the marble side tables; trollies; wardrobe racks; steel cases; tool kits; plastic crates and coils of thick, black cables. Magnificent, organised carnage.

'Where's the nearest 13 amp socket, love?' A red-faced electrician accosted her. 'S'alright, seen one.' and shot off in the opposite direction.

With the front door wide open, she noted Trevor and Sanjay chatting under the gazebo by the catering van. This was pitched in the carriage circle, next to a huge silver light reflector outside the Back Parlour window. Enter Ms Strawberry Blonde with a steaming disposable cup.

'Er sorry, no hot drinks in the House.'

Christ on a Walnut Whip, how many times do you need to be told?

The assistant grimaced and backed out. Despite her more pressing secret mission, Maureen was irritated by the overt flouting of this most basic rule. Then she bumped into a suited man with a bristly moustache. Another well-known actor, whom Maureen couldn't identify.

'What's the Wi-Fi password?' he demanded.

'They don't really have Wi-Fi here.'

Maureen felt the need to throw in a needless apology, as if this appalling oversight was down to her. Adding, 'I sometimes get a signal in the Orangery.'

Mr. Walrus Moustache grunted.

'Gonna hide in here before Martin collars me for an interview. Although, knowing him, he'll probably hunt me down on your CCTV.'

'That's unlikely, seeing as we haven't got any.'

'Okay, well I promise not to nick anything.'

Damn right, that's my job.

And with that, he plonked himself down on a chair tucked inside the Buttery and closed his eyes. This usually sparse room, lined with some of the oldest panelling in the House, was now crammed with furniture from the Gentlemen's Dining Room, together with more crates and fold-up chairs. The butler would have gone ape. Situated between the downstairs Kitchen and the Dining Room, the Buttery was where he would have checked all food dishes before service. And for any pilfering by the junior servants.

Not sure I could have got away with much under his watch.

Walking down the West Passageway, she bumped into Emma.

'Ah Maureen, now that you've had lunch, can you head back up to the Library Closet. They're still filming that scene in the Long Gallery and—'

'Er, I haven't—'

'As you know, everything's already been set up, but just in case they carry more stuff through the Library. Venetia, there you are! Been trying to radio you. I need to ask…'

And with that, Maureen was dismissed. As the two women swept back into the Great Hall, she paused for a few seconds, contemplating the animated chaos around her. Everyone engrossed within their assorted micro bubbles, trading insults and gossip, checking worksheets and phones. Here was her chance. Unnoticed, she turned and slipped into the office where the butler used to sleep. It had that Marie Celeste flavour: a contraband mug of coffee abandoned on a desk, drawers opened, half-drafted emails displayed on screens, hand-held radios spouting tetchy queries.

The floor by the filing cabinet heaved with myriad rucksacks and boxes. Shifting some of these aside, she extricated her plaid laundry bag stuffed with a single duvet. She'd waffled on about having collected it from the dry cleaners, not wanting to leave it in her car, due to the spate of break-ins down Ham Street, and it being too bulky for the Basement lockers. But Meera had been far too distracted by radio calls and demands from the crew, to register. Or care. Although cumbersome, its low tog rating made it lightweight, and amid all the turmoil, she looked unremarkable lugging it up the West Stairs to the first floor. She disappeared through the open door on the right, into a mellow, book-lined oasis.

The Library was one of Maureen's favourite rooms. It was like stepping back into the late 1670s. You could almost picture the Duke sipping a glass of claret, bent over his writing desk, immersed in some leather-bound tome, a fire crackling in the marble fireplace. Although, the fire extinguisher beside the cast iron grate shattered the illusion somewhat. From the cedar bookshelves, faux bronze figurines of those celebrated wordsmiths — Shakespeare, Milton and Spenser — observed her entrance. She advanced between the Duke's locked bureau and the mahogany table.

Neat rows of gold-leafed spines gleamed in the faint light yielded by the drawn blind. Inhaling that heavenly blend of polish and antique books, she gazed up at the plaster frieze of bay leaves and flower heads, dotted with berries. She marvelled at the plasterer's skill and patience in attaching each moulded piece. Her neck ached after just looking up, so that poor bastard must have been in dire need of an osteopath.

The red rope barrier safeguarding the furniture and more valuable books had been pushed right back. Placing her laundry bag near the guide's chair, she reappraised the room's other striking features, while she had it to herself. That large set of oak library steps — doubtless responsible for many a slipped disc. And facing her, a fetching pair of globes, evoking Tweedledum and Tweedledee. The terrestrial one perched like a giant, spherical egg in its stand, while its celestial twin sported a faded leather cover, like some oversized tea cosy.

Just as she contemplated standing on the guide's chair to vet the rarer books on the top shelves, Mr. Shaved Head sped through, carrying a steel case and a roll of cable, masquerading as a garden hose. Whistling tunelessly, he nodded at Maureen, dumped the case in the Library Closet and vanished. She needed to get back to business. The clock was ticking, and she still hadn't figured how to gain entry to the Green Closet. From then on, between takes, she chatted to the amiable Martin, peeked out into the Long Gallery, and tried to keep the faith.

Sunlight shimmered round the edges of lowered blinds. Indeed, it was one of those freakishly warm, golden days that made your inner demons applaud climate change. In the same way as you might savour the beauty of a flaming red sunset in the aftermath of a volcanic eruption, all too aware that the stunning ruby hues were caused by ash and poisonous gases.

Therefore, when Mr. Spiky Hair said they should break for lunch, there was a shameless scrum for the main catering van, next to the Orangery. Nearly all the cast and crew decamped on to the terrace in a laudably egalitarian fashion, with Simba, the Gardens' resident Bengal cat, soliciting for sausage, prawns and peri-peri chicken.

However, Mr Spiky Hair and Mr Supreme Hoody tarried on set to question a flummoxed Venetia. Unseen,

Maureen remained seated in the Library Closet, pretending to scroll through her phone. Discerning only snatches, her heart skipped a beat as she overheard mention of the Green Closet and saw Venetia scurry through the North Drawing Room. Minutes later, she spied the curator return with Emma, holding the Key of Keys. She heard the lift door slide open, presumably to switch on the Closet lights. There followed a familiar series of clicks, which signalled entry to that green-lined treasure trove.

From inside, she heard the men talking while Emma adjusted the blind and Venetia hovered in the doorway. Before long, the director and his sidekick emerged laughing and strolled off towards the Great Staircase to join their crew for lunch.

'He asked to look in here yesterday, but then that actress felt unwell, so they shot an outside scene instead.' Venetia made a peculiar horse puffing sound. 'Gave me a little break.'

'Relief all round,' said Emma, 'seeing as we lost the key.'

'What?'

'One of our guides misplaced it. He finally found it in his locker. Poor old duffer was mortified. Said he'd been distracted by *personal issues.* But you know, their memories start playing up at their age.' Emma locked the doors with swift expertise. 'Fun times.'

This morsel triggered both light and shade in the earwigging volunteer. Miffed that Sanjay had wangled two consecutive days on the rota, Maureen was also outraged at Emma's flippant ageism. Doubly so, considering Sanjay's wife. *Badly done, Emma!*

'God, I had no idea. Nightmare,' said Venetia, feeding off her colleague's omnishambles.

'All good in the end though,' said Emma. 'Anyway, can't see them filming in there to be honest. I know they've nearly wrapped, but it's their last day, so not enough time.'

'Hope not. It'd be super stressful, with it being so small.'

'Yep, awkward for the camera, boom et cetera. Anyhow, the alarm's off and we'll leave the lights on for now, but no point in removing the dustsheets unless it's a definite. You better take the key, in case they want to look in again. Can't risk a repeat of yesterday.' Emma broke into a high-pitched laugh, then checked herself. 'Radio me if you need help unlocking it. It's super fiddly. Guess we should grab a bite with everyone else.'

'Yes, what a morning.' Venetia pocketed the key. 'Must check out the catering van. The food looks seriously good.'

'Isn't it? Their mini doughnuts are lethal…'

Off they went, discussing abandoned diets, the latest synthetic resins for retouched paintings, and the red tape involved in exchanging artwork with independent charitable trusts. And as per usual, Maureen was left — unobserved, forgotten and quite alone.

But just this once, utterly elated.

Chapter 15
Petition to St. Martha

'I mean no one liked working with him and that actress, Emily Whatserface, you know the lead in — She told me he was dead creepy. Felt weirded out.'

'I know the one. Well fit. Anyway, curtains for his career. No one's gonna work with him now, the slimy perve.'

'This one seems alright. Super chilled.'

'Makes a fucking change.'

'Tell me about it. He's still out there eating lunch with everyone.'

Well, why the bally hell don't you get back out there with him then?

Rooted to the Green Closet parquet, Maureen resisted the urge to scream this out loud. If these eejits didn't bugger off pronto, she was royally screwed. Petrified on the spot, gripping two hundred and fifty grand's worth of art with her latex-gloves. There was no way she could old loon her way out of this one. Hysteria swelled within her. What would she say if Venetia joined these clowns and unlocked the door for Mr Spiky Hair?

'Er, I heard this noise coming from inside, and finding the doors ajar—'

'Open? But Emma locked them just before lunch.'

'How strange. Anyway, that's when I saw this painting had been removed.' Best not to name it or the artist. *'It was just lying on the floor here. I must have disturbed—'*

'What's that?'

She imagined Mr Spiky Hair pointing to the laundry bag by her feet. This was an absolute soup sandwich. While she could stuff the gloves in her pocket, there was nowhere to hide that wretched nylon holdall. Neither could she explain why, when investigating suspicious noises, she'd felt the need to bring a freshly laundered duvet with her. In case of an emergency nap? To incapacitate a dangerous thief? In fairness, it would be the last thing they'd expect — an old woman chucking a quilt over their head and wrestling them to the floor.

Outside in the Long Gallery, the pair bantered on. In desperation, Maureen eyed the Duchess's ebony table. From under the dust sheet, curved legs protruded in the form of topless bathing nymphs, their sinuous curves resting on lion's feet. She could try shoving the bag underneath, but there was no way to mask its shiny blue squares between those gilded paws. Plus, shit creek aside, she couldn't risk damaging any of the Closet's contents. That was a strict no-no. Even if the bag had been white and less garish, she couldn't spirit it away undetected. Her exit would be about as discreet as a one-man band.

When Mr Spiky Hair had asked to see the Green Closet, she thought she'd hit the jackpot. A double-edged bonus mind; although the alarms were off, the painting's disappearance might be discovered too soon. Or not, as her target was tucked away in the far corner. Just as she'd calculated after that portentous pub game, this was the only room displaying portable fine art, undisturbed by daily through-traffic. Her little *Blackbird* favoured the opportunist. Its removal wouldn't necessarily trigger alarm bells. None in fact, as they were all switched off. She banked on this, also aware that its absence wouldn't stay unnoticed for long.

In hindsight, it had all gone too well. Her duplicate key had worked a treat — hats off to that seasoned locksmith — and she'd perfected the knack of unlocking the Closet. Recalling the noise and hassle involved in unbolting it, she hadn't opened the left door. This meant that she had to enter sideways into the restricted doorway, squeezing the laundry bag in after. Double-checking the Long Gallery set remained uncrewed, she closed the non-bolted side.

This time, there was no hesitation as she crossed to the far alcove. While her target's position was convenient, it was also awkward, as she had to lean over a cabinet. Glad that its inlaid mother-of-pearl was protected with a dush sheet, she still feared contaminating it with her own DNA. In vain, she checked her fleece for hairs, as if she could control the shedding of dead skin cells, or the dropping of an eyelash. As her left arm brushed one of the green curtains in the corner, she reminded herself that she wasn't listed on any police database. Yet.

Another deep breath. Would her hunch from the test-run prove correct? Just in case, some wire cutters and a set of screwdrivers lay buried beneath the duvet. Minus any Ryman tweezers or springlock release tool. The moment of truth had arrived.

She didn't have to do this. She could walk away, and no one would ever know. But this was her one shot before the *Blackbird* was taken away from her. Otherwise, how often would she see it again? And hadn't she promised to look after it for Jodie? To give up now, after all this planning, the regret would eat away at her. And she'd had her fill of bitterness. Of stagnation. Sod all that, it was right there in front of her. How could she resist?

With tongue protruding from the corner of her mouth, she lifted the *Blackbird, Butterfly and Cherries* off the damask. As simple as that. Stock still, as if in a dream, holding the chalice in her latexed hands. As she drank in this dazzling gem, her elation surpassed any orgasm that she could remember. Well, it had been aeons. In that moment, she metamorphosed into the glossy blackbird — bill dribbling with sweet juice, gazing in wonder at the markings on the butterfly's outstretched wings. Like all highs, it vanished too soon, as she heard the numpties' premature return to the Long Gallery, buzzing like the fly which landed near the blackbird's foot. Only they were far less pleasing than Bosschaert's masterly insect.

As if in some Ealing Comedy, she froze, cradling her trophy, straining to hear the bants outside and praying they'd re-join their crew on the Orangery terrace. She also began to regret that second cuppa in the Mess Room.

* * *

Having commandeered the round table beneath the Basement window, Sanjay was hoovering a paper plate piled with croissants, macarons and chocolate dipped strawberries. He was in *very heaven*, as that sanctimonious bore, William Wordsworth, would have put it. Except Ham House being closed for filming hardly amounted to a New Age of Reason, and Sanjay's spring-chicken status had expired decades earlier.

'Have you seen how many lorries are parked out on the North Terrace? Conservation's flown out the window. Mind you, they must be minting it.'

He spoke through a mouthful of flaky pastry, and Maureen wasn't sure if he was referring to the filming company or the Trust.

'Mammoth crew. Like Piccadilly Circus up there.'

Preoccupied, she'd executed the appropriate nods and smiles, while swishing a Twinings teabag round her oak-leaf mug. Not wishing to queue at the catering van, she'd banked on the Mess Room being empty to brood over her assignment in peace.

'They let me watch one of their takes,' Sanjay had crowed. 'I was right on set. That famous guy playing Hastings — been on all the chat shows — kept fluffing his lines. Said his concentration went when the young actress suddenly felt dizzy. She needed a Lemsip or something. Meant they had to keep reshooting. Got a bit boring to be honest. The director seemed quite relaxed though. Said they were still ahead of schedule and should just plough on, so everyone could enjoy a decent lunch break.'

If Maureen had been a reptile dozing on a sunny rock to prime her sluggish blood, all three lids of one eye would have instantly receded on hearing this. A decent break. And her notional, forked tongue began to salivate at the prospect of a very different form of lunch.

* * *

There was laughter outside now. More crew were drifting

into the Long Gallery, after a far from *decent* recess. Maureen's hopes faded as the noise levels grew. She placed her treasure down on the veiled cabinet, right beneath the glaring expanse of green silk, flagged by two gilt hooks.

Above this naked rectangle, the 4th Earl of Arran eyed her with grave suspicion over his lace ruff. Like the albatross round the ancient mariner's neck, the *Blackbird* had become heavy, and she couldn't risk holding it for too long. Neither could she trust her trembling hands to re-hang it.

Now she identified with the hapless cherry that lolled on the sunny table ledge, its stem trapped beneath the blackbird's yellow talons, waiting to be pierced and devoured by that merciless beak. Do blackbirds have talons, she found herself wondering. Surely that was only birds of prey, like eagles.

What, in Fanny Fart's name, is wrong with you? Now is not *the time to worry about correct ornithological terms. There must be some way out of this. Think!*

But Maureen could only envisage Laura's face as she answered the Met's transatlantic call. Finding that image too painful, she gazed down again at the plucked fruit. Jodie loved cherries. And cherries were supposed to be eaten, weren't they? That was, after all, their botanical function: to enable their seeds to be dispersed over a wide area and thus ensure successful propagation. But she wasn't meant to get caught. That served no useful purpose at all. She didn't regret her plan; she merely lamented its failure. Defeated, she felt like emptying her bladder in protest. Except that would only double her humiliation. And ruin the parquet.

'...Not sure what's happening now. Do you need me to open up the Green Closet? I've got the key.'

Maureen's pelvic floor constricted. With primal reflexes, all her muscles braced for fight and flight, as she registered Venetia's harried tones the other side of the door. Not for the first time, she lamented her own loss of faith. Yet, like the old man in the small sixteenth-century Flemish oil to her left, still she prayed.

Her mother had always sworn by St. Martha in a crisis. In fact, Bernie had her own celestial directory of patron saints. Lost an earring? St. Anthony of Padua was your man. Car won't start? Try St Frances of Rome. Got a sore throat that gargling with TCP won't shift? St. Blaise would soothe it. Overdrawn again? You need St. Matthew the Apostle.

But according to the gospel of Bernie, St. Martha outshone them all with a five-star reliability rating. *Normal* women identified with Martha. And as if her mother had witnessed it all, she would go on to explain how Martha's work-shy sister, Mary, just sat fawning at Jesus's feet, lapping up his incessant preaching. Typical, it was left to Martha to skivvy around and prepare the food. Peeved that her sister wasn't offering to help, she protested to Jesus. He replied in customary patronising fashion, that Martha shouldn't be distracted by all the little things. 'Like feeding everyone, for Christ's sake,' Bernie used to say, without a whiff of irony. He Godsplained further that Miss Goody-Two-Shoes Mary had chosen *the better part.* Namely, hanging off his every word. Maureen often reflected how irritating Jesus must have been, showing off about the size of his father's house, but on balance, worth hanging with, in case he pulled that nifty water-to-wine trick again.

So, Maureen begged St. Martha for help and copied in St. Jude, patron saint of lost causes, for good measure. She promised to reject sin, to be good and never feel sorry for herself again. Although even now, as the single horse's hair holding the Sword of Damocles over her head began to fray, she didn't promise not to steal the painting.

'Okay, right you are then,' Venetia replied from the other side of the wall.

Maureen heard the curator step back, and gave a spiritual standing ovation to St. Martha, along with a nod to the spirit of her comedic mother. Was this some sort of acoustic mirage, or was the volume dialling down in the Long Gallery? She tiptoed across and put her ear to the gilded swirls of foliage blinging the white door panels.

'What's going on?' First Numpty voiced her very question.

'They're doing a walk-through of the stairway scene. We've all got to go and watch.'

Thanks a million, Second Numpty. Or rather, thanks a quarter of a million.

She detected multiple sets of footsteps and diverse threads of conversation travel past the Closet's south wall. Evidently, the crew were filing through the North Drawing Room into the Round Gallery and on towards the Great Staircase. After several minutes straining to hear above her thumping heartbeat, she perceived, well, nothing at all. Wonderful, manna-from-heaven silence.

This was her only chance. She had no idea how long this walk-through would last, but she guessed not for long. Now for crunch time: would her folding practice pay off? She unfurled part of the duvet from the top of the holdall, so that it created an open flap. This exposed a padded crevasse running the length and depth of the bag, lined with sheets of glassine.

The PH neutral paper rustled as she inserted her gloved hands, pressing back the duvet to widen the gap. Then, biting her lower lip, she lifted the painting off the dust sheet and lowered it, inch by inch, into the bag's cushioned cavity.

In no time, the carved scroll on the frame's lower left corner snagged on a plumped square of duvet. She paused to release it, smoothing it back out. Now, a delicate protruding frond on the right. Somehow, the magical waxy paper remained intact. There must be no damage to the Bosschaert. She was pretty sure that only the painting itself required protection, but just in case, she swathed it front, back and sides. If only there was a handy website with *Top tips on how to package stolen art.*

The picture was getting heavy; she needed more hands. Hers were sweating, and condensation had formed in the clammy creases of her latexed palms. No turning back now. A third of the painting had disappeared into the cushioned ravine. Then, half was no longer visible. She must watch out for the carved puttis. Like infant sentinels clasping verdant garlands, their chubby curves jutted out on both sides, one tilting his head outwards, as if in response to a noise. On cue, loud applause drifted up from the inner hall, where she'd encountered that sepulchral apparition a few months earlier. Afterwards, she'd interpreted it as some sort of sanction from Her Grace. But now, with the all too tangible prospect of being caught red-handed, she read it more as some prophetic warning.

Despite her panic, she'd manoeuvred the widest part of the frame into the quilted abyss. The rest of the painting slipped down with ease, just leaving the floral coronet sticking up. She prised out some spare paper and, with more unnerving crackles, tucked them over the top, followed by a slip of duvet. Now her plunder was fully concealed in the zipped nylon holdall.

Even with the extra weight, the bag was still manageable. She deposited it by the doors and listened again. All quiet. Opening the left door a crack, she peeked through, past the floor lamps, side tables and potted ferns. The set appeared empty, although the peacock-feathered screen hid the writing desk from her line of vision. She risked opening it wider. Not a soul in sight. As the King himself used to croon to her smitten mother on Pick of the Pops, it was now or never.

As if about to plunge into a murky, underwater tunnel, she took a large gulp of air and shuffled out sideways holding her breath. Her ears hadn't deceived her; the Long Gallery was deserted. No time to offer further gratitude to St. Martha. The crew could return at any minute. Holding her breath, she hauled the laundry bag after her through the constricted exit, which proved only just wide enough.

Setting it down, she twisted the ornate brass ring noiselessly and closed the door. Perspiration formed on her upper lip as she fumbled for the duplicate key, but its serrated edge hooked on her pocket liner. Yanking it free, she heard material rip over her thudding heart and more applause rippled round the Great Hall. The violence of her tug made her drop the key. It bounced on the floor. Cursing her clumsiness, she knelt on the hard wood to retrieve it. Geriatric offenders with weak hearts need not apply, she thought, wincing as she hoisted herself back up. Just when the white noise of laughter and raised voices might have offset locking the door, all fell quiet downstairs. The actual walk-through must be in progress. Now she was in trouble. It may have worked like a charm earlier, but the newly cut key, didn't oblige when turned anti-clockwise.

Cheap trick, St. Martha, to forsake me now.

Gritting her teeth, she made one last attempt. In her haste, she pushed the key that bit further into the gilt escutcheon and was rewarded with a sweet double click as it rotated twice. She mouthed thanks, raising her eyes to the ceiling — unadorned apart from smoke detectors. Its tired surface, bumpy and cracked with flaking paint. But the Trust's lack of maintenance wasn't her prime concern right now. She needed to navigate the set and reach the Library Closet, without being seen toting this alien holdall. This was bound to be the first question police would ask potential witnesses:

'Did you see anything out of the ordinary that day — anyone behaving oddly?'

'Nope. Oh, except for some old lady carrying a laundry bag around.'

Key thrust into other pocket, she grasped the bag and strained to listen. A resounding burst of applause and chatter signalled the crew's imminent return. Bracing herself, she crept down the other end. Pausing midway before the open doorway, she stuck her head forward, like a vigilant tortoise craning its gnarled head to scout for predators and lettuce.

She peered left, past the empty North Drawing Room. Through the mayhem of tripods, TV monitors and sound equipment that cluttered the Round Gallery, she spied heads and torsos emerging onto the first-floor landing. They were on their way back up. Alive to her vulnerability, she scuttled a perilous criss-cross over the Persian rug, skirting round props, careful not to stumble over any cables. That would be sod's frigging law, if she was apprehended, sprawled face down on her crushed booty.

Footsteps, directives and chitchat nearly upon her now.

'Are we done in here then?'

'Anyone seen Mandy?'

'Shit, my radio's dead… try WhatsApp…'

'Yeah, tell them we need more blood.'

'Reckon it'll be a late one…'

With a final spurt of adrenaline, she panted into the Library Closet a nanosecond before the crew spilled back on set. In her haste, she nearly chucked the bag down.

Instead, she stowed it in the corner, then collapsed on to the guide's chair with heaving bosoms, splayed legs and a big sigh. Exhausted but stoked. It wasn't over yet, but she had made it to Base Camp. By the skin of her stained, crooked teeth.

Chapter 16
Of All the People

'Are you alright Maureen? You look as though… Well, you look peculiar.'

Leaning on her stick in the Library doorway, Grayson Perry scarf fastened with cameo brooch, Thelma studied her with a chilled cocktail of curiosity and disdain.

What fresh hell is this? Of all the people, of all the volunteers, it had to be her walking in right now.

'Sorry, must have nodded off. Had the strangest dream.' Casual yawn. 'Couldn't tell where I was for a second.'

A fumbled save, but the best she could scrape together in the circumstances. Thelma remained sphinx-like. It was only then that Maureen woke up to a serious own goal. She was still wearing latex gloves.

Dummkopf. Distract her quick.

'Did something fall over in there? Thought I heard a bang, or maybe I dreamt it?'

As Thelma turned round to scan the Library, Maureen whipped off her gloves. Seizing her handbag from under the chair, she stuffed them inside and extracted a scraggy tissue.

'Nothing out of place that I can see,' said Thelma, directing her frown once more on to Maureen, who dabbed at her dry nose, bare-handed.

'Must have come from the Long Gallery.'

'Anyway, Emma asked me to find you. I can take over now.'

Had her nemesis spotted the gloves? At least they were see-through — thank Friar Tuck she hadn't bought blue ones — and the lowered blinds worked in her favour. Maureen stretched, reluctant to stand and expose the holdall behind her. Now, also aware of an urgent need to pee.

'Okey doke. Sounds like they've finished the walk-through.'

How the hell do I shift this bag from under the beady Eye of Sauron?

'Yes, Emma was surprised you didn't go along to watch.'

Sadly, I had a prior engagement in the Green Closet.

'Thought I had to stay here. Not to wor—'

'They're doing one more take in the Long Gallery before they move on to the Great Staircase. Can I sit?'

Thelma began folding up her floral stick.

'Hi ladies.'

Emma bustled through, taut smile, frayed requests spewing from her radio.

'Right Thelma, before they start shooting again, let me show you the bit of parquet Venetia's concerned about.'

Angel of mercy!

'Do you need me to stay here Emma?'

And piss myself in front of a stolen painting?

'No thanks Maureen, we won't be long. You can go home now.' She held the radio up to her mouth. 'I'll be down shortly, Trevor. Just briefing Thelma about the floor damage. Over.'

And without a backward glance, she exited on set, pursued by a gender-neutral Dark Lord.

Maureen waited until they were out of sight, leapt to her feet and surveyed the Long Gallery. Synchronised pandemonium had resumed, various crew absorbed within their own conflabs and allotted tasks, no interest in some doddery volunteer. Once again, Maureen rejoiced in her powers of invisibility.

Handbag slung cross-body, she retrieved the holdall from behind the chair. Checking both directions, she shifted across the Library. A devil to avoid bashing her grab against the desk and globes. She stopped sharp on the threshold to the first-floor landing. The upper stairs were devoid of traffic, but she could hear heavy footfall below. About as good as it was going to get. Plus, the Dark Lord could return any minute.

The West Stairs comprised a wide, wooden flight that wound from the West Door, past a small office, all the way up to the second floor. Trodden over the centuries by family and servants alike, it was now used by staff and volunteers, apart from the odd guided tour. In any event, they were tricky to descend in a hurry. As the staircase twisted, the treads narrowed to treacherous slivers towards the central bannisters. A blu-tacked notice urged *Please take care when going down these stairs* and *Keep to the left.* Dutifully, she pressed her hand on to the pocked wall, clasping the laundry bag, alert to any disastrous missed footing. From one floor above, she heard a door slam and identified Venetia's fretful tones and another voice. Less verbose, more assured.

Shitting Nora, it's The Enforcer. Didn't think she was in today. Forget about Poirot, what with her and the Dark Lord, they should be filming Godzilla vs. Kong. Hurry! Don't trip. Mustn't trip.

She pictured Lorna standing over her lifeless body, spread-eagled at the bottom of the stairs. Or worse, spine-crushed - a paraplegic detained at His Majesty's Pleasure. Maureen wasn't just in the glass-half-empty camp, she was an inspired catastrophiser.

Yet now, she hardly recognised her adrenaline junkie self. Was this all some kind of wild insurrection against years of hypervigilance?

As she rounded the last few steps, Ms Strawberry Blonde whizzed past to the West Passageway, clutching cold remedies and a bottle of Smart water. Arsenal Cap hot on her heels, pocketing his vape.

'Mate, you should have seen his face. Priceless…'

Neither marked her, and she didn't point out that both smoking *and* vaping were prohibited *everywhere*, including the Gardens.

Through the open door, Mr Walrus leant against the sundial, as one of the crew daubed more stage-blood on to his dress-shirt. By now, Lorna and Venetia had reached the first floor.

'I simply don't know whether this is a recent scratch, or—'

'Let's assume it's new damage, shall we?'

Maureen halted at the foot. As though kerbside on a busy road, she looked both ways, then dashed over to the business support lobby. Someone was talking inside the office, door pulled to. And by joyous fluke, the adjacent lavvy was free. Sanctuary at last.

Life's simple pleasures are very underrated, she pondered, her eyes half-closed as she peed in a hot, protracted torrent. Just as well the mirror was fixed too high to reflect her own undignified euphoria. Wetting yourself was not the best stealth strategy.

Far too close for comfort. In more ways than one. Proof that those pelvic floor exercises have paid off.

Apparently, Laura's Pilates teacher evangelised on the importance of these little squeezes: 'do some whenever you wait at a red light.' Maureen had started to practise when driving, eyebrows raised in unison. These miraculous clenches soon lessened the perils of coughing and sneezing.

She remained seated on her porcelain throne, savouring the relief. This convenience was really meant for staff but guides often nipped in to avoid the grim windowless toilet outside the Mess Room. An attempt to redeem the Basement one with artificial flowers, only increased its grot factor. In contrast, this was the Hanging Gardens of Babylon. For starters, the radiator was often on, which made it a snug retreat in winter.

Centuries earlier, this loo and next door's office had been a bedroom for Elizabeth's lady-in-waiting. From here, she would have observed the cloth caps' daily grind in the Dairy, Laundry and Bake House over the courtyard, her own back warmed by a fire in the corner grate. This now bulged with a yellow, plastic bag, while the mantelpiece served as a charging station for handheld radios.

In fact, this lav functioned as an all-round depository. Suspended from a long cable, the glare of a single bulb highlighted the jumble; velvet cushions piled by the collapsed wheelchair and first aid kits dumped on a cupboard, beneath an emergency eye wash unit. The lady-in-waiting would have been appalled.

Shunning the noisy hand drier, Maureen wiped her hands on a paper towel. From force of habit, she eyed the stacked loo rolls, before recalling the more valuable item stashed in her bag. Several voices drifted in from the lobby, and she pinned back her ears. One of them belonged to Emma.

'No, I *definitely* gave it to her. Is she not there? Thought I saw her go up with Lorna. Okay, I'll radio her. This stupid bloody key's doing my head in.'

The voices trailed off. Maureen's brief respite was over. There was only one key that Emma had handed over, and that could only mean one thing. They were about to open the Green Closet. She needed to leg it back to the car park asap. Plaid bag in tow, she unlocked the door. As if about to weaponize the cricket bat propped outside, she hesitated. In the office, the head gardener was on the phone, lamenting time spent doing admin, as opposed to what she loved most — literally getting her hands dirty.

Maureen couldn't afford to dally, so she turned left and had just started down the last few stairs, when she heard her name being called.

Fuck that for a game of soldiers.

'Maureen.'

Selective deafness — another senior superpower. Head lowered, keep going. I can't see them; they can't see me. But the voice became louder, more insistent, until she could no longer ignore it.

'Must catch you before you leave!'

Glued to the bottom step, she imagined bolting through the open door. Or wielding that cricket bat. But

Emma had already pounced, tapping her shoulder. Maureen was toast. Her time was up.

Chapter 17
The Shining

Best out to lunch smile, Maureen turned round, half expecting to be handcuffed. But catching her breath two steps above, Emma hunched over, hands pressed on her thighs.

'Well, I've certainly hit my ten thousand target. Been up and down these stairs all day. Wish the director would make up his piddling mind.'

Unusual for such pre-arrest chit chat. Unable to speak, Maureen's jaw slackened as her hijacker launched a sporadic mickey-take:

'Can we look in there? We want to shoot a scene in this room. It needs to be unlocked NOW. Can we move all the pictures out? God no, we can't film in this green room. Appreciate the offer, but it's way too cramped…'

As Emma ranted on, Maureen's mind galloped in all directions. This was good. Very good. Green Closet as yet unopened. Immediate calamity averted.

'… behind schedule. We'll shout if we need you. I mean, give me strength. If it wasn't for all the cash…'

But it was also bad. What with her standing right under the House Manager's nose, clutching the spoils in an eye-catching holdall. Slowly, she shifted the bag behind her. 'Did you want me for something? I ought to head off.' Toot-bloody-sweet.

'Yes. Can you come in again tomorrow? Usual time. The House will be open again, so we need guides for the ground floor. This lot won't be long, and when they are done we can start putting everything back upstairs. Always a total mare.'

She screwed up her eyes.

'Think I've put my lenses in the wrong way round. Everything looks a bit fuzzy.' Then, laughing at her own gag, she added, 'You look beautiful Maureen.'

'Yes, yes, of course. No probs. Right, better—'

But Emma started conversing with her radio, backing up the stairs. Twisting round, she pointed to her handset, grimaced and gave Maureen a thumbs-up.

Seizing her chance, Maureen darted out into the bright afternoon. A bored security guard in a yellow High Vis tilted his plastic chair against the Still House. Didn't even bother raising his head from his phone, as she emerged, blinking like a timorous mole.

Ms Luvvie, rocking a hairnet'n'rollers with velour dressing gown, cackled with Mr Walrus, elbows resting on the green crusted sun dial.

'Honestly, talk about hammy delivery. Excruciating. Where the hell's Mand? I need bickies and my phone. When are we shooting the next scene again?'

'Don't ask me. I'm the last to know what's going on around here.'

From only a few feet, she swerved past, head down. But both seemed oblivious to the old dear with the lanyard. As was Ms Strawberry Blonde, who appeared, genie-like, at that moment, to hand Ms Luvvie her mobile and a plate of Hobnobs.

'Thanks sweetie, where's Tom?'

'He's showing Poppy how to walk downstairs.'

As the actors exchanged looks, Maureen remained a background blur. Like a basic wage extra, her exit remained peripheral to the movie plot of their own lives. How little they knew.

On entering the walled garden, she realised her mistake. It would have been prudent to take the more shielded route; leave the courtyard via the second-hand bookshop and scoot round the Ice House. But in her haste to dodge the thesps, Maureen had indeed chosen the path of least resistance.

Then again, the Fountain Garden was glorious. Right now, its pristine beds of rich soil were peppered with bluebells, blending into violet tones of muscari. Sheer bliss on long sunny afternoons. You could retire on benches against the crumbling, coral walls, and contemplate the tangled grass, dotted with wildflowers and lemon trees. Maureen lingered a few seconds, its woody scents soothing her close shave. Hugging its secluded calm, she psyched herself up for the final leg.

Through to the North Forecourt, she scampered over black rubber mats. Her approach masked by the giant silver reflector still blocking the Back Parlour window. A couple of crew, backs turned, stood chatting outside the open front door. Maureen slowed, until they chucked paper cups into a large barrel and disappeared indoors. Even while absconding with a stolen painting, part of her applauded their sticking to the no-hot-drinks-in-the-House rule.

Although the path ahead was deserted, she felt way too exposed. Once down the steps however, she was covered by the line of yew trees and an empty trailer stranded on the carriage circle. Another large refreshment stand had been set up east of the main gates, in front of the Cherry Gardens. Her heart sank as she clocked Trevor and Sanjay squinting at the menu. Now what? But they seemed hell-bent on sampling the gourmet fare, so Maureen risked a mad dash. At the gates, a security guard was directing a lorry to a parking space. Grateful, she scuttled through the smog of fumes. No banalities or eye contact required with the second Mr High Vis. Her back twinged in complaint, and she swapped the bag over to her other hand.

Nearly there. She veered left on a footpath parallel to the avenue of limes, planes and sycamores. That thoroughfare was busy today, and she wanted to avoid all the couriers, taxi drivers and crew shouting into their phones. Instead, she trod the less frequented, flattened trail through the meadow. Soon she outstripped the ha-ha flanking the North Terrace. So nearly there. Teasing her, the dusty track seemed to go on forever. Once or twice, she looked back, half expecting to see the House licked by Daphne du Maurier flames, but its projecting bays and gables met her anxious tabs, implacable and resolute.

This stately home had withstood revolution, civil war and The Blitz. It wasn't about to be ruffled by filming and some petty theft. Not that petty. Apart from a screech of parakeets that flashed yellow and pea green among the treetops, all seemed quiet as she passed the tall brick chimney of an outhouse. At last, she joined the Ham Street entrance, by the Black Lab poster, touting that four legs were now welcome in the Gardens.

More production trailers were stationed opposite on Ham Fields, where only a few weeks earlier, a group of travellers had camped. Maureen snuck left, side-stepping the desiccating horse dung. Once past the bedraggled stables, — now a riding school — she crossed the road into King George's Field.

Since January, on-site parking had been declared a capital offence against the jewel on the Thames. Mutinous grumblings quashed by lofty citations of aesthetics, conservation and safety. Not to mention the pain-in-the-arse factor for Visitor Reception, forever admitting the unpaid help. This enforcement was waged with the standard iron-fist-in-velvet-glove. Attentive lip service was paid to consultations, lengthy meetings with reps, while the Mess Room flowed with chocolate Digestives. In truth, management were under no illusion about the volunteers' physical prowess. And although vastly outnumbered, hedged their bets on the staff annihilating them, if actual violence erupted.

King George's Field had become the parking spot of choice, unlike the muddy verges on Ham Street. Or the river car park, officially designated for visitors, and unofficially for doggers. This had a remote, Wild West feel with its red warning flood sign and dusty expanse of potholes. By contrast, King George's Field comprised a green pitch, bordered by allotments and a playground. A stone heraldic plaque ushered drivers to tarmacked parking bays. One side shaded, the other chain-link fenced by tennis courts.

Flaunting bare, sinewy torsos in the perverse February heat, some teenage boys goofed around, slugging balls over the net. Maureen wasn't about to stop and ask why they weren't in school. Instead, she made a beeline for her faithful red Micra down the end, by an overflowing bin and discarded fridge. A fly-tipper's paradise. She took her time arranging the laundry bag into the vacuumed trunk.

'You doing your weekly wash at Ham House now?'

Maureen stood bolt upright, just missing her head on the open boot, and swung round. Right behind her — a beaming Deirdre alongside Rhona, eyebrow arched. But for a split second, all Maureen could see were the twins in The Shining.

Chapter 18
For Tomorrow We Die

Maureen drove much slower than usual. For once, she heeded the 20mph limit through Petersham. Not risking any jolts to her precious cargo, she took the speed bumps with care. Besides, she didn't want any unwelcome attention. A year ago, she'd been stung by police officers in an unmarked car. Clearly, with nothing better to do than lecture an old woman.

'Madam, have you any idea what speed you were doing? Exactly how much protection do you think your little tin box would provide in a collision?'

Suppressing a sarky riposte, she'd forced out a few tears. Doubtless her age and the crush of yet more paperwork had saved her from a fine, plus points on her licence. Or, one of those ghastly speed awareness courses.

For once, bowing to the Highway Code soothed her. Calmed the nerves dousing her glory. Despite her Unsung Hero status, she experienced not one twinge of guilt. Quite the opposite. She revelled in having pulled off this remarkable theft, against all the odds. No, her only worry lay in the dread prospect of getting caught. And this had become more tangible following the shock encounter with last minute subs, Rhona and Deirdre. While they'd bought the same flimsy story about dry cleaners and car break-ins, she'd over-egged the Yorkshire pud. Classic rookie error. Jabbering on about cleaning the spare duvet, should Jodie fly over as an unaccompanied minor during school hols.

Nor could she hide her flustered reaction on bumping into them, almost as if she'd been caught in flagrante. And it was not the right car park for that sort of malarkey. But she'd left them suitably distracted, strolling up the avenue. Deirdre gossiping about the cast and Rhona whinging about Sanjay's raid on the catering van. Also, griping why Thelma had turned up like a bad smell, despite not even being listed as a stand-by on the sacred rota.

Her thoughts turned again to those wretched latex gloves. Had the Dark Lord noticed? As a rule, nothing got past that harridan, but she would have said something, surely? Thelma wasn't shy in pointing things out and seemed to luxuriate in others' discomfort. Maureen decided that on balance, this blunder didn't matter. Yet still it nagged.

All appeared quiet as she turned into her road. The usual lull before school pick-up. Rick-with-the-silent-P, who sometimes worked from home, was heading off on his bike, kitted out in too-much-information lycra. He nodded to her, clipping a fluorescent helmet over his bob, with the grim face of someone about to ascend the Swiss Alps, as opposed to circuiting Richmond Park. To be fair, there were a couple of steep climbs between Roehampton and Kingston Gates. Seema was nowhere to be seen, so she risked carrying the laundry bag inside. She was being paranoid of course; it wasn't as if her neighbour possessed X-ray vision. To any casual observer, it would simply look like she'd returned from a humdrum trip to the laundrette.

Before long, she cozied in front of *A Place in the Sun* with tea and a victory Wagon Wheel, unable to compute what she'd just stowed in the back bedroom. She gawped at the screen without tuning in, lost in pipe dreams of Scarlette showing her round Puglian trulli. Long siestas by the pool with Laura and Jodie, a lizard darting up whitewashed walls, the rustle of olive groves in a welcome breeze, toasting the sunset with chilled Prosecco…

A turgid electric guitar solo signalled the end of the show and jerked her back to reality. She turned off the TV and sat, head in hands.

Jesus wept, pull yourself together.

She knew full well that she could never sell the painting without it being flagged on police databases and art loss registers. That even if she found some dodgy dealer, as flaming-hot property she'd be lucky to obtain a fifth of its market value. Not that fifty grand was anything to be sniffed at. That suddenly splashing round loads of dosh would raise a lot of eyebrows. That she didn't want to sell it. That wasn't the point. Why had she done it then? To see if she could. To fool everyone. For the sheer hell of it. All of the above. But mainly, just to feast her eyes on that treasure.

And to stop it being sequestered to the corner of some draughty castle east of Peebles, unappreciated and forgotten. Then, why the Dickens was it languishing on the top of the wardrobe? She'd just pulled off a fine art heist in broad daylight, right from under everyone's noses. She may as well enjoy the fruits. Or in this case, the cherries. And as if to check the Bosschaert hadn't vaporised, she scrambled back upstairs.

Obviously, she couldn't hang it in the hallway, but she found the perfect place: next to her bedroom window, shielded from any direct light by thick curtains. It ousted an old mirror, peppered with black spots so redolent of Hogarth's syphilitic rakes. Anyhow, she wasn't on friendly terms with mirrors these days. Mere brutal reflections of her own mortality. So she dumped it on the floor, alongside scrumpled paper and gloves. Perched on the edge of her bed, she gazed up at the *Blackbird, Butterfly and Cherries* on her very own wall. Oblivious to the backdrop of screaming school kids, shouting parents and Britney yelping next door.

Deaf to it all, she sat entranced by the painting's irrefutable beauty.

Every time she looked at this deceptively simple scene, she saw something new. The moistness of the pale-yellow pulp oozing out of the skewered cherry, against the dryness of the Chartreuse green leaves, already curling in the sun. This was no accident. Bosschaert was injecting a puff of vanitas into the still life, with its cheery message — *memento mori* — remember that you have to die. She always found this somewhat ambiguous. Despite its warning against sinful indulgence, its call to nourish the soul instead, this symbolism of life's transience, swayed her more to the *eat, drink and be merry* club. Indeed, the blatant evidence for this confronted her this very moment.

For tomorrow we die.

And right then, hugging her knees, she was glad that this Dutch Golden Age gem graced her shabby little cottage. Ecstatic, even. In a strange way, she felt it belonged here, its wild fanciful frame offset by the faded wallpaper. No one else appreciated it like her. To Maureen, it possessed an almost magical quality. And later still, guzzling a bowl of Coco Pops, she sat, cloaked in her duvet, and marvelled at it. And in her own ingenuity.

Chapter 19
Houston, We Have a Problem
Tuesday, 6th February

'Someone's looking awful pleased with themselves. Did you get a lumber last night?'

Rhona had strayed into the Private Closet and found Maureen smiling up at Medea Casting Spells.

Oh I did way better than that. 'You know me, the usual drug-crazed orgy.'

Rhona followed Maureen's gaze. Even in daylight, it was hard to discern much above the shadowy corner fireplace. Only the furious witch leapt out, pointing her wand at the thick coils of her winged serpent.

'Wee bit nippy dressed like that. No wonder she's got a face like a slapped arse.'

Circe's niece was breaking that cardinal rule of flaunting legs *and* cleavage. Her whole right boob, in fact. Still, Medea wasn't renowned for following etiquette. Case in point, she was cradling her own dead baby in one arm.

'Not the cheeriest of paintings, right enough. I wouldn't want her nipple gracing my sitting room.'

Polar opposite to the jaunty blackbird currently sprucing Maureen's wall, that was for sure. 'I reckon you might. It must be worth a few bob.'

'Aye, it'd definitely get me a spot on the *Antiques Roadshow*,' said Rhona, as if sizing it up for that very purpose. 'Right, best drag my sorry arse back to the Volury. I can hear our Dee chatting up some punters in the Great Hall. A fiver says I can bore them longer than you. I can do my whole *you mean, you don't have a Volury in your house?* gig.'

'You're on,' said Maureen. 'Though they'll be moaning that the first floor's shut, what with everything being put back.'

On cue, an ominous thud sounded on the Verrio painted ceiling.

'Oops. Trevor'll be turning the air blue,' said Rhona, ducking back through the low doorway.

Alone again, Maureen gloried in her secret victory. With a pared-down crew filming mainly background and continuity, there was little danger of the Green Closet being opened today. Most of the cast had already moved on to another location. She could play Best Unsung Hero and relax. For now.

She considered Medea once more. It was curious that the Duchess had chosen this macabre scene for one of her favourite rooms. Maureen liked to think of her sitting by the window, pouring from the rare Chinese teapot displayed on the lacquered table. Bad-mouthed as a witch, maybe she'd glimpsed herself in the vengeful priestess, as she sipped her precious brew. *Underestimate me at your peril.*

'We've come all the way from Maidstone, and we're not even allowed upstairs! It doesn't say anything on the website.'

Yes it feckin does.

The woman in the floral Pac A Mac had a face on much like Medea's, although her mauve-fleeced friend yawned affably behind her.

'I'm sorry, they're finishing off some filming and everything's been shifted round up there.'

'What are they filming?' asked Mauve Fleece, perking up.

'I'm not really supposed to say,' said Maureen. Which wasn't strictly true, but it would help butter them up. 'It's a Poirot, and you didn't hear that from me.'

'Ooh I love a good crime drama.' Floral Mac mollified now.

Me too, sweetheart.

Recalling her friend's wager, Maureen shone her torch on to Medea's nipple and rattled through her Greek mythology blurb:

'… She certainly lives up to the adage, *hell hath no fury like a woman scorned.* Because not only does she murder

Jason's princess by sending her a poisoned dress, she also goes on to kill her *own* two children by him.' Maureen highlighted the stiff, waxen baby. 'I guess it's the ultimate revenge story.'

She couldn't help but empathise with the jilted sorceress. It was very painful to be cast aside for another woman — younger, prettier, more fertile. Although, the infanticide was a little OTT.

Purple Fleece rounded her eyes. 'Blimey, not one to mess with then.'

But Floral Mac pursed her lips, as if Medea was front page Daily Mail. 'Well, we better crack on if we're going to have lunch before the garden tour.'

Good thing the first floor's not open then, thought Maureen, knowing that they wouldn't get past Rhona so easily. Floral Mac disappeared, while her friend gawped at a bare-breasted Mary Magdalene floating on the ceiling. They were surrounded by Stuart soft porn. Maureen was about to offer Purple Fleece a mirror to view the fresco without straining her neck, when she trotted off wordlessly after her boss.

Not one to mess with.

Neither was the Duchess. After all, hadn't she held on to Ham House against all the odds? Following the Duke's death, she spent years fighting his brother over the will. So maybe that canny old crow was proficient in the dark arts. As not only did she leave the House to her eldest son from her first marriage, but it passed down that family line for the next three and a half centuries.

'You seen that fuckwit Venetia?' A sweaty-faced Trevor stormed in from the servants' passage.

'Er, no I—'

'Just looking for her now, Emma.' he lowered his voice into the radio. 'Yeah, no one goes into the Long Gallery…' Stepping through to the White Closet, he added, 'Scrub that, stop anyone going upstairs…'

Houston, we have a problem.

Heart in her mouth, Maureen followed him round and watched him race down the south front. Next room along, Rhona was in full flow with Floral Mac and sidekick.

'…Comes from the French word *volière*, meaning aviary. We still have the joiner's bill from 1672 to supply bird cages outside this window. Wee bit confusing, you see this was originally the Duchess's Bedchamber…'

Clocking Trevor's flypast, Rhona turned to Maureen and shrugged, allowing her victims to flee to the Marble Dining Room, where the Dark Lord loitered with intent.

Maureen sidled up to Rhona on the replica carpet.

'What's going on?' Maureen asked, as if she had no idea.

'Dunno, but you owe me a fiver.'

The very next moment, like some cheesy West End bedroom farce, Emma swept past. Sticky-palmed, Maureen wondered who would appear next.

'Man alive, it's all kicking off today.'

They caught hissed snatches of her radio exchange: 'Yes, they're on their way…. Better keep this quiet… Oh God, someone has to tell Lorna…'

'This is turning into Glasgow after an Old Firm game,' said Rhona. 'Now heeeere's Dee.'

From the opposite direction, Deirdre nearly knocked Floral Mac out of Thelma's path, as she belted towards them.

Although no one else was around, she spilled the beans from behind her hand. 'They've closed the House and the Gardens.' She couldn't contain her excitement. 'Luckily, it's pretty quiet, but Meera asked Visitor Reception to get the names of all non-members on site. Something big's happened.'

'No shit, Sherlock,' said Rhona.

'Once we've cleared out all visitors from the House…' Deirdre spoke as if she'd just completed a triathlon. 'Emma says we're to assemble downstairs.'

Even amid her inner turmoil, Maureen conjured Floral

Mac's meltdown. *But we've come all the way from Maidstone.*

* * *

The Mess Room was buzzing. Rhona scanned the animated throng and pronounced, 'The game's a bogey.' Maureen wasn't quite sure what this meant, but it seemed to capture her deep-water status. 'I mean,' Rhona continued, 'you know something's up when the garden lot start talking to us.' She inclined her head towards Deirdre finger-combing her hair, as a brawny gardener quizzed her on the unfolding drama. 'Shameless hussy.'

But chewing her lip, Maureen logged out. How had they found out this soon? The staff had been flat out, so why bother opening the Green Closet? Unless one of the crew had requested it for background footage. Elbowed out of her maelstrom by Rhona, she was aware of a looming presence. The Dark Lord stood before her.

'Would you like a camomile tea, Maureen?' Thelma handed her a *We're All Mad Here* mug. 'You look like you could do with one.' Maureen was so stunned, she mumbled some thanks and took it, even though she loathed herbal tea.

'Are we in the upside-down?' asked Rhona.

As if to prove her point, a doom-faced Emma marched in with Trevor, clenching and unclenching his fists. Instantly, the babble ceased. Emma cleared her throat.

'Well, I'm sure you're wondering what this is all about.' Feeble smile. 'We can't say much at this stage, but there's been an incident on the first floor.'

A hand shot up. 'I used to volunteer for St. John's Ambulance, if that helps.'

'Thank you, er.' Emma flicked through her memory files.

'Penny,' said Penny.

'Yes, thanks Penny. But no one's been injured.'

Disappointed, Penny lowered her hand.

Emma continued. 'As you know, we've—'

'Is it an infestation of Huntsman spiders?' asked a Friday guide. 'I know it's early in the year, but what with climate change…'

It was fast descending into Twenty Questions.

'Ooh yes, I've read about this. My daughter lives in Sydney—'

'No, it's nothing like that,' Emma assured them, but looking very much like she wished it was.

'I mean, it's well known that spiders can't go downstairs, what with their eight legs,' said Rhona into Maureen's ear.

More hands in the air now, which, like a frayed supply teacher, Emma ignored.

'As I was saying, we've had to close the House and Gardens, so you should all go home now.' Raising her voice over the growing rumble, she added, 'but on your way out, Meera's going to confirm all your contact details.'

'Any idea when the House will re-open?' Thelma's pragmatism muting the room.

'Can't say yet, I'm afraid. We'll update you by email and you can check the online rotas. Okay, that's all for now. Except,' a pleading note in her voice, 'obviously we'd appreciate your discretion on this.'

'Suppose there's a first time for everything,' said Rhona. 'Hang about, where did Sanjay spring from?' Goggle-eyed, he'd slipped through the open door and shook his head imperceptibly at Trevor, who mouthed a stream of expletives as he followed Emma out.

* * *

'Head down Dee, it's the Feds.'

Sure enough, as they rounded the carriage circle, several police cars with flashing blues drove through the open gates, where Meera was stationed.

'Oh my God!' said Deirdre. Maureen swallowed hard. It had all gone pear-shaped way too fast. She needed to get back asap and stow the *Blackbird* out of sight. What if the police came banging on her door later today? Prize eejit leaving it exposed on her bedroom wall. Why not just display it on an easel in her front garden?

'If no-one's been slashed,' Rhona, going full-on Gorbals gangster, 'then—'

'Something's gone missing.' Behind them, a familiar voice completed Rhona's logic. It was Thelma. Also, Sanjay on the paved mossy path. Rubbing his chin, he shifted from one scuffed brogue to the other.

'You know something, don't you son?' Rhona stared him down. 'You were on the first floor, lugging furniture with Trevor.'

Sanjay blinked first. 'I'm not really supposed to say,' he said, echoing Maureen's earlier line.

They broke off to watch the uniforms follow Meera along the east curve past the river god and up the steps to the main entrance. The officer in charge scanned their faces and turned to Emma. Hands clasped, she ushered them inside the Great Hall. Next to her, The Enforcer, with a face like murder. As the carved wooden door swung shut, Sanjay blurted, 'It's the Green Closet.'

Chapter 20
An Urgent Set of Towels

Not quite the O.K. Corral, but a tense face-off in King George's Field car park.

'Why the sudden trip to Kingston? You meeting your dealer or something?'

'What would I want with a dealer?' Maureen snapped, her guilt prefacing *dealer* with *art.*

'Well in your case, mebbe some weed.'

The penny dropped. 'Look, I'm sorry about the change of plan,' she said, skating over her Freudian gaffe. 'But seeing as we've clocked out early, I want to nip to John Lewis before schools are out. I need a new set of towels. Been meaning to go for ages.'

Not very plausible, but it was all she could muster. She needed to race home without having to act calm. And without her friends dissecting the day's SNAFU.

'It's fine,' said Deirdre. 'I'm happy to get a 371. In fact,' she checked her watch, 'there's one due in eight minutes.'

Tapping her leather sneaker, Rhona looked anything but fine. 'You still owe me a fiver.'

As silent witness to this showdown, Thelma glid past in her yellow Mercedes Hatchback with a curt nod.

'Well, I'm heading your way, if you want a lift.' Under the horse chestnuts, Sanjay leant against a dented bonnet, splotched with birdshit. His craving for company outweighing the sticky dynamics.

'Thanks pal, as long as *you* don't need to buy towels.'

Ignoring the dig, Maureen noted her friend rally at this chance to extract juicy details. After his startling Green Closet leak, Sanjay had dodged further explanation. Instead, he started unburdening about his wife, aware this subject change was non-negotiable. How when he visited now, she often called him chacha, or uncle, because of his white comb over. How she blatantly flirted with her buff, male carer. 'You have to laugh,' he said, as they walked up the avenue. But none of them did.

Maureen juddered out of the car park, as if her Micra ran on kangaroo petrol. Having stalled twice, her undignified exit did not go unnoticed by the twins strapping themselves into Sanjay's Audi. No time to worry about that now.

Soon, she was burning rubber up Sandy Lane, but then the speck of Sanjay's silver estate materialised in her rear-view mirror. So wired, she'd forgotten they'd be heading the same way. No choice but to go right at the mini roundabout towards Kingston and watch Sanjay take the left instead. Cursing, she U-turned and parked up in a residential lay-by. After three hundred excruciating seconds, she could bear it no longer and floored it through Petersham, praying she wouldn't catch them up.

Past the Russell School — no enemy in sight. Round Tommy Steele corner and all the posh Grade II listed houses. Still all clear on the Audi front. After the mock Tudor Dysart Arms, the lights were just turning. Unsure if it was paranoia, she glimpsed a flash of silver heading up the leafy Star and Garter. Gripping the steering wheel, she ran the red light, taking the left fork down by the river.

Other than buses, there was little traffic on Richmond's one-way high street, but she remained on high alert. Once past Waitrose, she felt dangerously exposed on Paradise Road. What if Sanjay was on his way down Church Road to drop Deirdre at the station? This time, the lights were in her favour, and too scared to scope the cars queuing on her right, she throttled through the cross junction. Breathing out as she reached the Red Cow, she snuck into the compact side streets and cul-de-sacs of The Alberts.

Home at last, she cast a brief squint out of her bedroom window. No sign of anyone, other than that sullen codger down the road sponging his Volvo's hub caps. Every other day, he was out there buggering around with it. Life in the fast lane, she thought, and her glance fell back on the peacock butterfly, caught mid-flicker with skilled brush strokes. Alive to its vulnerability, she snapped back into heist mode and drew the curtains. After some lengthy faffing with gloves and fresh sheets of glassine, her *Blackbird* nested snug in its laundry bag on top of the wardrobe. This time, under a judiciously folded blanket.

With the gilt-edged, syphilitic mirror back in situ, she nursed a steaming mug of tea, NT lanyard still round her neck. Propped up on some pillows, she hatched various game plans, her mind ticking over in the empty silence of number fourteen.

She found herself on a TV quiz show. She knew all the answers, and stood to win thousands, but her buzzer didn't work. The host ignored her protests, while the other contestant kept gaining the points. Her rival stood behind her, and on turning round, she saw Thelma, convulsed with demonic laughter, pressing the buzzer again and again. She woke to frantic blasts of the doorbell, and Britney's crazed yapping.

Transiting that ephemeral threshold from snooze to wakefulness, Maureen sleepwalked to the top of the stairs. In those first few seconds, failing to register her plight, she grouched:

'Alright, alright. Give me a chance.'

It was only as she padded downstairs that it dawned. This could be the police outside her front door.

Chapter 21
Best Unsung Bloody Failure

Much worse than the pigs. It was the twins. Deirdre, no longer sunny side up, but edgy, checking up and down the street. Rhona, arms folded, thin-lipped.

'What's the m—?'

Rhona barged past her, followed by Deirdre, who grimaced in apology.

'No really, do come in…'

Rhona began pacing round her cramped sitting room. Maureen attempted a joke. 'You come to collect that fiver?'

But taking in Maureen's dishevelled hair and lanyard, Rhona fired back. 'Have fun choosing your towels?'

Maureen was about to dredge some excuse, but Rhona extended a palm. 'Talk to the hand. Sanjay told us all about it.'

'All about what?'

Maureen felt the blood drain from her face. She gripped the sofa in a desperate bid to remain composed, feigning confusion, buying time.

'What the hell's going—'

'What's going on? Nothing much. Oh, apart from a wee spot of larceny at Ham House.'

Deirdre translated. 'It seems there's a painting's gone missing from the Green Closet. That one you like Maur—'

'Aye, funny that!'

'The blackbird one…' Deirdre trailed off.

'Where is it then?'

Well, it's definitely not hanging on my bedroom wall.

Rhona's eyes darted around, as if searching for a corner of the carved frame from behind a cushion.

'What are you talking about?'

'I'm no glaikit, hen.'

Maureen had always suspected that her pal's roots weren't quite as blackened sandstone tenement as she liked to make out, but now, as Rhona's accent thickened with her savagery, she reconsidered.

'We were wondering,' Deirdre wrung her hands and took a deep breath. 'Well Rhona thinks, er, you might know something about it.'

'Come off it, you looked guilty as sin yesterday afternoon, foutering around in the boot of your car. All your blether about needing to get the spare duvet cleaned for Jodie. And then today, some guff about ditching us to buy towels. You couldn't get away fast enough. Your bum's beef and ye cannae eat it!'

Maureen didn't have the faintest idea what this last bit meant but was way too scared to ask.

'And let's not forget that whole New Inn episode — that game you started at our Christmas lunch. *The fire alarm's gone off in Ham House. So what you gonna steal?*'

Rhona made an absurd attempt to mimic Maureen, which in normal circumstances would have cracked them up. As it was, the accused remained silent, her mind scrabbling for a decent explanation. Mercifully, Rhona dropped her Dick Van Dyke routine.

'Then, only a couple of days later, I caught you right in the act — about to swipe a miniature in the Green Closet.'

'What?' said Deirdre.

'I told you; I was just comparing—'

But Rhona ploughed on with her bad cop schtick.

'Why exactly did you lug your laundry bag all the way to the House, eh?'

'I left it in the office because of all the break—'

'Do you think I came up the Thames on my bike?'

Rhona looked on the verge of bestowing a Glasgow kiss.

'You have often said how much you love that painting,' Deirdre intervened, also concerned that Rhona's interrogation might turn more physical.

If only she could press a pause button right now, pour herself a large early-doors gin and weigh up all the options.

Whether to continue hamming total bafflement, never mind protesting her innocence. After all, Rhona was going on pure hunch, curse her sharp nose. But she had no concrete evidence. Despite her nap, Maureen felt utterly spent. Why hadn't she grabbed lunch? A Nutella sandwich would have spiked her blood sugar levels. Rhona was one of her few close friends, and Maureen lacked the energy to combat her ferocity.

'Don't mind if I check upstairs?'

'Rhona!'

But DI McFarlane ignored her junior's reprimand, and Maureen froze. Like a dog after a bone, Rhona would sniff out that laundry bag in a trice, blanket or no blanket. Why keep up the façade? Besides, would she really grass her up? Deirdre's reaction was harder to predict, but it was safe to assume that she'd follow Rhona's lead. Time to trust her gut and fling herself on their mercy.

She sunk onto the mussy sofa. 'No, you carry on. You'll find it in the spare room, on top of the wardrobe.'

The DI halted on the bottom step. 'I knew it!'

'You're joking? Oh my God, oh my God, Maureen!' Deirdre's hands flew to her mouth.

'Maureen Goodwin — Best Unsung Hero. Who'd have fucking thunk it? You're as deep and dirty as the Clyde, right enough.'

And despite her fury, Rhona howled with laughter at the absurdity of her friend's crime. Fuelled by the relief of confession, Maureen couldn't help but join in. By now, Rhona had collapsed next to her on the sofa and the two women were bent double, screeching, their faces contorted.

'That is enough!'

Ashen-faced, Deirdre slammed her hand down on the teak coffee table, jolting the yellowed newspapers and making the convulsed pair jump.

'For fuck's sake, this is no laughing matter. You could end up in prison for this, Maureen. Is that what you want?'

It was more Deirdre's unprecedented use of an expletive, than the *P* word, that sobered them. They sat up straight, like unruly children being roasted by their teacher, Rhona's jaw hanging in disbelief and admiration.

'You've all gone radio rental.'

'She's right. You're right Deirdre. I know. I know this is serious.'

'Why? For Pete's sake, why did you take it?'

Oaths diluted, Deirdre raised both arms, as if trying to summon Peter, whoever the hell he was. Maureen groaned, hand over face.

'I don't know exactly. I don't know. Because I wanted to, okay? Because they're taking it away from Ham House, and no one else seems to care. Because… just everything in my life turns to shit. I'm bored. Lonely.' Her voice choked. 'Best Unsung Bloody Failure, more like. I feel… lost. Empty. I'm a pointless, dried-up husk.'

Not bothering to wipe tears from her blotchy cheeks, she crossed her arms in a solo hug, then raised her head. 'What am I going to do?'

The trio looked at each other, gripped by a weighty silence. Rhona was the first to break it.

'Right, get the kettle on, Dee. We're going to sort this out. But first, you need to stop greetin' and give us chapter and verse.'

'You're not,' Maureen sniffed, 'going to tell the police, are you?'

'Where I come from hen, you stick by your friends. End of. Plus, talk to the polis, and you're dead already.'

Deirdre got to her feet, chipper status resumed.

'Obviously, we're going to help you put it back.'

* * *

Sugared and caffeinated, the planning for Operation Save Maureen's Bacon began. With faltering steps.

'A wee bit like Thelma and Louise. Bagsy be Geena Davies, cos she got to shag Brad Pitt.'

'Then who am I going to be?' Deirdre woke to the

insanity of her protest. 'Anyway, it's not a game Rhona.'

Maureen rested her chin on steepled hands, astounded by her friends' unswerving loyalty. She had just spilled the whole sequence of events. How, on a crazed impulse, she had made a duplicate of the Green Closet key before returning the original. How she had banked on the chaos of large-scale filming to present the perfect opportunity.

Except, she hadn't quite 'fessed all. Too ashamed to disclose the full shebang, she had glossed over exactly how and why she had acquired the key in the first place — her whole reconnaissance mission. Instead, she claimed that newbie Daisy had dropped the key the night of her tour. That she'd picked it up with every intention of handing it over, but, panicked by the spectral Duchess, had driven off with it by mistake. This prompted a loud snort from Rhona.

Still, first rule of plausible deception, always fib close to the truth. Second rule, keep it brief. Unlike her verbal diarrhoea in the car park, on the day in question. Already, it felt like aeons ago. Full of remorse, she interrupted their squabbling:

'I don't think you should help me with this. I'm pretty sure you could both be charged with accessory to theft.'

'But you're going to give it back,' said Deirdre. Bless her naivety.

'No matter hun, a crime's still been committed by old Peruggia here, and in the eyes of the law, we should clipe on her right now.'

'Who's Peruggia, when he's at home?' asked Maureen, momentarily distracted.

'You know, that Italian artist who worked at the Louvre and lifted the Mona Lisa early one morning.'

Rhona spoke as if this, the most notorious art theft of the early twentieth century, had only made headlines the other week. Maureen made a mental note to include Rhona on her pub quiz team, before remembering she never went to any.

Disregarding Rhona's history lesson, Deirdre asked, 'Is it accessory, or aiding and abetting?'

'Dunno, let's make an appointment at Citizens' Advice and ask them.'

Ignoring her friend once again, Deirdre blew on her tea.

'Anyway, sod it. This is the most fun I've had in years.'

Rhona's mouth hung open. 'Who are you, and what have you done with Deirdre Hall?'

She took a large gulp and said, 'If Jack's death has taught me anything, it's that life is far too short.'

They couldn't argue with that, so Maureen kept quiet. Partly overwhelmed by their support and her guilt in endangering them, and partly because she agreed. Despite the gravity of their predicament — her predicament — she couldn't deny that it was kind of fun. She hadn't felt this alive in a long time.

'And another thing,' Deirdre blurted, 'I'm fed up with being called *sprightly*.'

'Bit random,' said Rhona, 'but I hear you, sister.'

'If one more person refers to me as *sprightly*, I'm going to… well, I'm damned well going to drop my knickers.'

Maureen and Rhona stared at her.

'Get you, Vivienne Westwood.' Rhona side-eyed Maureen. 'That'll be a treat for us all. I take it you don't vajazzle.'

* * *

They had nearly emptied the tub of rocky road. Maureen muted the TV, while Rhona WhatsApped Sanjay for updates.

'It won't be on the news,' said Deirdre. 'Emma told us to keep it quiet, remember. Terrible PR for them.'

'Fat chance of no leaks with our lot and the crew standing idle,' Rhona scoffed.

'Has filming stopped completely?' Maureen's eyes widened, as the enormity of what she'd done began to sink in.

'No, they've just carried on as if nothing had happened. Of course, it's stopped, ya eejit! Trevor told Sanjay there's this wee guy, all white-suited up, dusting for fingerprints in the Green Closet right now. The Feds have already interviewed some of the staff, and they reckon *someone* took it yesterday. They'll need to speak to us,' she nodded towards Maureen, 'that's for sure. Sanjay's already been called back in to give a witness statement.'

'How come we haven't been asked in yet?'

As if there was some pecking order, and as if that mattered.

'Don't get your thong in a twist. Sanjay was there all day, remember. Your turn on the thumbscrews will come soon enough.'

Maureen let their bickering wash over her. Apart from being busted by the twins, she had predicted a similar sequence of events, but now it was real. It was actually happening. All because of her. And her head felt pulled apart by the conflicting forces of shame and pride, like opposing magnetic poles.

Deirdre clapped her hands. 'Your ghost tour.'

'Riiiight.'

Ignoring Rhona's sarcasm, she continued.

'You've got a key to the Green Closet. Why not just put the painting back on your next tour? It's not for another week, the police will be gone by then, and they'll have to re-open. It's after hours, so the House'll be empt—'

'Yes, clean deserted. Oh, apart from twenty-six visitors, and a staff shepherd. Then there's the tiny wee detail of an alarm system.'

'As a matter of fact, the alarm was switched off on my last tour,' said Maureen. The two women narrowed their eyes at her. 'According to Daisy,' she added, examining her tea. *Well, no alarms were triggered when I broke in that night.*

'Either way, that won't look at all dodgy. The *Blackbird* miraculously back, safe and sound in the Green Closet, the morning after Maureen's tour. I'm sure they'll just draw a line and forget the whole thing ever happened.'

And on it went, Deirdre's brainwaves batted aside by Rhona's caustic sense. Like Maureen's own ideas and rebuttals being acted out in front of her. Finally, they agreed on a scouting trip to suss out the range of options. A dry run.

'We can't do anything 'til the House opens again,' said Rhona.

No one spoke for a while. The excitement had done a runner. Reality breaking over them now in a cold sweat.

Chapter 22

Ginger Nuts and High Thread Counts

Friday, 9th February

As it turned out, they only had to wait a few days. Deirdre's prediction proved correct. With forensics complete, most of the cast and crew questioned, all the filming had switched to another location. In a vain attempt at PR, Ham House opened up to the public in a *business-as-usual* show of bravado. Some of the tabloid columnists accused the Trust of cashing in on its own ineptitude, with predictably higher ticket sales. Not that far off the mark, thought Maureen, recalling The Enforcer's zero tolerance for missed targets. By some minor miracle, all three managed to secure shifts on the first day of re-opening. So now they had a plan. Of sorts.

When Maureen questioned why there were so many free slots, Rhona suggested that a posse of Friday guides were off skiing black runs in Chamonix, citing their radical feminist slogan: *Haven't we got enough now?* Rhona added, 'seeing as that lot are such thrill-seekers.'

'Not as much as us,' said Maureen under her breath.

* * *

The irony of a valuable artwork vanishing during filming of a detective novel by best-selling crime writer Agatha Christie, had not been lost on the press. It was an editor's wet dream. And much to the Trust's chagrin, it had taken place at a popular property, in the presence of illustrious actors with massive social followings. Indeed, Ms Luvvie had posted a costumed selfie in front of Ham House with the hilarious caption, *it's a fair cop guv* on Instagram. It was deleted soon after. Aside from some media-savvy members' outraged tweets on the apparent scandalous lack of security, this mini-heist had truly captured the public's imagination. Most, it seemed, bought the glamorous, movie myth of the art thief as a dashing, lovable rogue, who outwitted wealthy institutions or collectors, whom it was assumed, could afford to lose the odd piece. After all, it wasn't as if someone had been violently mugged. Maureen herself was seduced by this image, unable to face the pitiful truth.

In the thick of this feeding frenzy, the trio started down the avenue. Even at the Ham Street end, you couldn't miss the camera crews and hacks camped outside the gates. Deirdre scrabbled in her bag for some Rescue Remedy and squeezed a few drops on to her tongue. Rhona snatched the small brown bottle and downed the lot. The twins had been asked to give witness statements that morning.

'Don't worry about they scum. I'll sort them out, so I will.'

Her adrenals once again pumping on overdrive, part of Maureen couldn't help but glory in being the architect of this trainwreck. She also felt like a sitting duck — well, a walking duck — lugging this pesky nylon holdall. Rhona had insisted people get used to her being seen with one, as nothing out of the norm. Like some delayed cover for the laundry bag. Not plaid this time at least, but dark blue, and more to the point, stuffed with a large packet of Scott's porridge oats wrapped in a towel. They had all agreed that the weight and size of the cereal packet acted as an innocent stunt double for the stolen painting. A hare-brained rehearsal for the real McCoy. Way too risky to smuggle the actual *Blackbird* back into the House with CID sniffing round.

At least, that's what her fellow hustlers believed. But earlier that grey morning in a blind panic, Maureen had decided that this was too good an opportunity to waste. Besides, the Dutch still life was burning a hole on top of her wardrobe. And it wasn't as if the volunteers would have their bags searched, she had convinced herself. So, recalling Rhona's unpatriotic disgust for gruel, she ditched the cereal, and taking care to don gloves, swaddled the still life with extra sheets of glassine beneath a layer of bubble wrap. Last year, a thief returning a barometer to a National

Trust property, had been identified by his fingerprint on the bubble wrap. This time, having bought some for real, it was concealed in a brand-new bath towel.

'A towel's less bulky than a duvet, but still provides a cushioned disguise,' she over-explained to the twins, to distract from their impending ordeal. 'Bargain price from John Lewis, and excellent—'

'Wicked witch alert at 2 o'clock.'

And sure enough, following Rhona's co-ordinates, up ahead was Thelma, in a belted dogtooth coat, striding at a fair pace through the Meadows, forehand slicing the long grass with her walking stick.

'What's she doing here again?' Maureen muttered.

As it turned out, the she-devil served as a useful diversion. By the time they reached the gates, she was brandishing her cane at a bemused camera crew.

'Get outta here!'

Guarding Visitor Reception, Emma scratched the mottled rash on her neck. Her futile appeals drowned by Thelma's cries of 'shame' and 'parasites.' Defeated, she opened the rope. They scuttled through, unhassled, apart from Deirdre, who had a fluffy microphone thrust in her face.

'No comment,' she said, head down.

'Not sure you need to say that,' whispered Maureen.

Ratcheting her Glaswegian up a notch, Rhona plumped for the opposite approach, squaring up to a reporter. 'Whit's wrang with you lot? Do you think that the thief's just gauny walk back in carryin' the painting?'

At which point, Maureen's legs almost gave way. She grasped the handles tighter.

'There's not a lot we can do about them,' said Emma, chewing the tip of her radio antenna.

Sated at last, Thelma abandoned her protest and accompanied them to the West Courtyard. Cutting through the dead air, Deirdre asked Thelma if she was in for room guiding.

'I've already given my statement to the police, if that's what you mean,' said Thelma, sizing up Maureen's bag. 'No, I'm doing some more work on the storeroom inventory.'

'Lovely.' Deirdre ditched further attempts at small talk. Much to their relief, Thelma branched off to the shop.

Despite the drama at the gates, the House appeared calm, but then both Rhona and Deirdre were directed to the first floor by an absurdly young-looking detective. Their plan already unravelling.

On the plus side, down in the Mess Room, Maureen extracted some juicy info from Trevor, who was itching to dish the dirt. It seemed that the producer had been surprisingly sanguine about the whole unfortunate episode. Yes, the halt to filming had constituted a financial and logistical headache, but the press attention was generating lashings of free publicity, which had their investors salivating at the prospect of bumped-up box office returns.

'Might not be so mint when the police pin this on one of their employees,' Trevor added.

'Is that what they think?'

Maureen tried not to sound over-eager.

'Makes sense. Huge crew, loads of strangers walking in and out the House. All you need is a lanyard — no one bats an eyelid. Lorna's having a full-blown meltdown of course, taking it all out on us. If anybody speaks to the press, there'll be consequences blah blah. Cos there was no forced entry, the insurance are being slippery bastards, saying it was down to staff negligence. So, Lorna's trying to pin this on Emma being too free'n'easy with the Green Closet key. Meanwhile, Emma's in a right tizz, thinking she's a suspect. Total bollocks. So, she's passed the buck on to Venetia. I mean, how could she refuse to give the key to the fucking filming curator?'

Recognising a kindred foul-mouthed spirit, Trevor never patronised Maureen with social frills like *pardon my French*.

'But neither of them did anything wrong,' Maureen protested, a little too much.

'Silver linings mind,' he said. 'Despite the compulsory overtime and endless security reviews, I reckon Lorna's dead in the water. As far as Head Office is concerned, her watch has turned into a right shitshow, and they're not happy bunnies. Not happy at all. That said, ticket sales are way up for this time of year, even though it states on our website clear as day, that only the ground floor and Basement are open. No rubbernecking inside the Green Closet.'

Trevor's radio crackled, summoning him to yet another meeting. He performed an impressive, backwards exit, complete with mimed yawn and eyes raised heavenward. Maureen waved in empathy. To avoid emptying the dishwasher, she rinsed her mug out and tried, with little success, to steady her nerves.

With no time to wait for the others, she would have to tackle this without a lookout. After all, she'd managed on her own before. With towel-lined bag in awkward tow, she crept up the narrow servants' wooden staircase that wound all the way up from the Basement to the second floor. Catching her breath, she stopped on the tiny first floor landing. Satisfied no one else was around, she eased open the door which once led to the apartment of Elizabeth's younger sister, and entered the small, red flock wallpapered lobby. On her left, the servant's entrance to Lady Maynard's Bedchamber, now a humble storeroom. She listened for a minute but could discern no sound from inside. Straight ahead, another gilt-edged door opened into the former lady's maid cell. They had earmarked this as a potential, left-stolen goods facility: one of the few non-public but accessible rooms. Door ajar, she nudged it wide.

The chink of light between the shutters exposed shelves crammed with sharpie-labelled boxes and files. This was now known as the Bug Room; where all those pesky silk-munching moth larvae were stored, identified and recorded on quarterly spreadsheets, lured to their death in sticky pheromone traps. A Most Wanted poster illustrated the usual suspects of little blighters, from the common woodlouse, brown carpet beetles, wood weevils, white-shouldered house moths, to silverfish and harlequin ladybirds. What in God's name, she wondered, would the maid have made of her cherished sanctuary's conversion into some bizarre pest library? But more pressing, she reminded herself, where best to deposit her bag's smoking hot contents. Minus her new, fluffy bath towel.

'You okay Maureen?'

Meera had emerged from the stairwell, followed by Thelma.

Marvellous. Simply marvellous.

Unseen, Maureen slid her phone out of her pocket.

'Oh, hi Meera. My great niece is doing a school project on insects, so thought I'd send her a photo of this poster.'

Nice save.

She proceeded to take several blurry snaps.

'That brings back memories,' laughed Meera. 'Help yourself.'

That's the problem — I already have.

'You might want to switch on your flash,' said Thelma, deadpan, her eyes once again darting to the bag by Maureen's feet.

No one likes a smart arse.

'Good point. Still trying to get the hang of this thing.'

But both of them vanished into the murky depths of the storeroom, Meera's falsetto laughter now muffled in the shadowy, high-ceilinged mausoleum. Through the part-open door, Maureen glimpsed metal shelves, chairs shrouded in ghoulish covers, a gold-bordered spyglass with crackled glaze, and ornate frames stacked on their side. Even the shell of a fire handcart, with red paint flaking from the spokes of its giant wheels. And buried somewhere in there, the ebony cane used by the ailing, gout-ridden Duchess.

Along with a layer of dust, an air of melancholy enveloped these discarded treasures. Abandoned in this dingy setting, among stepladders and plastic-sleeved inventories, they whispered of grander days and forgotten stories. Maureen acknowledged a strange affinity with these dumped artefacts. Now that she'd been spotted in the vicinity, it was game over. Conceding defeat, she aborted the assignment and exited.

Back in the Basement, enroute to the lockers, she heard her friends' dulcet tones in the Mess Room. Impatient to hear about their encounter with the detective, she rushed in. Too late, she realised her mistake. Surprise, surprise, the Friday clique weren't heli-skiing in the Alps. Rather, they had hijacked the long table, and Deirdre was busy regaling them about her interview.

'… Didn't take long at all…'

Maureen aimed a slight shake of her head at Rhona, who rolled her eyes and passed her the biscuit tin.

'…honestly, she's really sweet. And she looks about eighteen.'

Maureen sneaked a couple of Ginger Nuts into her pocket, as Nigel's rubicund features emerged from behind the Telegraph. 'Did you think she'd beat a confession out of you?'

Deirdre's laughter rang hollow above the chorus of gales. 'By the way, how's your new bathroom coming along, Pam?'

An unsubtle but effective subject change from Deirdre, as said guide launched into a mind-numbing account of delivery delays and colour schemes. But as Maureen double-backed to the lockers, her accomplice stopped her dead.

'…Maureen was telling us she's just bought a set of towels, from the John Lewis sale. Did you go for the claret in the end? In fact, she's got one in her bag. Why don't…'

Misreading Maureen's rounded eyes, Deidre yakked on

about how Maureen wanted to co-ordinate the colour of her towels with a wool throw from the shop. Now, it was Rhona's turn to shake her head.

Pam started gushing over Deirdre's ad-libbed style tip. 'Using one of their throws over a bathroom chair — love it!'

This woman really needs to get a life.

'… always on the lookout for interior design ideas.'

'Oh, our Maureen certainly gives Linda Barker a run for her money. Loves combining precious antiques with modern comfort, so she does.'

Toting, as she was, a Dutch Golden Age oil, wrapped in an Egyptian cotton towel, Maureen experienced a severe sense of humour failure. She evil-eyed Rhona into silence.

'I might go for claret too. Can I have a peek?'

'It's taupe. I chose taupe.' Maureen continued to edge towards the open door. Rhona's frown deepened. Pam, far too self-involved to let it lie.

'Can I feel the thickness?'

At least Nigel had retired once more behind the Telegraph. Presumably, the highs and lows of Pam's new wet room were too thrilling for him to bear. Meanwhile, his harem was busy debating the role of Russian agents in the *Blackbird*'s disappearance.

'It's all part of Putin's plan to destabilise the National Trust.'

As a result, Maureen's reluctant show of compliance went unnoticed. As if unzipping a body bag, she opened a few inches of holdall and extracted an ear of oatmeal fuzz. A dawning realisation clouded Rhona's face, as her light-fingered pal made no attempt to move nearer. Undeterred, Pam walked over and fondled the corner of towel, inspecting its thread count through half-moon glasses.

For the love of God, it's just a towel!

'So soft. How large are their bath sheets? Can I see—'

Maureen's hand guarded the zip pull, as though her very freedom was at stake. Which it was.

'Sizes are shown online,' Rhona growled.

'Maureen won't mind.'

I wouldn't mind throttling Deirdre right now.

'Er, I have to—'

'Maureen, there you are.'

Kerry, terser than usual over her clipboard, had snuck in behind her. Her face, the usual bag of spanners, had never been so welcome.

'Detective Adamu is waiting for you in the Library. So, if you could head up there, please. I'll update you on our security review after. You're down in the Kitchen today.'

With Rhona's whispered steer, 'mebbe don't take that bloody bag up with you,' ringing in her ear, Maureen finally stowed the holdall in one of the larger lockers.

The irony of being saved by a police interview wasn't lost on Maureen as she made her way up to the Library, aware that her mouth was filling with saliva. Throwing up over an officer from the Arts and Antique Squad was not the wisest strategy. So, ignoring any conservation-unfriendly crumbs, Maureen devoured a Ginger Nut, and tramped down the West Passageway, as if being led to the scaffold.

* * *

Never underestimate the restorative powers of a biscuit, she thought, as DC Adamu introduced herself. Straight away, Maureen clocked that the detective was nobody's fool, noting how, just like the onset of grey hair and wrinkles, the guise of youthful inexperience can also provide an invaluable smokescreen.

Kitted out in unfussy black trouser suit and suede ankle boots, an abundance of rich brown curls framed her poker-face, adorned only by a silver nose stud. Behind her perfunctory smile, a pair of keen hazel eyes scanned the senior volunteer up and down, assessing her faded smart ensemble of long, grey cardie and cords. Maureen had the distinct feeling that she had been categorised and labelled in the DC's notebook within seconds.

The police are used to members of the public, even the law-abiders, acting nervy in their presence. A gratifying perk, Maureen imagined. And as they trudged up the West Stairs, she performed some cheery prating, aware that Adamu would consider this standard behaviour. They entered the Library. Although the first floor remained off-limits to the public, (more for winter conservation reasons than the recent excitement), the lights had been switched on and shutters pulled back. Adamu indicated the stairwell door.

'And this was left open all day?'

The detective already knew this of course, but doubtless, she needed to check. Besides, Maureen took it as a classic ploy — always start with easy questions to loosen up the witness.

'Yes, so crew could carry equipment through to the Long Gallery via the West Stairs. Less potential for damage,' Maureen added, with a needless laugh.

They stepped through into the Library Closet, and Maureen showed where she had been stationed on the guide's chair, to keep an eye on through-traffic from both directions.

Maureen then ran through the sequence of events that day, making sure to correct herself a few times, and trying not to sound like she had rehearsed this ad nauseam. Crucially, she also followed Rhona's advice to miss out the part about stealing the painting. Despite the arctic temperature, she soon began to feel sticky under her layers.

Unlike her vivid nightmare sequence in the early hours, Adamu didn't ask about the laundry bag. Either Meera hadn't considered it relevant, or she'd forgotten. Or, St. Martha had intervened on her behalf. At any rate, Maureen's sugar rush was receding, and her nerves were beginning to show, judging from the DC's penetrating stare. Despite her casual manner, the routine questioning was drenched in don't-fuck-with-me tones.

'To recap, during the run-through on the main stairs,

you were in here the whole time, and you didn't see anyone enter the gallery? Anyone at all?'

Maureen stopped herself from clarifying this with, *the Great Staircase* and *the Long Gallery*, when an eighteenth-century print caught her eye. The Field of the Cloth of Gold. This famous scene depicted the meeting between religiously fluid, wife-snuffing Henry VIII, and the long-snouted, arty-farty Francis I of France. A meticulously planned encounter just south of Calais, intended to ratify an Anglo-French peace treaty. With retinues looking on from the crest of opposing hills, the two kings embraced as brothers under a gold cloth tent in the valley below. Predictably, this soon descended into a tiresome dick-swinging contest, to see who was better at jousting and who could flash the most cash.

It was all about putting on a good show.

And with that, Maureen decided that the moment for confession had arrived.

'Well, it's a bit embarrassing, to be honest. I wouldn't want the staff to find out.'

'Go on.'

'Er, I think, I mean… Well, I might have dozed off for a bit. You see, I often have a nap after lunch these days and it had been quite an early start. I only woke up as the crew returned to the Long Gallery.'

Adamu's lips twitched as she scribbled in her notebook. This explained the old dear's jitters. It was clear she'd slept through the whole episode and was about as useful as a chocolate teapot. Probably did this all the time. One step away from a care home. Maureen read all this in the ghost of a smirk, blessing the younger woman's ageism.

'I understand,' replied the detective, and flicking her notebook shut, she glanced at her watch.

'Right, I've got a meeting with the manager. Lorna Richards?'

Maureen decided this did warrant correcting. 'Lorna

Richardson.' Then asked, 'you don't need me anymore?'

'No, that's it for now. If you do think of anything else, call me. The smallest detail might prove useful.'

With a final scan, she handed Maureen a card and strode out to the West Stairs. Once out of sight, Maureen rested a hand on the Closet's dark stained panelling. Her Godfrey routine from Dad's Army had paid off. For the time being. But right now, she felt like racing down to the shop and glugging some of that special offer sloe gin.

From downstairs, an abrupt clatter of bolts signalled that Kerry was opening the front door. On the surface at least, normal service had resumed. Maureen slunk down to the dank Kitchen, knowing full well that it wasn't over yet. Not by a long chalk.

Chapter 23
Captain Mainwaring

'You tosspots! You had one simple job.' Rhona banged her fist on the table. 'And that was not to bring the actual painting along.'

'Why am I a tosspot?' asked Deirdre.

Following the day's botch-up, they had regrouped at Maureen's to thrash out Plan B.

'*You're* not. It's a line from Ocean's Eleven,' said Rhona.

'Er, don't you mean tossers?' asked Maureen.

'This is so ridiculous,' Deirdre turned to the tosser in question. 'Seriously Maureen, you should've told us you had the painting in your bag. We're all implicated in this now.'

Deirdre was right, and Maureen felt ashamed of acting on impulse. Hadn't she learned by now this was a risky strategy?

'I'm sorry. Just wanted it out of the house. But I agree, it wasn't fair.'

'Especially as this one nearly dropped you right in the jobby. Blethering on to Pam about towels: *Did you go for claret in the end?*'

Deirdre sniffed. 'At least our witness statements went well. And look, we're just going to have to wait *'til the right moment.*' Her tone was firm. Then, with less conviction, 'they'll never suspect us.'

'Me, you mean. I'm the one who took it.'

Rhona looked up from tutting over Word Trip.

'Let's have a butcher's then.'

'Sorry?'

'Show us the Blackbird, Midge and Whatsit. May as well reap some rewards before we're all incarcerated.'

Pre-empting an earful from Deirdre, she added, 'Joking. Not about seeing it, mind.'

Maureen felt that she owed them this. Particularly after

their rollercoaster shift. So she traipsed up to the spare bedroom, then with some involuntary grunts, retrieved the holdall from the top of the wardrobe. Back in the sitting room, Deirdre had cleared the coffee table, switched on a couple of lamps and was drawing the curtains on a salmon-flecked sky. Rhona was rummaging through a bucket bag for her specs.

Unzipping the holdall, fully this time, Maureen donned a pair of gloves. She ignored Rhona side-eyeing Deirdre through a pair of streaky glasses, and instructed them to hold open the sides, as she extracted the painting. With theatrical delicacy, she placed it on the table, unfolding the bubble wrap. At last, she peeled off the crinkled glassine. And there it lay gleaming, its incongruous surround of greige towel still visible beneath the translucent paper. In unison, the trio inhaled and knelt over it, as if paying homage.

At this sudden exposure, the blackbird looked startled, fixing them with its wary left eye. Now, the feathered predator seemed rigid with fear, while the butterfly flitted unconcerned, and the bluebottle snatched a second's rest. The cherries just sprawled, candescent in the sunlight.

'Guess it's no so bad, after all,' Rhona conceded after a minute's lapse.

'It's beautiful.' Deirdre continued to pour over it. 'And this frame…'

'Still think Wyck's *Alchemist* in the Duke's Closet is way better.'

'Can't think why didn't I take that instead. It's only about ten times bigger. It would have been so easy to cut it out of the seventeenth-century panelling. No one in business support would have heard a thing.'

'Alright Catherine Zeta-Jones, I was only say—'

A sudden shrill blast of the doorbell killed their spat.

'Dee, quick. Go keek through the curtains for any panda cars,' Rhona hissed.

In a futile gesture, Maureen pressed herself flat against

the wall. Deirdre crept to the window, then shook her head. Maureen exhaled invisible cigarette smoke.

'Who is it then?'

'Couldn't see.'

The doorbell rang again.

'Pretend you're not in.'

'I can't. It might be Seema, and she knows I'm here. It'll look odd if I don't answer it,' Maureen whispered back.

'Well, keep it casual like and get shot of her then.'

This time, Maureen remembered to remove her gloves. Deirdre started to cover the painting, but Rhona motioned her to leave it.

'Not without those,' she urged under her breath, pointing at the discarded gloves. 'Just leave it. It's no like she's inviting anyone in.'

Bracing herself for more of Seema's baking experiments, Maureen opened the door.

'Thelma!'

Stapled-on smile, violent wave of nausea.

Fantastic, it's the Effing Dark Lord. Maybe SO19's round the corner waiting for The Enforcer to abseil down from a helicopter.

'How lovely to—'

But it appeared that Thelma was not in the mood for any social pleasantries. For the second time that week, an uninvited visitor shoved past Maureen at her own front door. Except on this occasion, her left ankle received a warning tap from that lethal walking stick — a wordless directive to give way. In Matrix-style slow motion, Maureen lurched after Thelma, dimly aware that the word, '*Noooooo*' was issuing from her lips.

Too late. Thelma had reached the sitting room. Not surprising, given the shoebox dimensions of her cottage. The scene that greeted them was reminiscent of that old Mannequin Challenge craze. But here, accompanied only by ominous silence, knelt Rhona, all frozen snarl, glaring over her glasses with appalled wide eyes, while Deirdre stooped over the table, petrified in the act of shielding the quarry. This now lay half exposed, so that the blackbird was betrayed only by its yellow beak, jutting out from under the shaggy taupe.

'Thought as much,' said Thelma, plonking herself down on the sofa, propping a cushion behind her back.

'Nice of you to come visit with us,' said Rhona, still paralysed.

'But how did you work—?' Maureen heard herself squeak.

Thelma launched into full Miss Marple. 'For starters, there was that hideous laundry bag you were trying to hide in the Library Closet, on the last main day of filming. And you were a bundle of nerves when it was discovered missing.'

Maureen had banked on her heebie-jeebies going unnoticed in the general commotion but now recalled Thelma handing her a camomile tea in the Mess Room.

'Then this morning, yet another curious holdall you felt the need to take up to the Bug Room.'

'See?' Maureen raised an exasperated hand in Rhona's direction.

'Plus, in the Library Closet, these were a bit of a giveaway.' Thelma flicked the scrumpled ball of gloves with the end of her stick. Rhona and Deirdre had lost the power of speech, which had to be a record for them.

'Right, so what's your next move?' Thelma eyed them in turn, still grasping her wizard's staff. Waiting for a reply, she collapsed it, so it assumed the proportions of an officer's swagger stick, which she deposited with care on the unhoovered carpet. And just like that, the Dark Lord morphed into Captain Mainwaring.

Still mute, the twins ogled Thelma with dropped jaws, maintaining their poses, as if keeping up the Mannequin Challenge to a silent hip hop soundtrack.

It was Maureen who broke first.

'You're not going to report this?'

'Whatever you think of me, I'm no grass, Maureen.'

'Snitches get stitches,' nodded Deirdre.

Rhona couldn't have looked more astonished if a diminutive spaceship had landed on the writing desk.

'We've been trying to help Maureen return it,' explained Deirdre, with an unspoken, 'honest, Miss.'

'Well, that's patently obvious from today's shenanigans. Besides, it's not as if you'd be able to sell it. Although, I expect it's worth a decent sum, given that frame and its provenance.'

Thelma spoke as if she shifted stolen art every other day. Maureen felt her legs buckling and sat down next to her.

'You have got a contingency plan?'

Again, Thelma scanned the raw recruits and perceiving they hadn't the faintest essence of one, continued. 'Well, Ham House is out of the question. Even though SOCO have finished up, not sure what you were thinking with all the press sniffing about and the staff so jittery. Doubtless, the police will want to talk to us again. Especially you, Maureen. Seeing as you were *around* when it happened.'

Even in her state of shock, Maureen could have sworn those pearly lips flickered into upturn.

'Seeing as she's the actual tea leaf,' said Rhona.

'Not helpful,' said Maureen.

'There's a staff strategy meeting this Thursday. You could take it back then,' Deirdre suggested.

'Genius. Why not just walk up to Lorna and hand it to her?'

'Thank you, Rhona.' Thelma, already the head teacher.

'I meant put it back without being seen.'

'Too much of a coincidence. Like I said, returning it to the House is out of the question now. Attention would immediately focus on everyone who has access to the House. Such as, volunteers. By the way, I'd murder a cup of tea, Deirdre. Earl Grey, if there's any.'

'I only have English Breakfast,' Maureen announced, as

if in a trance.

'Ooh yes, top me up as well, hun.'

'I'm not the paid help, you know,' said Deirdre, as Maureen remained ossified to the spot. Nevertheless, she collected the assorted mugs and headed for the kitchen, grumbling, 'This isn't even my house.'

As involuntary hostess of this surreal lawbreakers' convention, Maureen knew she should leap up and offer refreshments, but maintained her role as couch potato, stupefied at what was unfolding in her sitting room.

Thelma snapped her out of it. 'This needs to be put away, now.' She motioned to the half-hidden painting, no interest in viewing it with work to be done. In auto mode, Maureen picked up her gloves and re-swathed her precious *Blackbird.* As she tucked it back in its prosaic hidey-hole upstairs, an alarming thought struck her. Back in the sitting room, Maureen shared this with her gang over scalding mugs of fresh tea.

'If you've all figured me out in a matter of days, surely it won't take long for the Met to piece it together?'

'Dear heart, you're forgetting your own insignificance. We're all doddery old farts in their eyes, and this makes us invisible. But not to each other. We see each other, even if nobody else does. They underestimate us at their peril.'

A respectful silence followed this shrewd insight from Thelma. Once again, Maureen conjured the Duchess gazing at Medea Casting Spells.

'But then, who's to say other volunteers won't work it out?'

'Sanjay was the only other guide there, and he wouldn't have a scooby,' said Rhona.

'Anyroad,' Deirdre piped up. 'If the House is out of bounds, what about the Gardens?'

Maureen noted the plate of biscuits being handed round. Clearly, Deirdre had rifled through her cupboards to impress their new captain.

'Brilliant plan, seeing as the Gardens are in a *completely* different location. No police, press or staff to worry about.' Rhona threw up her hands at her friend's crass logic. Clean forgetting that this afternoon's failed mission had all been her initiative. Best not remind her of that right now.

'That's not a bad idea.' Thelma leant forward, eyeing her new star pupil. 'Not bad at all, Deirdre. Dogwalkers stop off at the Orangery every day.' She frowned. 'Usually members though, so cards would be scanned.'

'Which means the Feds would have a record of all visitors entering the grounds, as well as that day's staff and volunteers' rota. Like I said, same difference.' Rhona dunked a malted milk with such force that some tea slopped out.

'You don't have to be a member,' said Deirdre. 'Anyone can buy a ticket at the gate.'

'With cash, so no digital trace,' said Maureen, nibbling round the biscuit's edges, saving the trademark cow for last.

'Aye, but then Visitor Reception press-gang them into membership.' Rhona ditched a wad of brown, sodden napkins on to the tray. 'No escape for the fresh meat.'

'Didn't Meera email for extra help with some big coach parties next week?' said Maureen, wondering from where Deirdre had procured napkins.

'Yes, the Bookham Bees W.I. — their burlesque dance routines are pure amateur,' said Thelma, with a dismissive wave.

'Oh aye, tell us more,' said Rhona, brows peaked.

Thelma ignored her. 'And the Effingham History Society, I believe.'

Rhona spooned a mouthful of soggy biscuit. 'The very underbelly of organised crime.'

'A useful decoy,' Thelma went on, impervious to Rhona's bants. 'All those extra bodies to distract VR and a long list of suspects for the police.'

'True,' said Maureen, playing with the hair on her chin.

'So *where* exactly in the Gardens?'

Deirdre's hand shot up. 'The Orangery.'

'Far too busy,' said Thelma, reappraising her Star of the Week.

'Er, by Bacchus in the Cherry Gardens.'

Again, Thelma squashed this. 'Too exposed. Deirdre, it's not a game.'

'No Dee, it isn't,' said Rhona, enjoying her friend's fall from grace. Deirdre snatched the last biscuit.

'There's always The Wilderness,' suggested Maureen. 'Now that's secluded.'

This was a less formal area south of the grass plats. Hornbeam-lined paths radiated from its centre, criss-crossing hedged enclosures.

'With those wee wooden huts.'

Alongside medicinal plants and flowers, these geometric hedges also screened small summer houses; rotund shelters in which to contemplate nature, seventeenth-century style. Mainly, they were bagged by gardeners to escape the elements.

'Yes, they're being used for that Silent Spaces thingy.' Deirdre was back on form, quoting the Bulletin: '*Providing an opportunity for solitude and reflection.*'

'That and the odd sneaky crack pipe,' said Rhona.

'It appears we have our plan, ladies.' Authorised by Thelma. *Not quite the man from Del Monte,* thought Maureen, *but the Captain from Cobham, she say yes.* 'We'll carry it out on Thursday. All go in for our next shift, as per normal.'

'Aye, just your average Thursday, returning stolen art in broad daylight.'

Chapter 24

Not a Fingerprint Worth a Dab
Tuesday, 13th February

'Listen, I don't even need to know if you took it. Ninety-nine times out of a hundred, you're best off saying nothing. And that's my advice at this stage — keep schtum.'

'But won't that make me look guilty?'

'Doesn't matter. You don't have to prove your innocence. It's up to them to show you any evidence.'

Maureen nodded, unable to process any of it. Earlier that morning, her brain had imploded as she answered the phone. It was DC Adamu. Would she mind coming down to Twickenham Police Station for a quick chat?

'We just need to clarify a few details on your witness statement. All routine stuff. You'll be in and out without any fuss. Nothing to worry about.'

Nothing to worry about! Bet she loves saying that.

'Of course, if you want, you're entitled to free legal advice, but there's really no need. Entirely up to you.'

Desperate to speak to her comrades-in-arms, Maureen craved a dose of Rhona's dark wit, infused with Deirdre's breezy optimism and their captain's curt no-nonsense. Thelma had a master's in being right:

Doubtless, the police will want to talk to us again. Especially you, Maureen. Seeing as you were around when it happened...

For the first time, she longed to hear those detached, clipped tones. But in her jumpy paranoia, she imagined herself under some sort of surveillance. Clueless of the legal niceties, she even wondered whether they'd tapped her phone. It was like living through some far-fetched ITV drama. One thing she did know, the police couldn't hack into WhatsApp exchanges. Something about end-to-end encryption.

*'I've been asked to go to Twickenham Police Station to answer more questions! What the flying f*** do I do now? Help m—'*

Her forefinger hovered over her phone's keypad, then she pressed *Select All* and *Cut.* They might not be able to read the actual content, but could they trace any phone numbers she messaged? She couldn't be certain, but on balance, decided it wasn't worth the risk. She was on her own.

Then again, there was Frank. Now, he would know someone. He always did. How could an east-end-boxer-turned-antique dealer not be on first name terms with a criminal defence solicitor? Of course he bloody was, he told her, unperturbed by her request. As if she'd phoned for his signature lamb tagine recipe. He would sort it and not to worry about the cost, it was on him. End of. She was family. No wonder Kathy had loved him so much.

Unlike on the telly, this one wasn't fat, bald and scruffy. Or male. Her cerise suit sported impressive shoulder pads, and *just call me Stace* was clearly no stranger to the gym. Like Frank, she spoke with a strong estuary accent.

'From what you've told me, they've got nothing. So, to reiterate, you should say bugger all. Let me do the talking.'

Sitting in a café near the police station, Maureen watched a couple laughing outside the Italian over the road. Not a care in the world.

'… like I said, I don't need to know anything.' She ignored her buzzing pocket. 'But one thing I will say,' lowering her voice, she glanced round. 'Whether you're a drug dealer, or… it's always the phones that'll fuck you in the end. Sorry, I always swear.'

Maureen waved this away.

Trust me, this is the perfect fucking time to swear.

'… some of my clients have been caught by not destroying their phones. And I don't mean just removing the SIM card.' She looked Maureen straight in the face. 'And *everybody* involved needs to get rid. But Section 32 only applies if you're under arrest. And you're on a voluntary — a Caution Plus 3 — so don't worry.'

She may as well have been speaking Russian.

'On that subject, I see you've got an iPhone. If they ask you, don't let them have your PIN number. They can't force you to hand over a PIN, so do *not* give it. Clear?'

Maureen hadn't even considered that. She pushed away her half-drunk tea with such force it sloshed into the saucer. Stace combed diamanté nails through her hair extensions and stood up.

'Shall we go then? Trust me, you'll be fine.'

* * *

It began with a loud, monotone. Beeeeeeeeeeep. On and on it seemed to go, until Maureen almost caved into hysterical laughter. Everyone else remained stony faced. Which then made her want to sob.

'It's 2:07pm on Tuesday, 13th February. My name is Nikki Adamu; I'm a DC in the Met's Art and Antiques Unit. Also present is PC Steven Ray. As you know, I'm going to interview you under caution, so for the tape, can you state your name and date of birth…'

Maureen obliged, unable to supress the tremor in her voice. No need for her few-crumbs-short-of-a-biscuit routine. She was entirely out of her depth here, in this cold, windowless room. Where was the two-way glass?

'You do not have to say anything. But it may harm your defence…'

She'd heard this umpteen times on telly. Now it was being addressed to her. For real. Shielded by the grey table, she clutched the sides of her unforgiving chair.

Sad choices, Maureen. Stupendously sad choices.

'… and you're free to go at any time.'

Stace leant over and in a low voice, added, 'But of course if you try to leave, you're no longer a voluntary, so they'll arrest you.'

Excellent news.

'So that we're clear, I'm going to explain to you what theft is. It means you've dishonestly taken property belonging to somebody else — in this case, a valuable painting owned by the National Trust — and your intention was to keep it, to permanently deprive them of it. Do you understand?'

Maureen wanted to reply that despite being over seventy, she still possessed a basic grasp of the English language but stuck with 'yes.'

Adamu broke in. 'Okay, I'll briefly run though the circs…'

Maureen was distracted by a plastic disc on the ceiling. Smoke detector or camera?

'… On Tuesday sixth February, a seventeenth-century oil painting was discovered missing from Ham House. All the evidence suggests this was taken the day before, when the property was closed to the public. We know you'd volunteered to help as a conservator during a filming project. You accept you were there on both Monday fifth and Tuesday sixth February?'

Maureen nodded.

'You need to speak for the tape please,' the bald uniformed officer reminded her.

'Yes. I was in Ham House both days.'

At least, she could answer this without her pants catching fire.

'Notice anything or anyone suspicious, specifically on Monday fifth February?'

A nice, easy icebreaker from Bald Sidekick.

'No,' Maureen paused, as if to rack her brain. 'But it was absolute chaos. Very large crew, people coming and going, carrying equipment.' Employing her bird brain to deflect. 'Quite exciting, I'd never been on a film set before—'

'We understand that this particular painting,' DC Adamu made a careful show of checking her file, 'The *Blackbird, Butterfly and Cherries*, was your favourite.'

Under the table, Maureen dug her nails into her palm, as Adamu staged pouring water into a plastic cup. She hadn't expected to be blindsided by Bad Cop quite so soon. Clever tactic, but more to the point, who the hell had blown the whistle on this? Rhona would rather eat her own tongue. Even Deirdre would know better, surely?

'It's *one* of my favourites, I suppose.' Maureen did her best to sound offhand. 'But I also love Lely's portraits of Elizabeth Murray, particularly his final one of her in the Round Gallery. Then of course there's Isaac Oliver's miniature *A Man Consumed By Flames*. Now *that's* probably my favourite. It's very intriguing,' she rambled on, while Adamu clicked her pen on repeat. 'No one's quite sure who the subject is and what it symbolises —'

'You're very well informed about all the contents.'

Adamu sliced through Maureen's bore-the-pants-off-them strategy.

'I ought to be after ten years.'

'Impressive,' Adamu smiled. 'Ten years is a long time. You must also be very familiar with the running of the House by now.'

Where's she going with this?

'Well, that changes all the time. We just interact with the visitors.'

'But still, you know all the staff and exactly how the House is run.'

'Where are you going with this, DC Adamu?'

Stace drummed her nail art on the cup-ringed table. Adamu didn't answer. Instead, she changed tack.

'What do you recall about events that Monday?'

'Ooh. I've just remembered!'

'Go on.'

'I'm also very fond of Francis Wick's bird paintings in the Volury. And Thomas Wyck's portrayal of *The Alchemist* is frightfully good. I don't think the artists were related, though.'

Adamu narrowed her eyes.

'Monday fifth February — the day we believe the painting was stolen.' She wasn't buying this doddery old dear routine. 'What do you remember, Maureen?'

Once again, Maureen stumbled through the bones of

her previous witness statement, while the detective sat back and studied her, pouncing on any hesitation or inconsistency. Much like how Pepys toyed with the odd mouse or fledgling. Circling round her movements, the timings, who she saw, who had keys to the Green Closet, did she have a key. On and on it went, with Stace consistently advising her not to answer. Frustrated, Adamu bared her claws once more.

'Did you really fall asleep in the Library annexe, while the rest of the cast and crew were rehearsing a scene on the main stairs?'

Jeeze Louise, it's the Library Closet and the Great Staircase.

'Yes.' Best appalled face. 'Like I said, it was an early start, and I generally nap after lunch. You need to at my age.' Slight chortle. 'There's a lot of scientific evidence that it's—'

'A very conveniently timed nap.'

'Cut your ageist sarcasm, detective, and stick to the questions.'

Go Stace!

Unfazed, Adamu changed course.

'Tell us about the game you instigated at your Christmas lunch.'

Maureen took a gulp of water. *Barbara. Of course. That conniving, bouffant little Judas. Snitches get stitches alright.* In the meantime, best top-drawer puzzled face.

'What Christmas lunch?'

'Oh, I think you know.' Adamu caught her solicitor's eye. 'You and your fellow room guides at the pub on Ham Comm—'

'And how is this relevant?' Stace hit back.

'Apparently, Maureen asked what item her colleagues would steal from Ham House, in the event of a fire.'

'So, not relevant at all. Don't bother answering this.'

'With respect, as we're investigating a serious theft, this little *what would you nick?* game devised by Maureen, is very interesting. This didn't just come out of nowhere.'

Maureen swallowed hard. 'Just a bit of fun, that's all. I was trying to relieve the boredom.' Crossing her legs, Stace kicked her under the table.

Shut up, shut up eejit!

Adamu smelt blood and went in for the kill.

'*Relieve the boredom.* Now we're getting somewhere. Here's what I reckon Maureen — you've been bored a long time. Isn't that the truth? All these years, same old routine. Lots of time to play *what if* games. You were craving some excitement, a renewed sense of purpose. Maybe you got bored that day and saw your chance during the filming?'

'That's not true!'

Maureen blinked away non-crocodile tears.

'Isn't it? I think I'm bang on the money—'

'As you well know DC Adamu, what you think has no relevance to this case whatsoever. Where's your evidence that my client was in any way involved? You've clearly got no forensics — not a fingerprint worth a dab. Zero witnesses, and a total lack of CCTV. Yes, Miss Goodwin happened to be in Ham House on the day you *say* the painting went missing. Along with God knows how many other volunteers and staff. Oh yes, not to mention the whopping great cast and crew. My client stands by her earlier witness statement. She's fully co-operated, but I think we're done here, don't you?'

At which point, Maureen wanted to fling her arms round her sinewy, designer-clad saviour, but instead, silently lauded her brother-in-law's dodgy past. And breathed.

* * *

'Didn't I say you'd be fine? You've got my number. Anyway, good to meet you, Maureen. And don't sweat it.' With phone glued to ear, Stace clicked her heels round the corner to her black Audi TT Roadster.

Maureen couldn't help herself. She went straight to look up custodial sentences. Not exactly straight away. She ambled across to Waitrose, and shilly-shallied at the pet food section, as if deliberating over Sheba, Felix or Gourmet. At last, having judged that the mother with the screaming brat and the bleary-eyed teenager restocking her aisle were not undercover CID, she shoved some tins of Whiskas on top of her Radio Times and snatched a packet of Liquorice Allsorts.

Still checking for potential tails, she nipped out the back entrance. Past the pigeons scratching at the mangy grass, past the vaping school kids and the red-faced man nursing his can of cider. Along the path to Garfield Road and the Grade II listed building with its sculpted roundels of former local residents, Pope and Tennyson. Yet another visit to a library. Twickenham, this time. Worth the council tax alone, she thought. That and refuse collection, but definitely *not* policing.

She logged on to the Sentencing Council website and, chewing a pink jelly button, assessed her larceny as Category 1 with High Culpability. That could mean six years. She knew Stace would laugh this off, what with her age, her clean record and the absence of intimidation or violence — however much she'd wished to pummel certain people, aka Barbara. But Maureen liked to rehearse worst-case scenarios. So, all she read was six years. Six years! Maureen doubted she could cope with six days. Prison mattresses would wreck her back, and they probably didn't serve blood orange marmalade with thickly buttered toast for breakfast. She might not even live out her sentence.

Now she replayed a *Panorama* report, exposing virtual anarchy in larger prisons. With the constant threat of drug-fuelled violence; smashed windows plugged with towels or flattened milk cartons; mindless boredom; catatonic zombies high on Spice; disgusting food; shouting.

Back home, with Pepys rumbling on her lap, she concluded several things all at once:

1) Less *Panorama*, more *MAFS*.
2) It was more important than ever for the *Blackbird* to fly home.
3) Liquorice Allsorts are murder on your teeth.

Chapter 25
Operation W
Thursday, 15th February

'Then we went over my witness statement *again* and she kept asking about keys. Who has access to the key cupboard, do any of the keys ever go missing? Next, it was alarms. What do volunteers know about the alarm system, has anyone shown a recent interest in—'

'That's 'cos Babs cliped on Nige, so she did.'

'What?'

On Thelma's insistence, they had convened at the far end of the Orangery Terrace. Huddled under golf umbrellas, their steel chairs were lined with Ocado bags, courtesy of Deirdre. No other guides had braved the elements and despite the pissing rain, Maureen was more than happy with the arrangement. She'd experienced many a hard-boiled eye and back-handed whisper that morning.

Despite her earlier resolution, she'd been on the verge of cancelling her shift. In the end, she'd decided that would garner even more suspicion. After all, the police hadn't charged her, and as her new bestie, Stace, had so emphatically stressed, they had not one shred of evidence. Not yet. As well as briefing her gang on Tuesday's nightmare, it was now critical to enact Plan B. They'd be all over the *Blackbird* in minutes, if they searched her place. It was hardly some Tudor mansion dotted with priest holes. Last week, Deirdre had offered to stash it *chez nous*, before remembering that Gary had threatened an early spring clean. Touched by her generosity, Maureen pointed out this would also risk a custodial sentence for handling stolen goods.

She pictured the neighbours' reaction to a police raid at number fourteen. Seema would self-combust with excitement as the TAGs WhatsApp went into meltdown, and Face Ache would probably pass out. Not to mention the press infestation of The Alberts. Britney would go demented.

Spurred by this alarming prospect, she'd turned up business-as-usual for her shift, as if she'd merely visited the podiatrist a couple of days earlier. Head high, ill-gotten spoils in tow, like some veteran badass. But as she ferried her smoking holdall across the courtyard, the insanity of this slapped her in the face. What had she been thinking? Especially as news of her joyous police encounter had run riot. When Maureen scribbled her name in the Visitors' log, Emma had blanked her and sprinted up the West Stairs. While Trevor, bless his holey hiking socks, had just winked on his way past.

* * *

Deirdre translated Rhona's update: 'Well, Barbara 'let slip' that Nigel seemed very interested in how the alarms work round the House. And seemed to know a lot about how valuable paintings are secured.' True to her previous declaration — *'This is the most fun I've had in years'* — Deirdre appeared to be relishing every second. 'Plus, he *misplaced* the Green Closet key during filming.'

'Oh, that was Nigel,' said Maureen. 'I heard Emma mention someone had lost the key the day before I—'

'Committed larceny?' said Rhona.

'Sssh.' Deirdre put a finger to her lips and scanned the deserted Terrace. By special request, the Bookham Bees were being corralled round the House before it opened to the great unwashed.

'That would explain why they called him in for questioning,' said Thelma from under her Scandi Noir waterproof.

'He's furious, apparently,' Deirdre continued. 'Threatening to sell his story to the Telegraph. Says he has contacts there.'

'In his dreams! Poor wee bastard. Result for our klepto pal here, right enough.'

Rhona did have a point. Nigel's interview took the heat off her and made it all look more routine. On the one hand, Maureen was relieved that another guide had been netted. In fact, it made the police look desperate. Still, she felt unable to crow in chorus. Poor wee bastard indeed, she thought, reliving that cold bead of sweat trickling from the nape of her neck right down to her apple catchers. A drop of pure saline terror.

'Anyway, I thought the Art and Antiques Squad were based at Scotland Yard,' said Deirdre, as if this was the crux of Maureen's ordeal.

To be fair, Thelma dignified this with a sensible answer. 'Well, I expect they prefer to use a local base to interview suspects.'

Suspect! I'm an actual suspect in an actual police investigation. Scrub that, I'm an art thief, an actual bloody art thief. Who might end up in actual bloody prison.

Recalling the DC's razor-sharp insight, Maureen experienced a sudden urge to both laugh and cry all at once.

...you've been bored a long time. Isn't that the truth?

Adamu had her number, sure enough. With supreme effort, Maureen maintained composure, aware Thelma was now speaking in low urgent tones.

'Maureen, you were wise to bring this in today, as planned.' She nodded at the blue, zipped bag. 'They could easily get a warrant to search your house.'

'Doubt even the brilliant Stace could haul you out the jobby if that happened.'

Maureen had rhapsodised over her solicitor's spiky talent. By now, she had assumed near goddess-like proportions. But Rhona was right; if the police came knocking, she was sunk.

'...simply can't afford to wait any longer.'

The twins were also hot to trot. Having divulged all the legal advice, Maureen sensed that they were part motivated by Stace likening phones to a homing device.

'No way am I ditching my new iPhone,' said Rhona, as if the very suggestion violated her basic human rights.

Thelma combed the rain-soaked Gardens for any lurking informants before giving the nod. 'Are we all set for Operation Silent Spaces?'

'You can't call it Operation Where-You're-Going,' said Rhona. 'Defeats the whole object. I mean, they didn't call it Operation Normandy Landings.'

'Operation SS?' Deirdre offered.

'Slightly bad taste,' said Maureen.

'Give me strength!' Thelma cast her eyes up at a pocket of blue sky nudging the wall of grey cloud. 'Operation W, then.'

'What does *W* stand for?' asked Deirdre.

'Wilderness.' Maureen and Thelma replied in unison.

Rhona piled on the upspeak. 'Hello, that's our destination.'

'Enough.' Their exasperated Head reasserted authority. 'The Effingham History Society will arrive shortly, and we have thirty minutes before our pre-shift briefing. So let's,' she stood up with surprising abruptness, 'just do it.'

Scraping their chairs on the wet gravel, Rhona muttered something about Nike patents. Bracing herself, Maureen picked up the holdall.

The rain had eased into mizzle and skirting puddles, the gang trooped down the path beyond the Kitchen Gardens. After a quick shufti, they slipped through the wrought iron gates opening on to the northern edge of the Wilderness. They were in luck; the grassy path lay sodden and vacant before them. Beetling out of view through the network of hedges, they squelched through the first gap on their right into a secret haven. Lemon primroses vied with brazen daffodils, and even the odd pink lungwort poked out from the evergreens. At last, came a celestial blessing and the wet shrubs glistened in the emerging sunshine. More Garden of Eden than Wilderness.

'It's so peaceful here.'

Scarcely had Deirdre uttered these words, when two things happened in quick succession. As they approached the wooden hut, Thelma raised her cane to stall them. Tucked inside on a bench, a man lifted his pallid face from his hands.

Nigel.

'It's over,' he told them. Drained, impassive. Speechless, they circled the summer house, Maureen's hands glued to the nylon handles. How the hell had he worked it out? Were the police already on their way?

'What do you mean, Nigel?' As if speaking to a Broadmoor fugitive, Thelma kept her voice neutral with a hint of concern, but Maureen noticed that she pressed her stick hard into the muddy turf.

'There's nothing left for me now,' he choked.

'Is this about the police interview, son?' Rhona's relief was palpable. Except for Nigel, who nodded, then buried his face once more, dousing Maureen's inner whoops. This wasn't the strutting, mansplaining brag, who whinged about snowflakes and woke-gone-mad, who made her want to whip off her greyed bra and set it alight. Although truth be told, it could do with incinerating. No, this was a new Nigel, one she'd never seen. A broken man.

Following Thelma through the hut's arched entrance, they sat round him on the semi-circular bench, like some awkward self-help group.

My name's Maureen and I'm a fine art thief.

'I've just had a meeting with Lorna, who told me I'm not allowed to volunteer anymore,' he said.

'How no?' said Rhona, in chorus with a thrilled 'What?' from Deirdre.

Nigel took a deep breath. 'Not while I'm prime suspect for stealing that painting. It seems innocent 'til proven guilty doesn't wash with the National Trust.' He twisted his hands together on his lap. 'I didn't do it, by the way. You do believe me,' he said, searching their faces with bloodshot eyes.

'That we do pal, that we do,' said Rhona, glancing at the blue bag pushed under the seat.

The real culprit couldn't resist. 'Let's face it Nigel, no way could you pull off a fine art heist.'

Frowning, he regarded Maureen, trying to place this familiar echo. His confusion interrupted by Thelma. 'Whyever,' she asked, unzipping her raincoat, 'do they think it's you?'

Nigel's chest heaved. 'Because I've been a total moron.'

Then he divulged all. How one of his former City pals had sold him a slam dunk investment scheme. A total scam which had wiped out his savings. Maureen had often panned his staple red jeans, striped shirt and wax jacket. Now she saw that like her, new clothes were very low priority. Now she understood all his bluster was a desperate front. He had very much been drowning, not waving.

'… They went back through my bank accounts, you see. Saw all my losses. That and me asking Trevor about the alarm system — just cos I was interested. Then like a dozy prat, I went and left the Green Closet key in my locker during filming. Forgot I put it there. I guess with all the press interest, they're under pressure to make it fit.'

'They're making two plus two equal five,' agreed Thelma.

'Exactly,' he said. 'At least, you lovely ladies trust me.' Despite his usual cringe factor, the gratitude was pitiful. 'Funny, everyone else is too busy to return my calls.' Ditched by his Friday fan club, which wasn't funny at all. 'Anyway, I'm heading for the hills. Well, until Tuesday. Going for a long weekend in York to see the grandkids. I've been *granted permission*.' He uttered a sharp 'huh.' 'Providing I'm contactable and don't leave the country, it's fine apparently.'

'That'll be nice,' said Deirdre, mouthing 'What?' as Rhona threw her daggers.

Nigel hung his head. 'What am I going to do? I love coming here — it's all I've got.'

'You're going to hold fast,' said Thelma, as Deirdre

patted his shoulder. Maureen gazed out at the shimmering Gardens, too wretched to speak.

'Trust us Nige,' Rhona added. '*You* are definitely not going down for this.'

* * *

Maureen's shift passed in a nauseous blur. Other than to confirm a crisis meeting the following afternoon, she barely spoke to the others on her way out, and she couldn't look Rhona in the eye. As if on some regular commute, yet again, the *Blackbird* lay tucked in the boot of her Micra. Once or twice, Nigel's plaintive face flashed in her rear-view, and she nearly turned to check he wasn't stowed away on her back seat.

Snap out of it, woman.

Nimbly reversing into a tight space, she spotted some neighbours outside her gate. Her heart sank; no way could she muster banal small talk right now. But crossing the road, she caught Will's concerned face, the tears in Seema's eyes. It took a few seconds for the jumble of words to register. For their meaning to sink in.

'... been trying to call you... left voicemails...'

'It's Pepys ... just found him by the side of the road... runover.'

'... to the vet... tried but it was too... late.'

'... so sorry, Maureen.'

Chapter 26
The Exact Opposite of Fine

It was exhausting being fine. Assuring her neighbours that she wasn't on the brink, and that Pepys was *only a cat.* Authorising the vet to dispose of his remains. No, she didn't want the ashes. Trying to get rid of Seema, who'd come over with some homemade fruit cake the consistency of granite. She couldn't face telling Jodie, even though she owed Laura a call.

When her landline rang, she answered it on automatic pilot. She heard Frank, asking how she'd got on with Stace. Cursing herself for not checking caller id, she spilled about Pepys, partly to distract from the police interview and the whole Nigel fiasco.

Under strict instructions from Kathy when her time came, it was Frank who had deposited that daredevil ball of fluff in her siting room, over ten years earlier. Bittersweet, Pepys had represented a present from beyond the grave and losing him felt like the painful inflammation of a re-infected wound. She kept her voice steady, but she couldn't fool Frank. Kathy had been adamant that he get himself a kitten too — a fat ginger called Ziggy, after her favourite Bowie album. So, Frank knew that Pepys wasn't only a cat. He was family, and it wasn't fine at all. In fact, it was the exact opposite of fine.

The cottage felt desolate, with the cat flap swaying in a raw easterly, ruffling its fur-lined edge. Those clumps were all that remained. That and the muddy paw marks on the French windows. She would never clean those off. Not much of a sacrifice. Neither was putting off the hoovering. Unthinkable to suck up the fluffy residue coating the sunken sofa. The smell of his half-eaten Whiskas had forced her to wash his food bowl, painted by Jodie, his second biggest fan. It lay propped on the draining board, surplus to requirements. In her anguish, she felt a certain affinity with this piece of extraneous earthenware. What was the point of her now? Other than to put an innocent chump behind bars, even if he was a smug prat.

Half listening for a mewl, she poured herself a glass of that rosehip gin she'd bought from the farmer's market near Richmond Bridge. No, Pepys hadn't been only a cat, he'd been her housemate and companion for a good decade. Without him, her sense of isolation and insignificance assumed hopeless proportions. Maybe he wouldn't have lived for much longer anyway. After all, in cat years, he'd been approaching the eve of his life. Just like her. But it had all been so sudden, so violent, and she wasn't ready. Although she knew that there was no such thing as being ready for despair.

There is a sort of madness to grief, and it felt as though she'd lost Kathy all over again, however much she tried to rationalise it. She might convince other people, but she couldn't kid Frank, and she couldn't kid herself. So, it was both a relief and a scourge to be on her own. She no longer had to pretend, but neither could she escape the darkness that closed in on her.

She took another slug of the syrupy liquid, which, despite its floral aroma, tasted more like cough mixture. That didn't matter; it was precisely its medicinal effect that was required. Now slumped in front of the TV, she found herself hypnotised by a repeat. *The Repair Shop* team restoring a matchstick replica of Big Ben. WTAF, as Jodie would say.

Hugging a cushion still flecked with black and white strands, she closed her eyes. Over the genial TV commentary, Maureen revisited another dark day, the tang of sweet-sour roses on her breath.

* * *

Dusted with flakes of dead skin, a cushion propped up calves so distended that it was hard to recall their former elegance. Sandpaper flesh repulsed her fingers, as she dabbed some saccharine body lotion up to the knees. But no further. The thighs had wasted away, so their circumference almost matched Maureen's wrists.

'Lovely,' came a whisper.

From under the loose sheet, a clear plastic tube coiled into a mercy-dispensing pump. It was hard to recognise this bird-like creature, with its weeping sores. Skeletal apart from grotesquely bloated stomach and calves, she weighed scarce more than five stone now.

Kathy no longer had sufficient flesh to close her eyes, so that when she slept, the only clue to her fraying thread of life, was the irregular heave of her tiny rib cage. As her body consumed itself in a desperate scavenge for calories, she hacked up globs of phlegm, and it took all Maureen's willpower not to retch with her into the slimy basin.

But there had been moments when she had metamorphosed out of her pain and Diamorphine haze, back into her big sis. The whites of her eyes had receded, and she'd stared at the vase of roses on the dressing table. Plucked from a friend's garden, several greenflies still patrolled their velvet terrain.

'Which one would you choose?' Kathy had asked in a low voice.

'Not sure. They're all beautiful.'

Maureen studied them. The dark red one was too obvious, while the orange seemed too garish to be real.

'Yellow,' Kathy murmured.

She was right. Her chosen rose was lemon yellow, edged with a faltering, dusky pink. It had reached its zenith. One more day, and its petals would begin to curl brown. This imminent decay somehow added to the perfection. Its magic was heightened simply because the spell couldn't last.

'Oh look, the dressing table's dissolving.'

Kathy's voice was matter of fact, although her pupils had all but disappeared, so that her eyes were a moist, opiate blue.

'You can't see it, can you?'

'No.'

Maureen turned away to smell the yellow rose.

'You've had enough of this. So has Frank.'

Her rasping voice seemed to vibrate within Maureen's skull. Still, she couldn't look at her sister, but continued to inspect the flower so that its fragrance began to make her feel light-headed. Because it was true. She wanted this nightmare over. She craved normality, but above all, she wanted to get some sleep. Shame and grief, powerful and sickly as the scent of those cut roses.

'Don't be daft. You mustn't worry, I'm fine. We're all okay.'

'Mo, you could never lie to me. You're not fine. I know you can't take it anymore.'

Kathy had decided that it was time. She had squeezed her little sister's hand over and over. With surprising resolve for such a withered claw.

'Look after Loz.'

Still, Maureen refused to accept its meaning, unable to face the unspeakable full stop. Two days later, while Maureen was out collecting yet another prescription, Kathy had died in Frank's arms.

* * *

A haunting cello score, a creaky weathervane and the wind rustling the trees; the show's bucolic interlude made Maureen more wretched than ever. She turned it off and drained her glass.

She thought of Deirdre. How in God's name had she coped with the loss of her son? How had she found the strength to get up every day and just keep on keeping on? Was her grating cheerfulness merely a coping mechanism — a sort of fake-it-till-you-make-it mask? Or maybe, once back in her 1980s townhouse, she collapsed into a wailing heap. Somehow, Maureen couldn't picture this. Then why did she still feel so raw at the loss of her best friend and sister? Kathy's absence had assumed a looming presence in her life over the years. But now, Pepys' death created a double vacancy, and K's comforting shadow had deepened into a sunless void.

Then there was Nigel's hell to consider. He'd lost his last shred of dignity. No more Ham House and potentially, no more liberty. All because of her. She pined for her old, safe routine. Too late now. Delving into her mind's darkest niches, she drilled her rebellious motives. Reflecting on her mad, selfish act of defiance.

There had always been an insurrectionary streak coursing through her veins. As a child, she'd kept her head down at school, treading the delicate tightrope that most kids navigate, between surviving the playground and handing in homework on time. She'd chosen the safer path of vocal dissent, scorning the rigid precepts. Like the absurd one-way system, which at times meant circumnavigating the whole building, just to move to the neighbouring classroom, while the teachers, exempt from this fascist lunacy, could just pop next door.

Of course, she'd joined in the standard pack tactics; the intimidation of the soft supply teacher, with the slow inching forward of desks, every time the hapless woman turned to write on the blackboard. But new teachers were always fair game, and anyway, it would have been suicide to conscientiously object. No, it was Kathy who smoked fags in the bogs, before going on to win the eight-hundred-and-eighty-yard run.

On the whole, Maureen was good. Unexceptional. But inside, a furious demon festered and railed at all the petty injustices, shredding the corrosive virtues of respectability and conformity, like cheap paper doilies.

Now, in what was nauseatingly labelled her twilight years, she had taken some satisfaction in delivering a giant, two-fingered salute. After all, hadn't she been abandoned by everyone she loved? Treacherous fly-by-nights. And for the first time in many years, she sank to the floor with loud bosom-heaving gasps and sobbed.

Drained at last, she broke off with a series of short, stuttering breaths. Aware that she was hungry, she wiped red puffy eyes and gloopy filaments of snot on her sleeves. After banging open and shut various kitchen cupboards, she foraged a stale tea cake, further speckling the butter with toasted crumbs. She poured herself another gin and wallowed some more.

After all these years, she still stewed over John. In the aftermath of his betrayal, she had often, like Salome, coveted his head on a plate. More Bastard than Baptist though. But she'd also longed for him. Physically ached. No one else ever came close. In truth, she had never allowed them. She just couldn't trust men after that. Half of them were mean little shits, and it was hard to separate the wheat from the chaff until it was too late. Even now, recalling certain brutal encounters, she trembled with rage and shame.

Her parents. How hard they'd worked, lining their little nest with cherished antiques. On retirement, Stan had splurged on a VW campervan and lovingly restored it. How excited they'd been, pouring over Ordnance Survey maps. But he was six feet under before their first road trip. Bernie's coffin placed on top of his before the year was out, with their beloved *silver hippy bus* sold on.

She thought of Kathy, and how much she still grieved for her. Always. What would she have made of this? Imagining those large, blue eyes, incredulous at her square little sister's delinquence. Half in awe, half fearful. Maureen was frightened too. For a while, she made a pretence of clearing up, but Radio 4 failed to muzzle the troublesome thoughts colliding round her head. Or that gut-wrenching image of Nigel, seated head in hands.

Grabbing the bottle of gin, she stumbled upstairs and kicking off her outer layers, crawled under the duvet into a foetal curve.

She thought of Laura and Jodie starting their new lives in the Big Apple. It had proved tricky keeping in touch, what with the time difference and her niece working all hours. Jodie was reaching the age when talking to your great aunt was more chore than choice. And that was just how it should be. But she missed them. So much. Sweet mother of God, if ever they found out. What had she done?

She felt so cold all of a sudden, as if the very marrow in her bones had frozen. Like those menopausal night chills that used to plague her. Alternating with vicious hot flushes, which had forced her to lean half-naked out of the bedroom window, past caring who saw her.

Finally, her blood began to thaw, and she straightened out. Despite her exhaustion, she thrashed around for ages. If only she'd hung on to Bernie's old bottle of Diazepam. For some reason, the day's events prompted a memory of her and Kathy watching *Porridge*. It had first aired not long after John had dumped her, claiming they wanted *different things*. Aka, that bottle-blonde trollop in accounts, who provided the sprogs that Maureen couldn't. Ironic, that she'd curled next to her pregnant sister in front of the telly to help nurse her broken heart. The prison sitcom had acted like a salve — laughing at Ronnie Barker's one-liners had made her forget. For a blissful half-hour. But actual prison life, she knew, was miles grimmer. More Ken Loach. No timid sympathetic officers like Barrowclough for Nige. In fact, very few staff at all, according to *Panorama*.

Now, she felt the shadows pressing down on her, so that she had to fight to breathe. In. Hold. Count to five. Out, slowly. Slooowly. Panic. Repeat. Stop thinking. Stop. Just repeat. Repeat. Panic. Repeat. At last, Hypnos, that benevolent Greek god of sleep, showed mercy and folded his wings over her throbbing temples.

* * *

And she was back, dragging after Bernie and Stan through cluttered, labyrinthine antique shops. Skulking behind Victorian button-back chairs, piled atop pedestal desks, she squeezed alongside Kathy and the brass-faced grandfather clock. She could feel the slow, somniferous beat of the weighted pendulum, resonating not only within the long, dark-grained case, but inside her head. As if marking a pause in time, like a needle stuck in a vinyl groove, repeating the same note over and over. Dust fairies floating in a shaft of sunlight, penetrating the damp air through a grimy fanlight. Kathy giggling as they pulled faces at the canny shop owner, absorbed in haggling rituals with their parents. What was his best price for a Georgian snuff box, a stuffed pheasant in a glass case, a pair of Staffordshire spaniels, or that print of a pipe-smoking woman perched on a barrel with her cat, titled *Single Blessedness*?

Her parents enacting coded gestures, signalling whether to feign disinterest and walk away, or snatch up the bargain with contrived nonchalance. Bernie standing there discombobulated, trying to recall what Stan's frantic nose scratching or chin rubbing meant. How they'd all laughed about it afterwards, her mother unwrapping and re-checking the bargain for scratches. Maureen's bare thighs sticking to the Ford Anglia's leather seats. Kathy's longer, tanned legs showing up her own pink mottled pins. Why did I have to inherit all the Irish genes, she wonders. But still, who cares, they're on the way to get fish'n'chips, with the promise of a decent mark-up at the next antiques fair.

John has already left. His side of the bed is cold, but there's more room now. Besides, Pepys has jumped up to join her, and arcs behind her back, purring himself to sleep, so she doesn't feel alone. She can hear Brenda asking John, was it beyond him to put a coaster under his Carlsberg? Chrissakes, he could see she'd just cleaned the glass coffee table, and if she'd told him once, she'd told him a thousand times not to leave his muddy allotment clothes all over their new shagpile. And does he have to spend so much time there? When all he brings back are a few, half-ripe, sodding tomatoes. She raises her shrill voice over whiny kids. Maureen hugs her knees, luxuriating in that warm glow of Schadenfreude. Kathy sniggering beside her on the sofa, raising her Campari Soda to salute the gratifying domestic.

Now Kathy clasps her little sister tight, making soothing sounds as wiped tears streak the Pan Stick on Maureen's bruised face. Promising not to tell anyone, not even Frank. He would annihilate the bastard. But then Kathy draws back, pale and retching. Squeezing Maureen's hand one last time before letting go.

Where's she gone? She can't find her big sis anywhere. She tries phoning, but she can't seem to enter the numbers on the keypad. Instead, she's distracted by Jodie who's joined her on the sofa, her ponytail teased through the back of a NY Yankees baseball cap. Squealing at Captain Mainwaring:

'Don't tell him, Pike! You stupid boy.'

Except already Jodie pronounces it *stoopid.*

Laura's there too. She throws back her head and belly-laughs just like her mother. Now she's demonstrating Pilates, how to sit on an invisible infant toilet and hold the perfect static squat. They're all trying it now, except Maureen, who just watches because it'll hurt her knees. Rhona almost perfects it, but then collapses backwards, pulling Jodie down on the rug with her, chanting, 'Why are we so good?'

Splashing amid such carefree rivulets of blithe semi-consciousness, Maureen catches the Duchess's icy gaze in the Stairwell. The starless, shadowy abyss of delayed grief. Anything but that, she protests, unable to move. Brimful of despair, those sharp coal eyes morph into Nigel's. Then she hears the endless clanging of fortified steel doors being shut and locked. Bang. Bang. Bang.

* * *

Maureen woke to the sound of rusty bin lids being hurled to the ground. The dustcart advanced down her street, like a Russian tank rolling in to crush The Alberts. She snuggled further down in a vain attempt to block out its grinding, screeching clunks. But she knew it was time for surrender. Her mind was made up. She would go to Thelma's that afternoon, as planned, and let the gang know. She owed them that at least. Then, she'd parcel up her *Blackbird* for the very last time, and hand herself in.

Chapter 27
Plan C
Friday, 16th February

'That would be ridiculous,' said Thelma from her patchwork Chesterfield, eyeing Maureen as if she required medical attention.

'Don't talk soft.' Rhona, also mincing her words.

'Not like you to be a party pooper.' Et tu, Deirdre?

Maureen couldn't help but feel cheated — her moment of heroic martyrdom overruled. It is a far, far better thing that I do, than I have ever done. Then again, it would be galling to cave to DC Adamu. To admit that she'd been right all along. And prison did sound like the absolute pits.

They were holed up in a timber-beamed sitting room down the mean streets of Cobham. Sipping a latte fresh from Thelma's Nespresso, Deirdre's pop-socked feet luxuriated on a Persian rug. Rhona reclined on a velvet chaise-longue, studying the rockery through black-latticed doors, her pose mirroring a water-coloured siren above her. Except Rhona sported mohair, joggers and slides, while the blonde was starkers. A natural blonde, so it would seem.

'Yes, Nigel's in a bit of a bind,' said Thelma, picking fluff off her cashmere jumpsuit.

'The wee diddy, falling for that scam. If something's too good to be true, it usually is, right enough.'

'Rhona, your compassion knows no bounds,' said Thelma.

'Aye, so I've been told.'

'The point is,' said Deirdre, replacing her willow pattern cup on its saucer, 'we're going to return the painting, and Nigel will be back at Ham in no time.'

'And how exactly are we going to do that?' Maureen snapped, nursing her dented ego, 'after our spectacular record so far.'

'Well, this is why you're all here,' said Thelma, reaching

for her iPad, 'to formulate Plan B.'

'Plan C, by my count,' said Rhona.

And so it began. Several coffees later, little progress had been made. Rhona's snark factor had increased and Deirdre's request for a guided tour had been ignored. Maureen was pacing the tongue and groove. 'I still think Sanjay might have his suspicions. Seeing as, apart from us, he was the only other guide around that day.'

'Och, his main focus was the catering van.'

'True,' Maureen conceded, recalling that epochal shift and Sanjay's pig-out in the Mess Room. *Mammoth crew. Like Piccadilly Circus up there.* And just then, she was also reminded of that radio interview. A former Scotland Yard art detective, she told them, had recovered Titian's Rest on the Flight to Egypt. Minus its frame but still intact, this multimillion Venetian masterpiece had been stuffed into a carrier bag and dumped at a bus stop outside Richmond station in 2002. That was it! Busy terminal, she argued. Countless people going in and out, armed with a range of bags and suitcases.

Her logic was reinforced by a recent spate of stolen artwork being deposited at stations all over London. Concerns had been raised at PMQs about shady Met-sanctioned deals between criminal gangs and top-notch art institutions. Of course, no ransoms had been paid, and said informants had no involvement in the actual theft. Honest, Mr. Speaker. But now, on the other veiny, arthritic hand, one more prominent heist had occurred. Although worth less than the paintings mysteriously surfacing in left-luggage facilities, she reasoned that the authorities would peg the recovered *Blackbird* as one more bargaining tool from the underworld. However, Rhona dismissed this with her usual tact — 'Does your head button up the back?' — on the grounds that Richmond Station bristled with CCTV.

'Well, I'd disguise my appearance. Say, with a wig and glasses.'

Deirdre enthused through a mouthful of Madeira cake. 'Ooh, that's a good—'

'Much as it pains me to agree with Rhona.' Thelma handed Deirdre a linen napkin. 'It's not worth taking the risk. As well as undercover officers, the police will be monitoring passengers with facial recognition. You know, the usual.'

Thelma spoke as if she was none other than Commissioner of the Met, but in that moment, Maureen was irritated by her pal's teacher's pet expression. Then she considered Rhona's loyalty. And all their courageous, if foolhardy, support. Besides, she knew they were right. Too dangerous by far.

After the Richmond Station veto, Maureen struck gold. Summoning Face Ache's slurred account of a Manet (crude forgery as it turned out), being ditched under a tree, she proposed Richmond Park. It offered multiple benefits: a regular destination within a short drive and no CCTV.

Much debate raged over the exact drop-off point. Abandon it under some random tree, and it could be days before it was found, ravaged by frost, rain and various feathered or furred busybodies. That bubble-wrap couldn't hold out forever. Then Deirdre, a left-field Machiavelli suggested King Henry's Mound in Pembroke Gardens. An ideal secluded but popular spot within the park. This received unanimous support. Before long, the prosaic bag would be found by an upstanding citizen, who would hand it in to Pembroke Lodge.

Ever the optimist, it suddenly occurred to Maureen. 'What if someone steals it?'

'What, steals the stolen painting?' Rhona, never slow with the irony.

Deirdre licked some yellow crumbs off her lips. 'We'll have to keep watch somehow.'

'What we gonna do, make a citizens' arrest?' snorted Rhona. 'Well, Your Honour, we all just happened to be in the area—'

'No one's going to steal it,' Thelma interrupted. 'It'll be barely visible under all that bubble-wrap. So, we're decided — King Henry's Mound it is.'

Maureen was beginning to warm to Thelma, grateful for her calm authority. And the royal mound did feel like a more appropriate setting to discard a Bosschaert.

But then, M'Wee Lassy Brightside, chucked in her signature spanner. 'Hang about. What if they think it's a bomb? Under all that bubble-wrap.'

They sat, stupefied at the horrific prospect of Blackbird, Butterfly and Cherries being blown to smithereens in a controlled explosion. But, stacking the side plates, their unelected leader displayed her steely nerve. It was now several decades since the IRA had been active on the mainland, she reminded them. Far right extremists wouldn't target a royal park, and jihadists usually favoured a truck bomb or suicide vest. On which cheery note, Thelma concluded that, with the total absence of wires and batteries, it was unlikely that the Bomb Squad would be called in.

'Actually, the bigger problem might be that it could languish for weeks, gathering dust in Lost Property,' she told them.

Ever resourceful, Deirdre suggested making an anonymous phone call with a disguised voice.

'That's just asking for soapy bubble. They'll trace the call, so they will.'

But Deirdre wouldn't let it lie. 'Yes, but we'd do it from a phone box and dial 141, so the number would be withheld.'

'I'm pretty sure the police can still trace it,' said Thelma, again suspiciously au fait with the workings of the Met.

'Well, we could always use a phone box in another part of London.'

The wrangling continued over what to say, choice of accents and, crucially, who should make the call.

Whereupon, Rhona, who'd been hunched over her phone, squealed. There were all these brilliant wee voice changer apps, so they could record a message, then play it on speaker down a pay phone. The subsequent altercation between Rhona and Deirdre on whether to use robot or celebrity, and moreover, which celebrity, was finally quashed by Thelma, pronouncing it as far too dicey.

Here, Maureen, inspired by those nefarious pros, proposed attaching some sort of tag. According to news reports, the stolen artworks, deposited by stealth at various terminals, had been accompanied by cheeky notes stating that they were the rightful property of Such-and-such Gallery. Despite knowing they could never match the exact labels, this met with solid approval. It also led to an absurd argument over choice of paper and font, with Rhona threatening to clype on them if they used Comic Sans. In the end, Maureen agreed to stick a Times New Roman label on the bubble wrap, stating that its contents belonged in Ham House. At which point, she wanted to lie down in a darkened room. Sometimes it's hard to be a felon.

It was only then that she felt the kick to her guts. She'd been so immersed in Plan C, she'd forgotten all about Pepys. Her eyes smarted with guilt.

'You're not still sweating over Nigel,' said Rhona, raising her hands in exasperation.

Maureen shook her head, unable to speak.

Thelma leant forward. 'What's the matter?'

'It's Pepys,' Maureen whispered, and then she told them. Rhona's tight hug and Thelma's softness caught her off guard. And Deirdre, who had known much greater loss, took her hand and said animals had souls too. Overwhelmed by their kindness, she blew her nose on a creased napkin, and shrugged them off, saying they had business to conclude. But their compassion stayed with her. Warmed her, like the Ready Brek glow from that 1980s TV ad.

Outside, the sunset yielded to a crisp darkness. The

glare of streetlights no match for Venus, as she lured Jupiter ever closer, while myriad planets orbited glowing suns in the bruised canopy. Dots of light transmitted from bygone centuries, sparkled unnoticed above Thelma's Grade II gaff. The local news flickered on mute, texts from husbands were ignored, and stewed tea cooled. Regardless, the Musketeers plotted and squabbled over Google Street View, and a weather app's blue light reflected on Deirdre's animated face, as she recited the long-term forecast to their captain.

Now and then, sand-sized particles of frozen comet debris burnt up in the earth's atmosphere at mind-blowing speeds, dashing evanescent white streaks across the inky sky. Such ancient harbingers of doom had foretold assassinations, earthquakes, pestilence, famine, epic conquests and bloody defeats. Yet these messengers of death remained unheeded by the four women. As did multiple ungranted wishes, which vanished like the flap of an owl's wings over the treetops of Painshill Park, into the vastness of the cold night sky.

Chapter 28
The Dream Team
Monday, 19th February

It was an Inset Day. This and the recent mild spell, saw the car park already filling with shiny SUVs, negotiating the uneven stretch of gravel, jolting up and down its craters. Further from the kiosk and visitor centre, the car park's northern tip stretched dustier and emptier.

It was here that four older women stood chatting round the open boot of a red Nissan Micra. Nothing remarkable. If the one who'd capitulated to her grey hair was taking meticulous care with a hamper, topped with a blanket and packet of brioches, then nobody appeared to notice. Or care. Just some friends exploiting the unseasonably clement weather for an impromptu picnic in Richmond Park. It might have seemed curious to a casual observer, that these old biddies should choose to strain their stiff hips and knees by sitting on a rug. Indeed, the alpha with the chestnut bob and pale lipstick, carried a floral walking stick.

Odder still, as the white, wisteria-clad Pembroke Lodge, stood within stone chucking distance. In addition to elegant tea rooms, the Lodge boasted an attractive, paved terrace. On this popular suntrap, visitors could wolf sarnies, cakes, cream teas, Lancashire Hot Pot, lentil cottage pie and pious salads. Best of all, stunning views over the Thames Valley provided countless selfie opportunities. The reality, of course, was its own tedious circle of hell. The carnage of sharp elbows in sluggish queues, scrummage for highchairs and the few vacant tables outside. Plastic trays dribbled spilt tea, a stiff breeze snatched at paper napkins, frazzled parents mopped up baby sick, and kids chased scrounger pigeons, while their morose older siblings moaned about the lack of phone signal. Maybe those four women had the right idea after all.

'No, I only saw cameras round Pembroke Lodge itself. But inside, they were *everywhere.* Gary and I went for lunch there on Sunday. We walked in the gardens afterwards. There's this lovely tunnel of trees that—'

'Oh aye, Laburnum Walk that leads to Poet's corner. Did you sit on that Ian Dury bench? It's got these metal plate thingies that you scan and listen to *Reasons To be Cheerful* and his interview on *Desert Island*—'

'Ladies please, we need to focus.'

Rhona pulled a face behind Thelma's back, but her compliance betrayed a newfound respect for their latest comrade-in-arms, once written off by them all as a snooty battle-axe. Slamming the boot shut, Maureen picked up the hamper and they passed a feral mob of Mini-Boden models pushing each other off some felled tree trunks. Two by two, the women moseyed down the path, alongside the galvanised wire fence enclosing Pembroke Gardens.

On their left, ornate chimneys and an incongruous glass cupola extended from a thatched roof. The Cottage, one of the park's private residences, was shielded by a verdant barrier of holly and rhododendrons. Buds quivered in the February sunshine. Deirdre whipped off her grey Jack Wolfskin and folded it over one arm, exposing a noxious lavender lining. She began fanning her face with her free hand.

'You better up your dose of HRT,' said Rhona.

'No, I decided to come off it. Been on it too long, and it was making me feel anxious all the time.'

'Really? It's a lifesaver for me. Couldn't face those night sweats again, meltin' away to a greasy spot.'

'I just use those oestrogen pessaries now: Vagi-something. Makes sex much easier.'

'Dear God, please stop.' Rhona put a forefinger in each ear.

'Well, vaginal dryness is a serious issue.'

'Mebbe, but that's pure mingin', and now I've got

images in my head I can't shake. Anyhow, why on earth do men think we still want it?'

'I still quite enjoy it now and then,' Deirdre continued, ignoring her friend's faux gagging. 'Plus, you have to keep them happy.'

'What is this, the 1950s?'

Their bickering stalled as Thelma and Maureen caught up, unsure how much they'd heard. All of it, judging from Thelma's news flash.

'Personally, I always preferred to bat for the girls' team.'

'Say again?'

'I like sleeping with women. I'm not averse to men, but mainly they just fart and make the place untidy.'

'I have to confess that I'm seeing you in a whole new light, Thelma.'

'Not all of us wear flannel suits and brogues. Really Rhona, you're quite conservative, despite your own dyke crop.'

Singling Rhona out was a little unfair, as both Deirdre and Maureen were staring, mouths agape. However, Rhona conceded Thelma's point. As if to counter this, she added, 'I often pretend to be asleep when David comes up to bed. These days, I need a three-cherry spin on my fruit machine.'

She stopped and began counting on her fingers.

'If I'm not cream crackered, don't feel like a crinkly sag bag and had me a couple of wee bevvies. Then and only then, David might get lucky. But usually, he's on tae plums.'

They laughed and strolled on, bonded by this unexpected frankness. After years of prescribed self-sufficiency, Maureen couldn't help thinking that any chance of jiggery-pokery would be a fine thing. Although she had to admit that all cravings on that front, had largely dried up, much like Dee's nether regions.

'Hang on.' Rhona stopped in her tracks. 'That explains

why you've been sniffing round Carmella, you crafty wee cougar.'

Said cougar sighed. 'Yes, Carmella's very easy on the eye, but mainly, she just makes me laugh. To be honest, now I'm through the whole menopause saga, I'm no longer a slave to any lust. No more rollercoaster of envy and pining. Like being unchained from an idiot.' She paused, as a grey squirrel weaved across their path in a series of stilted leaps. 'So liberating.' Maureen wondered if she was referring to the fluffy-tailed squirrel, but Thelma went on, 'I love living on my own. Nothing better.' She glanced at Maureen. 'Don't you agree?'

The art thief, who had never considered her loneliness a blessing, was spared having to reply as they passed a middle-aged couple walking their Westie in the opposite direction. In silent accord, they halted and pretended to study a notice on a nearby gate.

'Well of course, if your sister says so.'

'She's only trying to help.'

'Is that what she calls it? Frankly, it'd be more helpful if she kept her big nose out.'

The couple disappeared out of earshot, having perfectly illustrated Thelma's point on the cons of cohabitation. They turned back along the path, except for Rhona, who remained studying the notice.

'So, here's the thing: dogs, bicycles, ball games *and picnics* aren't allowed in these Gardens. But the good news: it doesn't say anything about stolen art.'

'Buggeration!' Maureen's nerves shredded by the last few days. 'That's our cover blown.'

'Why didn't I see that?' Deirdre berated herself. 'I was so busy checking for cameras without alerting Gary, I didn't even notice these signs.'

'Well, they're easy to miss, so they are.'

'We'll be fine,' sighed Deirdre, as much trying to reassure herself. 'We can still go in, so long as we're not caught picnicking. Here, I'll take these.'

She reached down and grabbed the packet of brioches, stuffing them out of sight into her Cath Kidston tote. The irony of their concern over a minor Parks' infringement, when Maureen was guilty of theft, and the rest, of perverting the course of justice, was lost on them in that moment.

'I doubt anyone would notice, but we mustn't draw attention,' said Thelma. 'Anyway, there's no choice. We can't afford to delay. Not least, because this dry spell can't last for ever.'

She was right. The pressure was building. Not just in meteorological terms, thought Maureen, shuddering at the memory of Nigel's despairing face in the wooden hut. Having reached their appointed entrance, past a small brick outhouse, the women scoured the other side of the mesh. Beyond, the pathway appeared deserted. With an unsettling clank, Rhona slid back the iron latch, and they entered the Gardens.

'Right, we best not all walk up. Rhona, Deirdre, go scout it out,' Thelma instructed in a low voice. 'We'll hang about here. Text an emoji when there's no one else around.'

'Which emoji should I use?' asked Deirdre, as if this was crucial.

Thelma delivered Captain Mainwaring's withering stare, rendering *You stupid boy* superfluous.

'Thumbs-up'll do, you daftie. Though maybe the aubergine, in your case, missus.'

Deirdre looked baffled, but they split up without further debate. Maureen watched the pair disappear beneath overhanging branches, as they spiralled up the path to the top of a small hill known as King Henry's Mound.

Legend claims that King Henry VIII stood on this summit in 1536, waiting for a rocket to be fired from the Tower of London; the signal that Queen Anne Boleyn had been beheaded for treason, leaving him free to marry Lady

Jane Seymour. A juicy spinechiller, but in fact, the merciless Tudor king had dined in Wiltshire that evening.

More famous for one of eight protected views across the City of London, the mound's pruned greenery created a giant keyhole, framing a tree-arched sightline through Sidmouth Wood. Then, beyond Barnes Common, over Stamford Bridge, past Brompton Cemetery, Sloane Square, St James's Park, once more crossing the Thames over Waterloo Bridge, to rest on the iconic dome of St. Paul's Cathedral. A tad blurry, but still visible to the naked eye. There was also a handy brass telescope to view Sir Christopher Wren's masterpiece in tantalising clarity.

Ten miles southwest of this famous landmark, Maureen and Thelma ambled around the ancient barrow, nigh on carefree. It was such a glorious morning that Maureen almost forgot what lay concealed in her hamper. Almost.

At Thelma's, there had been further parley on how to package this contraband. It needed to be cushioned, untraceable and waterproof. Deirdre checked that the outlook remained dry, with threats of a spring hosepipe ban if this untimely drought held. Maureen refused to use yet another holdall. Instead, she shrouded the *Blackbird* with extra layers inside a spanking new plastic bag for life. This got Thelma's vote, with the caveat that Maureen wear latex gloves when wrapping it. Like she needed to be told. Nevertheless, she indulged their new ally, still dumbfounded by her conversion to the dark side. Also, it was pleasing to watch her trump Rhona on having the last word.

'I know you're not on any police database Maureen, but—'

'Yet.'

'Very droll, Rhona.'

Indeed, despite the warmth, Maureen wore leather gloves. Just to be sure. Nothing noteworthy; everyone knows that geriatrics feel cold all year round.

They halted at the Mound's low-fenced base to absorb

the splendid panorama over Petersham Valley. From the red Gothic spire of former All Saints' Church in the foreground, all the way to the hazy control towers of Heathrow. On the lower slopes, almost due west from their vantage point, the unmistakeable, flushed grandeur of Ham House rose above a line of cedar trees. Possibly, it was the Stuart mansion's more aerial perspective that prompted Maureen to ask, 'Why are you doing this?'

Her companion, struck deaf, pointed to the horizon with her stick. 'That must be Windsor Castle over there.'

A grunt of hoodies skulked past the other side of the wire fence below them, and a distinctive pungent odour wafted up.

Maureen tried again. 'I mean, why are you helping me? You barely spoke to me up until a few weeks ago.'

This time, Thelma acknowledged the question. She turned black oversized sunglasses towards Maureen, reflecting the latter's sceptical, grey-eyed gaze. Leaning on her stick, she brushed a leaf off her camel cape. The urgent *tchacks* of jackdaws, a man's futile calls to his screaming kids and the jagged breakbeats from the teens' portable speaker, peppered the low white hum of traffic. Thelma drew a slow deep breath, as if her answer required extra oxygen. Or possibly, a drag on that joint.

'Because it was only a few weeks ago that I realised who you were.' Spurred by Maureen's knitted brows, she added, 'Or rather, who your sister was.'

'You knew Kathy?'

'I was her tennis partner many moons ago.'

'Shut the front door!'

'1974 Ladies Doubles Champions for Surrey. Those heady days when my hip joints were titanium-free. With my serve and Kath's volleys, we made mincemeat of our opponents.'

'Bloody hell, you're Tee. She talked about you all the time. I was never very sporty, and it's deathly dull to watch. Unless it's Wimbledon, of course.'

'Like I said, we made a pretty good team—'

'Kath was crazy about tennis. Loved showing off her legs.'

'They were worth showing off.'

Maureen threw her a sharp look.

'Behave,' Thelma replied. 'She was besotted with Frank, and besides, she wasn't conversion material. Still,' she broke off and scanned the horizon once more, adding with a discernible quaver, 'I did grow very fond of her.'

Maureen remained silent, struggling to compute all this. After the past few months' self-inflicted drama, nothing should have surprised her. But life's random convergence and entanglement; the coincidences, the chains of acquaintance, these freakish six degrees of separation that bind us all, short-circuited her overloaded mind.

'It's funny how we never met then. She mentioned you a lot,' Thelma continued while they both contrived to study the vista. 'She called you Mo, which is why—'

'Kathy refused to waste more than one syllable on anyone's name.' Maureen let out a half-laugh, then her turn to falter. 'She was the only one allowed to call me that.'

'She used to worry about you. Said you went into self-destruct after The Bast… your fiancé left…'

Maureen retrieved blurry Piña Colada-fuelled nights in sweaty discos, followed by grappling sessions on the suede seats of Ford Capris, infused with hairspray and Old Spice.

'… and then your father died. You look a lot like him, though you've got your mother's colouring. I've got this sweet photo of you as teenagers on holiday with your parents. Found it in an old Angela Carter paperback she lent me that I forgot to give back.'

Thelma bit her lip. 'Except I didn't. Forget, I mean. To be honest, I just wanted something of hers. She'd underlined her favourite quotes and well, she didn't seem to miss it. Anyway, a few weeks ago, sorting through some books for the second-hand bookshop at Ham, I came across it again. That's how I worked it out. Someone had written *The Goodwins at Trebarwith Strand* on the back. I only knew Kath by her married name. So then, after all this time, I realised you were, you *are* Mo.'

Another pause, then: 'You can have her book back. And the photo, if you want.'

Maureen shook her head, trying to process it all. As if she'd just fished the missing jigsaw piece from that coin, button, earring, cork and crumb debris-strewn universe that resides beneath the cushions of any respectable sofa. This explained everything. The identity of the mysterious brunette in that photo, smirking up at her sister from under her sun visor. And of course... that strange modification of the letter *K*, also comprised *T*. It turned out that Thelma, *yes Thelma*, was the other half of *The Dream Team*.

And now, after all these years, it seemed that Thelma was looking out for K's little sister, still faithful to the memory of her one unrequited love. Maureen hadn't the heart to tell Thelma that it was her Angela Carter copy that Kathy had swiped and therefore, her own selected quotes which Thelma had treasured all these years. All part of life's twisted fuckery. As was the fact that Thelma had been at Ham as long as she had. Longer. If only she'd known, they could have shared memories of Kathy. Perhaps, united in grief, they might have become friends.

But as it happened, Maureen wasn't the only one who economised on the truth. One balmy summer night all those years ago, Thelma had learned the hard way that Kathy wasn't conversion material. Misread drunken signals during celebrations of yet another Doubles' triumph. Her clumsy lunge, K's instant recoil, still scorched onto her memory disc. The stinging humiliation, despite her tennis partner's repeated assurances that there was no need for Thelma's awkward apologies, it didn't matter and that *she* was sorry. But it did matter to Thelma. It mattered very much, and she could never retract it. Everything had changed. Despite Kathy's best efforts, Thelma became cool and offhand in the following weeks. She couldn't help herself. In the end, she had faked an ankle injury to cut short the season. She never returned to the club, or even played another game. K's phone calls and invitations remained unanswered.

Thelma had kept the final Christmas card, with *I miss you* penned in that distinctive sloping hand beneath the printed Yuletide cheer. In the years that followed, she'd thrown herself into work, batting aside male colleagues. And in her love life, lobbed her own grenades. Enjoyed her own conquests. Some perfunctory, some fun, some clandestine, some lasting longer, some other hearts broken. She'd folded the K episode away like an old fragment of Venetian lace, so delicate that it ripped further with every handling.

Then, one bleak morning, she'd read the obituary notice. A single stark paragraph sliced right through the decades, so that she found herself back on court, watching K leap to volley-smash their helpless opponents. Once again, heard her cries of triumph, her oaths, her whispered tactics, her filthy laugh. That stabbing pain once more, the wound salted with guilt and regret. Unable to face Frank and Laura, she'd snuck in late to the packed church. Choking on Amazing Grace, she'd stumbled out before the final prayers. Past the crooked, mossy graves with their sunken ivy beds, cursing her stubborn pride and all that pointless, wasted time.

A submarine dive's klaxon shattered their parallel regrets. Checking there was no one around, Maureen answered Rhona on speaker. 'You're supposed to send an emoji.'

'Aye right, like GCHQ are listening in.'

Thelma shook her head and Maureen tried not to laugh.

'You're on speaker by the way,' she warned.

'Bloody Americans hogging the telescope. Going on about how *awesome* it is. Over and over.'

This was followed by an extended snore. 'Had to stop our Dee from chatting them up.'

'Well, let us know when they lea—'

'Finally. Dee's waving. They're heading down now. Towards the gate where we came in. Come up the other side. Go go go!'

As Maureen snatched up the hamper, Thelma muttered, 'think Rhona's enjoying this a bit too much.'

But the smile that now graced her pastel lips remained unseen. The absurdity of it all, the danger, didn't matter. Guilt alone, she had decided, was mere self-indulgence. Something more meaningful was required. Reparation.

And so, chaperoned by clusters of bobbing snowdrops, the two women chased their shadows, which, like their unconscious cravings, stretched out before them along the gritty path below King Henry's Mound.

Chapter 29
McFuckity Face

Other than a couple performing mouth-to-mouth at the entrance to Laburnum Walk, the coast was clear. Around the entangled duo, slim trunks and pliable branches curved over the tunnel's metal frame. Despite hellebores and dwarf irises emerging through their roots, the laburnums displayed no signs of the pendulous yellow blooms that would erupt in May. One of nature's many warped gags; every part of this alluring tree was Grade A toxic. Blissfully unaware, the pair continued to exchange saliva, like some allegory of doomed love.

Meanwhile, the stick-tapping, hamper-lugging miscreants turned sharp right and legged it up the gentle incline. On one side, a low rail hemmed bushes flaunting lemony specks. Gorse, Maureen presumed. Straight after the info sign, which sprouted from an ivy-choked tangle on their left, they arrived at the top. Rhona sat glaring down at them from a bench near the abandoned telescope, hands rammed into her shacket, tapping a Hi Top trainer. Deirdre stood on anxious lookout over the other path, gusts of wind teasing her thin bronde layers. They issued simultaneous greetings. One stating the bleeding obvious, the other, frothing with antsy sarcasm.

'Oh good, you're here.'

'Dinnae fash yersel; we've got all day.'

It was crunch-time. Maureen snapped back in control. She told Thelma to wait by the sign and feign interest in the gripping geographical data; eyes peeled for any unwelcome sightseers.

'Good plan, I'll start coughing if I see anyone walk up this end.'

'And if people come up this side, I'll activate my ringtone as a signal, as if someone's calling me,' said Deirdre, raising her voice with girl-guide zest. 'It's *Don't Look Back in Anger*,' she added, over the low, distant whine of a strimmer. 'You know, that Oasis one.'

The others stared at her.

'It was Jack's favourite,' she explained. 'My daughter set it up when Gary bought me the phone as a—'

'Another time Dee.' Rhona's sharpness betraying her nerves.

Throwing caution to the chill breeze, Maureen extracted the bag for life. She scaled the steps, edged with giant teeth-like stones, and reached the mound's crest. Rhona thrust out her palms in a fierce shrug. Maureen spun round to the fuzzy profile of St. Paul's. Wooden benches flanked the arched sightline, engraved plates fixed to their slatted curved seats. She read one: *For your rest in the views east and west.* Adding in unspoken rhyme: *But which bench would be best?*

'Eh, we're in a bit of an Andy Murray here,' said Rhona, foot tapping resumed.

Maureen tried to block out the increasing hum and keep a level head. Clearly some sort of handheld stonecutter. Either that, or an indignant swarm of bees. More furious than indignant. Trouble was, these benches had no backs, and she didn't want to lay the bag flat, in case some dope sat on it.

'Fuck, McFuckityface!'

Horror was etched on Rhona's upturned face. Maureen's stomach lurched, as she also looked skyward, her worst fears confirmed. High above, a mutant quadcopter hornet whirred, silhouetted against the cloudless blue. Over the drone's mad buzzing, Rhona yelled, 'We need to skedaddle Maureen. Leave it!' Just as it reached critical mass, a classic Mancunian anthem blared that Sally knew it was too late.

Plumping for the *East to St Pauls* bench, Maureen propped the carrier bag upright against its metal leg. Maybe Sally could wait, but they couldn't.

'Yes, I'll come and meet you,' Deirdre shouted into her phone with as much subtlety as a flying cowpat. Even amid the panic and frenzied whiz of that McFucking drone, Maureen noted their gain was definitely not MI5's loss. Wild-eyed, Deirdre kept up her am-dram. 'I'm heading down to Laburnum Walk right now.'

Speed-walking past the bird's eye map, she bore down on Thelma, who'd begun to retreat. In their crazed flight, they legged it down the path in a freakish single-file stampede. As if replicating some weird bus-pass holders' take on that Abbey Road cover. Except down King Henry's Mound, not a zebra crossing in NW8. Also, the Beatles had been unencumbered by picnic hampers, and Macca had been holding a fag, not a walking stick. In fact, barring the single file and the trees, nothing like it, but they made a noteworthy spectacle that early spring morning. Not least, from above.

'I meant abort, not dump it there. We're being watched, in case you hadn't noticed,' said Rhona.

'Too late now,' Maureen shot back.

'It'll be okay,' said Deirdre.

'Aye right, who you trying to kid?'

It wasn't until they were halfway down, before the triple path junction, that they fanned out over the grass, trampling the crocus shoots and daffodils. Then the humming began to recede, as the drone dipped south behind some leafless treetops.

Deirdre patted her chest. 'Thank God for that.'

Thelma stopped sharp, her voice low and tense. 'Ah, so that's why it's gone.'

'Mammy, Daddy, it's the polis.'

'What, have the Met got us under surveillance?' Deirdre's question a mix of terror and incredulity.

'Don't talk daft.'

'You're only supposed to operate drones on the Flying Field and presumably, the parks police were called to investigate,' said Thelma, the font of all knowledge.

'Where's Flying Field?' said Deirdre.

'Off Sawyer's Hill, at the turning to the White Lodge.'

'What? The Masons have a base in Richmond Park?' sputtered Rhona.

'No, it's the Royal Ballet School.'

'Never mind all this, they mustn't see us!' said Maureen, exploding at the improbable obstacles that the universe was hurling, quite literally, in their path.

Sure enough, two uniformed constables were strolling past birch trees, towards the far side of Laburnum Walk, the truncated voices and spluttering static of radios audible even from their end. The heavy petters had long since scarpered. Maybe to get a room. Or a cup of tea. Or both.

With no pretence of calm now, the gang of four swept right. Breaking into a pitiful jog along the empty, mulch-strewn path, back towards their entry point.

'I suppose this is one way to test-drive my new hip. My physio did say I needed to up the ante,' Thelma panted.

'Do you think they saw us?' Maureen asked, as they slowed down to a sedate, butter-wouldn't-melt amble, shielded by a strategic clump of rhododendrons. She peered back over her shoulder. No sign of the Woodentops yet. 'Reckon we got away with it. Just.'

'Now I wish I was still on my HRT,' said Deirdre, flapping the waistband of her Breton top. 'Can't remove any more layers.'

'No please don't frighten the bairns.' Rhona wasn't joking. Then, in a hissed alert, 'Not this gate — too many people.'

Maureen's heart sank as she registered a team of runners, sculpted in branded active wear, swigging energy drinks and stretching quads, but most of all, blocking their escape route. The fewer people who noted the four of them this morning, the better. This lot, it seemed, were too engrossed in taking the perfect group selfie and comparing heart rates, to register the vintage quartet scuttle past the other side of the gate.

Aping Deirdre's earlier speed-walk, they doubled back towards Pembroke Lodge, skirting tall immaculate leylandii, past a flower bed and some bird-bath-planter affair. Still no sign of the Filth behind them. Even though the sweeping expanse on their right exposed the drone pilots; Maureen recognised the teenagers from before, stuffing Exhibit A into a backpack. She watched as they absconded across the valley below and once more, her eyes were drawn to the distinct gables and chimneys of Ham House.

'Clatty wee toerags,' Rhona snarled after the juveniles.

'Let's lie low in here,' suggested Thelma. Up ahead, a fret of mothers pushed laden prams past some grandparents chasing a Ribena-stained toddler.

They slunk left into a large rose garden, laid out with pergolas and herringbone-bricked paths, which weaved between sprawling perennials. Although the wooden frames were twined with bloomless climbers, and the beds displayed no more than scrubby bushes, it provided sufficient cover for the senior desperadoes. Only a few shrubs proffered pollen to the odd, groggy bee. Like some amuse-bouche for the riot of heady red roses and vampish foxgloves that would explode in a few months.

Thelma and Rhona slumped on to a bench. Behind them, the scrolled gingerbread trim of The Cottage's thatched roof loomed above the thicket. The bench was dedicated to a couple whose weathered names were faint in the sunlight. Below some tribute, there was a visible mention of Ganesh, the popular, elephant-headed Hindu god, Deity of Good Fortune and Remover of Obstacles. If only he could lend one of his four hands right now.

Judging it best not to sit together, Deirdre and Maureen loitered on some secluded steps at the garden's perimeter, ignoring the PRIVATE RESIDENCE notice on the tall, wooden gate. Sheltered by thick holly hedges, they lurked in this corner, ears cocked for any radio squelches and splats, above the squealing tots and Disneyesque birdsong.

Deirdre threaded her jacket through her tote. 'Do you think they filmed us?'

'Not sure. Depends which way their camera was pointing,' said Maureen, in a valiant attempt at glass half-full status.

'I think we have to face the possibility that they did,' countered Thelma, inscrutable behind her Jackie O sunglasses. She had wandered over to join them and made a point of examining the crab apple-sized buds on a shiny rhododendron. Rhona remained seated, head swivelling, scouting for Old Bill. They fell silent, absorbing Thelma's ulcer-fuelled prognosis.

At that moment, two little girls raced zigzag up the central brick path. Giggling, they squeezed under the bench next to Rhona, the soles of their sparkly, pink trainers flashing fluorescent lights, like some acid lighthouse code. As if they were no less than the Grim Reaper's junior assistants, Rhona shifted with impressive speed.

'What are we going to do?' Deirdre asked, as Rhona materialised next to them, her furtive casing reeking of pensioner street dealer.

'Nothing. Just wait.' This time, Thelma's unflappability failed to appease. 'We don't know if anyone's found the bag yet, or handed it in. Even if they did film us, they'll probably delete it.'

'Aye, us four on some hill — we're no likely to go viral.'

'Speak for yourself,' Maureen joshed, masking her unease.

'We will, once they find the painting, mind.'

'Not funny, Rhona,' said Deirdre.

'Coming! Ready or not…'

A super-mum paced the lawn beyond, shielding her eyes from the sun. *'Where is everybody? I can't see them anywhere. Where are they? Hellooo…'*

'We're up here by the gate, hen,' muttered Rhona. 'Hiding from the polis.'

'Look, we can't stay here forever,' said Maureen, as the

two girls shrieked from under the bench, impatient with their mother's inept seeking skills. Fortunately, as their mother began another loud, tedious countdown, the youngest started to whine about her empty tum tum and they hurried towards the Lodge.

Talking of which, as Deirdre craned her head forward, Rhona whisked the packet of brioches out of her tote, ripping apart its cellophane wrapper. Thelma tapped her wrist and snatched back the crinkled package.

'I'm hungry. I wanna jeely piece,' protested Rhona, in a flimsy spoof.

'Well, I'd like some caffeine.'

'And I could do with something stronger, but we need to hang on,' Thelma said. 'We can't risk drawing attention to ourselves in the vicinity of—'

'Bugger me, that was quick.'

Deirdre's voice was barely audible, but there was something in her tone and the way her back stiffened that killed their squabbling. In unison, they edged out further on the step, squinting into the sunshine.

Sure enough, through the far pagoda's gallows-shaped arches, two uniforms emerged, walking towards Pembroke Lodge. The lanky constable was talking into his radio, while his female colleague grasped the handles of a familiar, bulky Sainsbury's bag for life.

Chapter 30
Lemon Drizzle

Again, Maureen stuck to the Park's speed limit with unusual rigour, her mind whirring much like that McEff drone. To be fair, she was tailing two Tour de France wannabes, cycling abreast with sublime disregard for other road users. For a heart-stopping second, Maureen saw Rick-with-the-silent-P, before realising that even he wouldn't stoop to pink and green lycra.

'A bunch of weed-smoking teens are unlikely to offer up footage to the police, and I think we can assume they don't have a licence to fly that thing.'

As she spoke, Thelma checked the car behind in the wing mirror.

'Aye right, no way were they eighteen. Bet they nicked it from one of their dads. Wee posh Neds,' scoffed Rhona, mouthful of brioche.

'God, I need a cigarette.' Deirdre lowered her window, as if a passing cyclist might hand her one.

'Get you, Fag Ash Lil.' Rhona spat out some crumbs.

'Oh, I haven't smoked for years. Decades even. Gary made me give up when I met him. Said it was like kissing an ashtray. But I have a sudden craving.'

'Sounds like a right charmer, so he does.'

'I've got some lemon drizzle back home,' Maureen offered, as a nicotine substitute. Although, despite her gastric reflux, she was hankering after a double whisky. 'My neighbour's practising for some W.I. competition. Keeps bringing over freshly baked samples for *honest* feedback.'

'Result.' Maureen watched in the rear-view, as Rhona pressed a licked fingertip down her front to secure the ejected crumbs.

'No, the less we're all seen together today, the better,' decreed Captain Sensible, who was now cleaning her sunglasses with a bespectacled owl-patterned cloth.

Thelma was right. Seema would note Maureen's visitors and bring over more cake as a ruse to meet them. She had mentioned road-testing a new red velvet recipe, which augured death by cream cheese icing.

Their light banter was all window-dressing of course. After having spied the Sainsbury's bag in the sweaty paws of the Royal Parks Constabulary, they'd slipped out of the rose garden. Sidled along the path to the Mound and exited towards the car park, in a wordless, bowed head automation.

The thoroughfare was busier now, but the hordes were consumed by their own compelling biospheres. Gesticulating in tearful phone-calls, intervening in kids' fights, trumping friends' anecdotes, and posting filtered snaps on Instagram. As they belted themselves into Maureen's dusty Micra, not a word was exchanged over the hooting contest for their space. The tension only spilled into backchat as they escaped the congested car park, with Rhona's motivational quip:

'Och well, as one door closes, another one slams in your face.'

In a way, it was a relief to know that the painting was back in safe hands, but it had all happened so soon after they'd fled the scene, and, as for that bastard, what-are-the-frigging-chances drone. This meant there was potential video evidence of them, or rather, Maureen, leaving the incriminating bag on the Mound. However blurry the focus, it would reveal the perps to be four older women. Then surely, even PC Plod would join the dots and zero in on Trust volunteers. Scrub that, DC Adamu would be all over her like a rash. Even Warrior Queen Stace couldn't extricate Maureen from that dollop of Barry White.

Yet, how soon would the Bosschaert find be made public? While it was in the Trust's interest to quash the bad publicity asap and increase footfall with the painting's return, the Art and Antiques Unit might keep it under wraps until they'd nailed the culprit. But wouldn't those kids have deleted the video by then? Not least, to wipe any evidence of their own infraction.

All these dark hairy prospects wafted round them like the silent-but-lethal fart in a lift. Best not acknowledge it out loud, muse about the ramifications of a spring drought, and breathe through your mouth.

Careful to deviate from her earlier route, Maureen dropped off her crew at various spots round Richmond: Deidre, just before the Bridge — Gary needed a new neck pillow. Thelma on the Green — she was meeting a friend at No.1a Duke Street. Last but not least, Rhona, opposite St Matthias's, the gothic mini cathedral on the Hill. She climbed out of the car. 'Maybe I should nip over the road and pray for our souls.'

'Thought you were a devout atheist.'

'Aye but reckon it's worth hedging my bets right now. Anyway, see you *as normal* in a few days.' She made air quotes with her fingers. 'Here's hoping Dee doesn't go all extra in acting casual.'

Maureen faked a cheery goodbye. It was only when she turned right on to the Sheen Road, that she realised she hadn't thanked them for their help.

Having agreed to make their own way to Ham House on Thursday and that, barring emergencies, it was best not to contact each other, she now had to shoulder her fears solo. They all would, as they stewed over the morning's surreal events. As Thelma had instructed, they just had to hold their nerve, keep an eye on the news and follow their usual routine for the next few days.

But Maureen dreaded those desolate, small hours tussling with the duvet as she clawed at an unrefreshing sleep. And while colonies of dust mites gorged on the flakes of skin that she shed along with her sweat into the lumpy mattress, waves of cold paranoia and prison doomsdays crashed over her semiconscious.

On the plus side, she did have some homemade lemon drizzle. And where there's cake, there's hope.

Chapter 31
Fifteen Minutes
Wednesday, 21st February

'You watching this?'

'Rhona, you know we're not supposed to call each other. I shouldn't even have said that.'

'Don't be a dumpling. Turn on the smelly.'

'Why?' Maureen was about to tuck into her faithful comfort snack — baked beans on lavishly buttered toast with a large dollop of HP.

'Do as you're told. The Beeb. Now.'

Sighing, she put the phone on speaker and switched on the news. And stared at the screen, slack-jawed. A blackbird with shiny feathers perched on a ledge, a cluster of cherries at its scaly feet, its keen yellow gaze held by a hovering butterfly. Then the camera panned out to the Great Hall, with a flushed Emma posing beside the easel.

'It's back,' said Maureen in a half whisper.

'Hello? Remember Monday?'

'...this simple vignette was painted by Dutch artist, Ambrosius Bosschaert...'

As she delivered her blurb, a caption flashed up: *Emma Doherty, House Manager, Ham House.*

'...quite rare because live songbirds rarely featured in still lifes of that period...'

'Told you,' preened Maureen.

'...recorded in an inventory drawn up when Elizabeth Murray, the Duchess of Lauderdale...'

'This isn't frigging *Mastermind.* It's a major news story — caused by us.'

'...brought here around 1670 by her second husband, a close confidant to King Charles II. The Duke probably had this naturalistic oak frame made in the same style as some of the larger paintings on our famous Great Staircase...'

'Nice plug Emma,' said Maureen, ignoring Rhona's tuts. Ignoring all the ramifications, elated that her little

Blackbird was starring on prime time. It had graced the front pages a couple of weeks ago, but the photos hadn't done it justice. You couldn't make out the pulp dripping from its beak, the butterfly looked amateur, the fly blurry and even the cherries had lost their gloss.

'…we're delighted that it's back in its rightful home, where it has hung for nearly three hundred and fifty years….'

'You're welcome,' said Maureen, more to herself.

'…thankfully, with no signs of any damage!'

'Well, I was very careful, you know.'

'*We*, you mean. *We* were very careful.'

'Sorry. Slip of the tongue'

She heard a loud sniff, then a grouched 'Freudian.'

'…we're reviewing all our security arrangements and upgrading where necessary, so that we can be confident nothing like this could ever happen again…'

'Almost sounds like a challenge, right enough.' It seemed that Maureen wasn't the only one getting a kick out of this.

'…this reason, Ham House will be closed from tomorrow. We'll continue to admit visitors to our gardens, but we plan to reopen the House next week, when the Blackbird, Butterfly and Cherries will be on view to the public. Details will be on our website. We apologise for this temporary closure, but…'

Maureen checked her Inbox and sure enough, there was an email from Meera confirming that all volunteer shifts were cancelled for the next few days.

'Holy shit. Lost our chance to get the low-down from Trevor,' said Rhona.

The reporter handed back to the newsreader.

'And here in the studio, we have DC Adamu from the Met's Art and Antiques Unit. Detective, what's the latest on this intriguing theft and return?'

'Ooh look it's your Five-O friend.'

Still black-suited and ice cool, damn her, Adamu was all lip-glossed up.

'The painting may have been returned, but a crime still took

place, and our investigations are ongoing to find the perpetrators involved. We believe the theft occurred during filming on location at Ham House. We're keeping an open mind at this stage, but I can confirm that currently, none of the cast or crew are assisting us with our enquiries…'

'Unlike the volunteers,' said Rhona.

'*… also following up on intelligence related to OCGs in the—'*

'OCGs meaning organised crime groups?'

'That's right, organised criminal activity in the area.'

'Not sure you're quite up to date with all the local gangs.' This made Rhona cackle.

'Do you think this painting's recovery is linked to the recent spate of stolen art recovered at various London rail terminals?'

'That's unclear at this stage…'

'As they haven't the foggiest.'

Maureen wasn't so sure. Neither was the newsreader.

'But this painting's return didn't follow the same pattern, did it? The Dutch oil was found by some walkers in Richmond Park, left by a bench at popular visitor attraction, King Henry's Mound.'

'Yes, it does appear to have a different M.O. but we're not ruling anything out. I should add that we're very keen to speak to the owners of a drone camera that was being operated in the area at the time—'

'Good luck with that, hen.'

'Contravening Royal Parks' regulations.'

Adamu ignored the anchor. *'Anyone with information regarding the theft of this painting should contact us on…'*

'Is there a reward?' asked Maureen.

'Thank you, Detective. Now, let's get the latest on this early Spring heatwave. Time to dust off our brollies, Tomasz?'

'That's your fifteen minutes,' said Rhona. 'For now.'

'Thanks.' Feeling queasy, Maureen pushed aside her plate of cold beans. Several arpeggio wolf-whistles chirped down the line.

'That's our Dee inviting us round to lunch tomorrow instead. Oh, and Thelma says it's fine to meet up, now the return's been made public.'

'How come I'm not getting these?'

'Easy tiger. Cos you were interviewed by your celeb Fed for theft.'

Maureen's phone pinged. Rhona had added her to the group Ham House Hags.

* * *

Washing up, Maureen surveyed her bedraggled yard, half expecting to see Pepys pick his way along the fence. Despite this sudden pang, she was still buzzing. Her *Blackbird*, hidden away for so long, had featured on national TV, for the whole world to see. Plus, it had a stay of execution; the Trust would want to cash in before it was carted off to Thirlestane Castle. It was famous. All because of her. And she saluted everything she'd engineered these last few months. In her own transformation.

Who'd have fucking thunk it?

Chapter 32

Eyes and Dyes

Thursday, 22nd February

'Jeez-oh, you risen again to feed the five thousand?'

Rhona had a point. The glass table in Deirdre's conservatory was groaning under quiches, mushroom vol-au-vents, coronation chicken, dips, breadsticks and potato salad. All neatly arranged in floral dishes with matching paper napkins.

Deidre waved a hand. 'Oh, it didn't take a minute.' The others exchanged looks; one hundred percent she'd been shopping, cooking and cleaning her heart out. 'Besides, Gary can eat any leftovers when he gets back from Bridge Club.'

'First rule of Bridge Club — don't talk about Bridge Club,' said Rhona, as she handed Deidre a clinking placcy bag. 'Here's my carry out.'

Foraging through her kitchen cupboards that morning, Maureen had chanced on a bottle of sloe gin liqueur, still in its oak-leafed brown paper bag. She stuck it behind Thelma's Veuve and Belgian chocs.

Their captain seated herself at the head of the table. 'Deirdre, this is very kind of you.'

Maureen, ashamed right then of her scruffy cottage and duff hosting skills, made noises of agreement, followed by perfunctory offers of help. Noting how Rhona and Thelma remained silent on this front. Predictably, she was dismissed, as Deirdre, now in her element, whisked off clingfilm and began dishing out. Like the proverbial yo-yo, she continued fussing up and down, while they gorged themselves stupid. Until sated at last, they could no longer ignore the elephant in the sparkling conservatory. Or rather, the blackbird.

Thelma leant back on her peach-cushioned, wicker chair. 'Well team, I think we can safely say, mission accomplished.'

'Can we really?' said Maureen, regretting that last devilled egg.

'Aye we can! Nigel's off the hook. The nuggit was in York on Monday. So they'll know it wasn't him on King Henry's Mound.'

'True,' Maureen replied, and she had to admit, the albatross did feel considerably lighter. 'But what about me? I mean, us.' Recalling Adamu's TV appearance, she felt the bare patch on her chin. She had attacked it with a tweezer after her bath.

'The painting may have been returned, but a crime still took place, and our investigations are ongoing to find the perpetrators involved.'

'Och, haud yer wheesht.' Rhona had made full use of her non-driver status with her wine intake. As had their hostess.

'What did your solicitor say again?' Thelma deftly popped the champagne's cork, making Deirdre squeal as she emerged from the kitchen with Maureen's bottle and some flutes on a tray. Thelma answered her own question. 'They've got nothing concrete on you,' she said, topping up Deirdre's generous slugs of liqueur with bubbles. 'Nothing at all.'

'And you can forget that drone. Any video will have been deleted pronto,' said Rhona, grabbing her Sloe Royale. 'I'm awful partial to a splash of shampoo in my gin.'

'Always popular in the shop, this one' said Dee, rosy-cheeked, distributing the rest of the dripping glasses. 'The gin, I mean. We don't sell Champagne.'

Never shy of stating the obvious, Deirdre plucked some National Trust cheese nibbles from nowhere, and well past the niceties of plates and napkins, passed round the packet. Then, slapped her forehead. 'What am I like? Almost forgot these,' she hiccupped, leant over and plopped a maraschino cherry in each glass.

Maureen raised eyebrows at Thelma. And in a moment

of historic import, Thelma's face surrendered to a broad grin.

'Eyes!' ordered Rhona.

In compliance, the four women eyeballed each other as they clinked glasses.

* * *

The following week, Maureen sauntered up Richmond Hill to that trendy new salon. In addition to a much-needed trim, she asked them to dye her longish, unkempt bob. As celebration of her secret triumph. After all, hadn't she single-handedly immortalised the *Blackbird, Butterfly and Cherries*? Okay, with a little help from her new gang, but she had kept her promise to Jodie about keeping an eye on it. Too close an eye.

Apparently, it had been big news the other side of The Pond, and Jodie expected the full scoop when Maureen arrived in New York. It was tempting to confide all and to enjoy lit Great Auntie status, but she doubted that Laura would be as chuffed.

But at least she could impress Jodie in other ways. At first, she had toyed with pink hair. Why the hell not? But then she recalled a courtier's description of the young Elizabeth Murray as a very good harmless virtuous witty little babe despite her unbecoming auburn deep-coloured hair. Sod it, she thought, and plumbed for an unapologetic bright red, in homage to that brilliant, unconventional Duchess.

Unfazed, the Australian owner examined Maureen's hair over big, round glasses, dropping phrases like deep cleanse in husky upspeak. With Vaseline smeared below her hairline against the oozing gunk, Maureen was regaled with a litany of Hinge horror stories over a thumping playlist. To avoid her unnerving reflection, she flicked through magazines, brimming with photos of Z-listers at various charidee events. Their side-on-knee-pop poses were set against pap shots of sneaky dates with lovers and fights with spouses. Celebs getting wasted, losing weight, gaining weight and heaven forbid, exposing cellulite — the shameful dimples circled in red.

Every now and then, Ms Caramel Curls came and poked at the goo with the end of a comb, and murmured 'coming on nicely,' as if she were a rising sponge. It wasn't until Helios's chariot had hauled the burning sun halfway across the sky that she was pronounced done. Dispatched to an area called the backwash, the nape of Maureen's neck ached against the basin's ceramic lip.

The result was astonishing. Lurid red locks gleamed back at her from the mirror. The whole salon cooed. Definitely makes you look younger and it really lifts your complexion.

Perleeze. You can't polish a turd.

Nevertheless, she bounced down the Hill, stunned by her own hair-swishing in shop windows. Next, on a crazed whim, she ventured into the scary cosmetics shop. A bored makeup artist pounced and before she knew it, she had splashed out on a tinted SPF 20 moisturiser and some mascara. She couldn't justify this on top of the eye-watering hair bill, but it was high time to dust off her building society book. Plus, on the QT, Sherin with the mesmerising, yes-honest-they're-real eyelashes, chucked in a sample lippy which doubled as rouge, and several eyeshadow testers. Off she floated back home, swinging her little black bag by its ribbon-tied handles.

No surprise, as soon as she rounded the corner into her road, she spied Face Ache and Seema deep in conversation, opposite her house. Both turned to ogle Rubylocks and on registering that it was Maureen (*Maureen*?), enacted a brief role reversal. The TAGs' garrulous chair remained slack-mouthed, while Face Ache actually addressed two words to her. Or at least, out loud, in her direction. 'That's brave.'

Then, the Looking Glass universe melted away, and Seema convulsed with laughter. 'Good for you, love.'

Face Ache tried to raise her eyebrows, then factory

reset to sour lemon. Grabbing her bags, she tottered into number thirteen. Meanwhile, Seema, wiping away tears, said she'd better check on her meringues. Presumably, code for WhatsApping the TAGs about Maureen's, *yes Maureen's*, severely delayed mid-life crisis. At any event, she scuttled down the road, shouting over her shoulder that maybe she would go scarlet too. Like that Loose Women presenter, whatsername, Janice Sweet-Porter.

Inside the bathroom of number fourteen, Maureen studied her startled face in the toothpaste-flecked mirror. Safe to say, her new barnet did not make her look younger, but she decided that looking zany was better than being invisible.

Her texted selfies (coached by Jodie), provoked mixed responses:

'Wow, your make-up looks lovely! Don't worry, I'm sure the red will tone down soon. Just keep washing it. You can always wear a hat. Deirdre xx.'

'who r u & what have u done with my pal Maureen *smiling face with sunglasses* better up my game *rofl emoji*'

'About time you had a makeover. Suits you. Kathy would have approved. Do NOT get a tattoo. T.'

Chapter 33
Memento Vivere
Thursday, 1st March

The 11:45 am briefing wasn't in its usual spot. Instead, the Thursday guides had gathered at the north end of the Long Gallery, near the Green Closet — scene of the dastardly crime. Silhouetted by light from the canted bay, the Dutch Golden Age tableau was showcased on a roped-off, alarmed easel. Alongside, Emma continued, 'and I'm sure you'll all agree, it's been an absolute rollercoaster these past few weeks.'

Tell me about it, thought Maureen, amid the consensual rhubarb rhubarbs.

'Really, I should open some velvet curtains. Like a proper unveiling ceremony, but it's not as though you haven't seen it before.' Broad, toothy grin. 'Anyway, it's back where it belongs, our prized *Blackbird, Butterfly and Cherries*.'

Everyone clapped. Some harder than others.

'Gaun yersel,' shouted Rhona. Deirdre could barely contain herself and Maureen knew she would have loved to broadcast her role in its return. Thelma's searching, dark eye-shadowed gaze met Maureen's. A trace of disapproval but still loyal. Shrewd. Calm.

* * *

They were flat-out that shift. The House at maximum visitor capacity, with queues outside the front door, snaking round the Jacobean arched loggias. Everyone desperate for a selfie in front of the notorious *Blackbird*. Strictly flash off. Rhona gave any non-compliant punter the hairy eyeball. They soon backed down; you had to when her switch was flicked.

Deirdre spent the first hour handing out laminated portrait lists, before skipping off to the shop. Blithe impervious to all the argy-bargy. That's what made her pure twenty-four karat.

Thelma was enlightening a group about the Bosschaert, although they were only interested in who stole it and how. *With great difficulty, some luck and a large pinch of brilliance.* Their captain enjoying being the expert, as usual. Then again, she often was.

Their tea break couldn't come soon enough.

* * *

'Maureen Goodwin, I'm arresting you for theft. You do not have to say anything, but it may harm your defence if you do not mention when questioned, something you later rely on in court.'

Slapping a hand on her shoulder, Sanjay blocked her path to the sink.

'Dropped yourself right in it with that game at our Christmas lunch.' He shook his head. 'Careless, Maureen, careless.'

The arrestee heard her own gulp, as if amplified on virtual speakers round the Mess Room.

'I've always wanted to make a citizen's arrest.' He released her, doubling over with hilarity.

'I think only the police say all that,' said Deirdre.

'Imagine Maureen as the thief!' Now it was Barbara's turn to crack up.

'Yes, imagine,' said Rhona.

'Dunno, reckon she's a dark horse, our Maureen,' Trevor grinned. 'What with her racy new hairdo.'

'I can testify to that,' said Rhona. 'But Babs, didn't you finger Nige as the prime suspect?'

'No, no, that was a terrible misunderstanding.' Barbara felt a sudden need to delve into her handbag. 'That detective really was quite manipulative.'

'Wasn't she just?' said Maureen.

'Oh yes,' Barbara rounded eyes at Maureen. 'I heard she gave you the third degree.'

'Well, it didn't help that you blabbed about my harmless little pub game. Oh, and let slip that the *Blackbird* happened to be my favourite painting.'

'I was only telling the truth,' Barbara patted her hair, 'as required by law.'

'Did ye, aye? We call it something different where I come from,' said Rhona.

'I didn't mean you stole it. That would be absur—'

'Any news on who actually took the painting? Assuming it wasn't Maureen.'

Deirdre's evil doppelganger flinched as Rhona jabbed her under the table.

'A few rumours about local gangs. Nothing confirmed,' Sanjay replied, serious now as unofficial spokesperson for both the NT and the Met.

'Nah, just some low life who saw an opportunity during filming,' said Trevor. 'I still reckon Venetia left the Green Closet unlocked. She was all over the shop that day — a walking waste of space. I didn't say that mind. Anyhow, this eejit klepto realised he couldn't flog it, and didn't want to get into deeper doo-doo.'

Rhona coughed, as Deidre blew on her apple and cinnamon tea.

As a matter of fact, fine art theft takes a lot of planning. I'd like to see any of you try it. Maybe she was making a point, and had no intention of selling it, Maureen had wanted to trumpet. Irritated at falling for Sanjay's clumsy gag, she conceded that Trevor was right about the eejit part, and the low-grade chancer bit. Plus, precisely what point had she made?

Her mixed broodings were interrupted by Thelma's entrance. Kerry had assigned Sanjay the Volury. Could he come up as soon as he'd finished his break. This, everyone knew, meant get your skates on.

'I better nip up as well, I suppose,' said Barbara, touching up her lippy. 'I'm in the Duchess's Bedchamber. No rest for the wicked.'

'Indeed,' said Maureen.

'Talking of which, Lorna's taking a *well-earned break*,' Trevor informed them. 'Official line is that she's got some holiday to use up before relocating to some other top post.

Total BS. Couldn't hack all the stress. Sad really.' He looked ecstatic.

'Good riddance if you ask me,' said Sanjay, despite the fact no one had.

'Aye, she'll be sorely un-missed,' said Rhona.

'Oh God, that'll mean a whole new set of managerial directives,' groaned Barbara, straightening the long service badge on her blazer.

'You're not wrong there,' Trevor continued. 'What with all the publicity, the *Blackbird*'s staying put now. No more *stately home, fine art game of Pokémon.* Huge members' protest — Bosschaert's painting was acquired by the Duke and Duchess, so belongs at Ham. Mustn't leave the Trust. Cultural self-sabotage and all that.'

'Really?' asked Maureen, a lump in her throat. 'That's the best news.'

'Unusual for common sense to prevail,' said Rhona.

'More like the money talking,' spat Trevor. 'What with this surge in visitors, they wanna maximise revenue. Emma says it'll make up for last quarter's downturn. As per friggin' usual, conservation goes out the window. Big increase in footfall up the Great Staircase and in the Long Gallery. And like today, we're going to need extra marshals. Well, you saw the email.'

'One thing's for sure, the *Blackbird* prints are flying out of the shop,' said Deirdre, enjoying her own cheesy pun, before reeling off sales figures and the minutiae of re-ordering tea towels and fridge magnets. Trevor leapt to his feet. 'Right, better head up and adjust the blinds, now it's clouded over.'

Visitors often grumbled about the gloom, for all the explanations about light damage on irreplaceable oils, tapestries and leather wall hangings. With a raised backhanded farewell, he followed Sanjay and Barbara.

As they exited, Thelma put a finger to her frosted lips. They waited until Ms Bouffant Snitch and the budding detectives clattered up the servants' staircase. The staff door slammed, then all went quiet.

'Apparently, Nigel's coming back,' Thelma told them, as she closed the biscuit tin. 'He's been called in today. Emma's making a formal apology.'

'Begging him not to sue, more like,' said Deirdre, restacking the dishwasher. 'Or give an interview to his friends at the Telegraph.'

'Och, his bum's out the windae. No way would he go public with being conned out of his savings.'

'Well, I'm glad he's allowed back,' said Maureen.

Rhona shifted her jaw to one side. 'Thought you hated him.'

'He's not top of my Christmas card list, but he was unfairly accused because of me. And this place means as much to him as it does to us.'

For once, Rhona had no comeback.

* * *

Grateful to be assigned the Library after her tea break, Maureen had hoped for some relative peace. Few would bother coming in once they'd viewed the returned Bosschaert. Wrong. She spent the last two hours fielding the back wash of amateur sleuths, crime bloggers and the odd, barefaced journo. With a cursory sweep of the tawny bookshelves, glinting with gold-leafed spines, all they wanted was more dirt on the recovered painting. Had she been at the House when it happened? *You could say that.* What was her theory on who had taken it and how? *Well, funny you should ask*. Had the National Trust paid a ransom? *Damn, why didn't I think of that?* Was it all a PR stunt? *Bog off.*

Maureen made them wait for her *anybody's guess*, while she enlightened them on the twin globes and ornate plastered ceiling. Plus, the eighteenth-century pole screens with their double-sided maps. The one which labelled Australia as New Holland, incorporating New Zealand, because European cartographers believed both were part of the same landmass before Captain Cook's famous voyage.

'Yes yes, but were ISIS involved in the painting's theft?'

Finally, Meera came to tell Maureen that the House was closed, and she was free to go. Leaving Meera to lock up, she stepped back into the Long Gallery. Now empty of visitors.

I am free to go. I'm free at last! Job done.

She nearly broke into a fist-pumping victory lap round the cordon. Instead, she stopped in front of her *Blackbird.* Hang about, it wasn't hers anymore. Or Jodie's. It was everyone's. Back where it belonged in the Duchess's childhood home. No longer tucked away hidden from sight, but out in the open. Valued at long last for its delicate, lively beauty. And cheeks glistening, she drank in every brushstroke.

'Your hair almost matches my jeans.' Nigel planted himself next to her. 'All that fuss over one little painting of a common and garden bird.'

Maureen shot him a glance. His red jeans hung a bit looser, his shirt cuffs frayed, but he was smiling. 'Kidding. It's a corker.' They studied it some more.

Maureen broke the charged hush. 'So, you'll be back volunteering Fridays again?'

'I let Emma grovel, although to be fair, it wasn't her who banished me. But yes, I'll be here tomorrow. Already had loads of texts. *We always knew you were innocent. It wasn't the same without you.* Fickle bastards.'

They both laughed and Maureen blew her nose. 'Well, it's good to have you back.' She turned away. 'Anyway, better dash — the others are waiting for me.'

'You're a tight little gang, aren't you?'

'I guess we are.'

And right then, Maureen realised that she wasn't alone anymore. Yes, she still grieved for Kathy. She always would, and she missed not having Laura and Jodie nearby. But she did have a new, tight little gang. Real friends, who had put themselves in jeopardy to protect her. And like the *Blackbird*, that really was priceless.

Nigel cut in on her epiphany. 'You know, I was wrong about you.'

She dug out the car keys from her Chanel bag. 'You were?'

'I reckon there's nothing you couldn't wangle, Maureen Goodwin.'

***

The Fearless Four meandered down the sun dappled avenue. Rhona handed Maureen a large, brown paper bag. 'We had us a whip-round.'

She extracted a mounted print of the *Blackbird.*

'There weren't many left, you know. I've already placed an order for—'

'Read the room, woman!' Rhona ruffled her hair. 'No one's interested.'

Nose in the air, Deirdre gestured zipping her lips.

'We thought it would help check any future urges,' said Thelma, decapitating a primrose with her stick.

'Why did you do that?' Deirdre's mouth already hanging open.

'Primula vulgaris — toxic to dogs.' Thelma picked up the offending bloom and gave it to Deirdre, who popped it into her buttonhole.

'Aye, sod the starving bees.'

Maureen examined the print, calculating where best to hang it in her hallway. 'It's perfect. Thank you, team.'

Thelma scoured the meadow and they continued brabbling over the raspy back and forth of a pair of magpies. Sidestepping some horse dung, Maureen tried to dredge up some guilt for her deranged actions. Tried but failed. Far worse, she thought, to stew in rancid regret.

Marking time, listening to the calibrated sway of the pendulum. The chiming of the hours, crossing off the days, all blurring into each other like smudged oil paint. Better to snatch that one sunny moment on a stone ledge, savour the sweetness of the ripe fruit. Worth risking that sharp, yellow skewer. What was your fragile, fleeting existence, without dazzling a little? Soaring with invigorated, outstretched wings. Hypnotise your predators, that's the key.

Better to feel alive. Better to feel the searing pain of loss, than the void of numbed suppression. Feel the Fear and Do It Anyway. Tell the fear to go fuck itself. Burn with passion, scorch the strangling bindweed of those neural pathways with a bubbling, chocolate honey hit of dopamine.

She knew it now. She'd always known it, deep down. Not *memento mori*, but *memento vivere.*

Remember that you have to live.

Epilogue
Monday 5th March

'Anything from forensics?'

'At the property — no footprints to speak of. Some sets of fingerprints — all matched to the staff. As for the recovered painting, zilch on the bubble wrap. A few strands of animal fur on the bag. Probably cat.'

'If only we had a pet DNA database.'

DC Adamu obliged her boss with a half-baked smile. He noted her effort and moved on.

'Anything at the drop-off point in Richmond Park on... When was it again?'

'The painting was found on Monday, nineteenth Feb. Forensics reckon it was dropped earlier that morning. Ie. no physical degradation to suggest it'd been there overnight.'

'Okay, nothing else from the bag?'

The office allotted to Detective Sergeant Fielding, Chief of the Art and Antiques Unit wasn't what you'd call palatial, but its choice location at the front of the Yard, afforded an enviable view of the Thames, albeit a grey sludgy expanse that afternoon.

'No, too much cross-contamination,' Adamu replied, after a slurp of disagreeable coffee. 'Couple of mums found it by a bench at...' Glancing back down at her tablet, she recited, 'At the top of King Henry's Mound in Pembroke Gardens. They handed it in to the Parks Uniforms, who assumed it was Lost Property.'

In response to his choice adjectives on incompetent clothes-hangers, she said, 'To be fair, last thing you'd expect to find in a supermarket bag. Only closer examination revealed the label.'

Fielding raised dark, bushy eyebrows at her. 'Nothing useful from that either' she added, and he resumed squinting at the forensic report on his monitor.

'As for Ham House, no CCTV nearby or in the actual

property,' he grimaced. 'And the side entrance was wedged open all day, so sod all on the buzzer camera. Okay, where does that leave us? Safe to exclude crew?'

Adamu nodded. 'No one leaps out from the interviews. No gamblers or dodgy connections. All old hands with location filming in stately homes. Why suddenly risk everything now?'

'What about staff? Volunteers?'

'That's my hunch, boss, some sort of inside job. We interviewed a few volunteers under caution, but—'

'Total lack of hard evidence. I understand one of them had a solid alibi for the nineteenth?'

'That's right. Nigel Herbert was staying with family in York at the time.'

Fielding puffed out his cheeks. 'Sorry Adamu, I know you're a TV star now, but I don't buy your volunteer angle.'

Adamu folded her arms.

'Far more likely to be an opportunistic pro taking advantage of the filming. All sorts wandering in and out the House throughout the day. He gets interrupted, grabs the painting and makes a snappy ex—'

'Yeah, but why that particular painting? Why not just stuff your pockets with all those miniatures?'

'Because,' Fielding growled, allergic to interruptions, 'There's no time. After a quick recce, he spots this flashy frame, gotta be worth some, and result — unsecured. Just hanging there. Unbelievable.' Rubbing his eyes, he opened a new tab and examined the *Blackbird* on the Collections website. 'Plus, portable in size and—'

'Hanging, tucked away on the far side of the fireplace,' Adamu studied the Green Closet's layout on her tablet, 'So not easily missed.'

'As I was saying,' Fielding raised his voice to reassert his senior status. 'Bitten off more than he can chew. Realises he can't cut a deal, dumps it and cuts his losses. Hoping we'll bracket it with the other returned art.'

'But boss,' Adamu, more deferential now. 'Totally different M.O. Why not at a mainline station like all the other returns linked to OCGss? Bit of a give-away.'

'Too much CCTV. Clearly not part of any third-party deal. I take it, you had a cosy chat with the usual suspects?'

'Again, all watertight alibis on both dates.'

Fielding tore open a sugar sachet. 'Any luck tracing that drone? No calls following your gig on BBC News?'

This time, Adamu grinned. 'Diddly, apart from the usual timewasters. Uniforms on the ground reckon it was just kids who scarpered. So, no licence. They wouldn't want to risk a fine. What is it, a grand? Or more to the point, being identified as informants. If they had any sense, they'd have deleted the footage.'

'Might not have filmed anything useful anyway. Nah,' DCI Fielding scratched his stubble. 'Time to wind this one down.'

'Sir? According to the insurers, the painting's worth around £250k!'

Slugs of the muddy liquid that passed for coffee dribbled over her cup's cardboard shell, as she slapped it down on Fielding's desk. She attempted damage limitation with a feeble excuse for a napkin. Her boss ignored the side-show.

'I'm aware, Adamu, but as it stands, I can't justify asking for more resources on this. We're already over-budget. The painting's safely back at Ham House. Insurers are happy. As are the film producers. Lots of sweet PR for them. Ditto, Ham House. And the Trust has dodged all the bad publicity of a court case. Best of all, the press are off our backs.'

Mirroring his DC's coffee spillage, Fielding sprinkled the papers on his desk with white granules, as he emptied a third sachet into his tea.

'Not to mention the DI,' he added, under his breath. 'Meanwhile, following these recent attacks on mosques, the threat level's just been raised to Severe. Not official yet, but NaCTSO need some extra bums on seats. So, NFA on this unless new evidence comes to light.'

Sympathetic to her obvious exasperation, he soft-pedalled. 'Look, my hands are tied. You know the score. As a small unit, we need to demonstrate flexibility and move wherever the need is.' He swore softly as a reminder pinged on his calendar. 'Got it? They're expecting you at Vauxhall ASAP. Thorpe's already there.'

Adamu groaned inwardly at this joyous prospect; hours of mindless tedium awaited her and other expendable suits low down the food chain. Trawling through endless CCTV footage, tracing, highlighting, eliminating, logging anything and everything. If only it was like those ludicrous TV dramas with their mythical central CCTV system, where they just zoomed in and cleaned up a blurred image to miraculously reveal a full car reg. People genuinely believed that shit was real.

'Yes sir.' Frenetic foot tapping under the table belied her passive tone. As did her freshly minted rank and pleasant demeanour, masking an inner rottweiler streak, fierce ambition and a bloody-minded aversion to shelving unsolved cases. Although she knew full well that her work in the Art and Antiques Unit, (aka the Tat and Old Junk Skive), was all about playing the long game, liaising with INTERPOL and other foreign agencies, as well as the Met's very own FALCON. Networking with dealers, curators, auction houses and exploiting under-used legislation to secure evidence from reluctant witnesses, blah blah, interminable blah.

But she was young and impatient, and there was something about this case that didn't sit right. Take that old, grey-haired bird she'd interviewed, nowhere near as dippy as she made out. For starters, she'd been smart enough to employ the services of a top-notch solicitor.

Adamu couldn't know that this particular old bird now flaunted bright red hair. And at this precise moment, roughly 3,500 miles west southwest, strolled in Manhattan sunshine besides the grass-filled tracks of the High Line, accompanied by what looked like her pre-teen granddaughter in cropped top and baggy jeans.

As she snatched up her tablet, the DS took a call, gesturing her to stay. Abandoning her caffeine dregs, she walked over to the tinted, reinforced glass window, and surveyed the crowd of tourists being fleeced by the three-cup trick on Westminster Bridge. Served them right. Hadn't Uniform just pulled those gangs, following some undercover filming by the BBC? Like that kids' game. What was it called — whack-a-mole? She scrolled down her tablet, seething with frustration over the slashed budgets and box-ticking bureaucracy that rendered the job pointless. Almost.

'I've attached the spreadsheet on that…Yep... She's on her way over, ma'am…'

Narrowing gold-flecked eyes, DC Adamu peered upriver. As if with magnified periscopic vision, she could scan westwards. Beyond the iconic chimneys of the gentrified Battersea Power Station, looping round Bishops Park and Barnes Wetland Centre, circumnavigating Kew Gardens, and finally curving further southwest, to rest opposite the kids' playground at Marble Hill Park.

There, through the trees on the facing bank, past the tour groups clustered round the wrought iron gates, she re-adjusted her mental focus on to the magnificent, gabled symmetry of Ham House.

A unique monument to seventeenth-century fashion and power. Home to knights marshal, earls, countesses, viscounts and baronets, with their entourages of extended family and servants. But most notorious of all, residence to a fatally ambitious Duke and his intrepid Duchess; its thick, red-bricked walls still harbouring restless ghosts, toting their triumphs, miseries and untold secrets.

Acknowledgements

Firstly, I want to thank JT, the first person who told me that I was a writer.

An early draft of this book was listed for the inaugural Discoveries Award, and I will always be grateful for the judges' validation. Thank you to Curtis Brown Creative, Curtis Brown and the Women's Prize Trust for establishing the Discoveries programme, a unique opportunity for aspiring female novelists.

I'm indebted to Viola Hayden and Lisa Babalis at Curtis Brown for their editorial input and their faith in Maureen's story. And to Olivia Barber, formerly of Hodder & Stoughton, for her generosity and acumen.

Thank you to criminal lawyer, Jamie Fisher, for his invaluable insights into how to avoid prison. This may prove useful if I'm ever tempted down Maureen's path.

Thanks also to Nicola for vetting Rhona's Glaswegian patter.

I owe so much to my cheerleading writer comrades, who share their wisdom, lend a shoulder and understand the insanity. Also, I want to acknowledge the excellent Failing Writers podcast for nudging me out of my writer's fug and making me laugh.

A massive thank you to Richard at Burton Mayers Books for his belief that *No Oil Painting* needed to be published and his commitment to seeing that through.

I wouldn't have finished this book without the loyal support of family and friends. Most of all from my husband, who read all my drafts and unlike me, never wavered. Not forgetting my brilliant daughter for checking that I hadn't turned into Jack from *The Shining*. It came close at times.

And to you, discerning reader, for picking up this book and stepping into Maureen's balding moccasins.

ABOUT THE AUTHOR

Genevieve Marenghi's writing uses dark humour to probe the difference between our perception of people and their true selves. The gulf between what is said and what is meant. While *No Oil Painting* explores themes of insignificance and loneliness in older age, it is mainly intended to entertain and offer a small haven in these dark, uncertain times.

No Oil Painting was listed for the inaugural Curtis Brown, CBC and Women's Prize Trust Discoveries Award. Genevieve's writing has also been listed for the Writers' & Artists' Short Story Competition 2024, and her flash fiction has featured on the acclaimed Failing Writers' Podcast.

With a degree in English and Philosophy from Exeter University, she worked for eleven years at the Weekend FT, where she helped create and launch How To Spend It magazine.

Genevieve lives in London's burbs with her husband. While she never tires of the Big Smoke, her soul lies on the wild north Cornish coast. She also enjoys visiting her daughter in Manchester — another great city. Fuelled mainly by chocolate, crisps and Prosecco, she values live music and laughing with friends. Recently, she has developed an alarming fondness for museum shops and fridge magnets.

OTHER TITLES FROM BURTON MAYERS BOOKS:

RED
ON THE
INSIDE
ELIZABETH KULIGOWSKI

www.ingramcontent.com/pod-product-compliance
Lightning Source LLC
La Vergne TN
LVHW091119080826
845145LV00008B/1982
* 9 7 8 1 9 1 7 2 2 4 1 2 3 *